USA TODAY Bestselling Author

LINDSAY McKENNA

brings you another action-packed,
emotion-filled story featuring the men and women of

MORGAN'S MERCENARIES

* * *

*When she saw the smoldering look in Gus's eyes,
Cam's mouth grew dry.*

The expression in his eyes was clearly readable.
He wanted her. In all ways. Swallowing hard, Cam
whispered unsteadily, "I—I wish I had the courage
to take what you're offering, Gus, but I don't...."

Then she turned and walked away, more scared
than she'd ever been. Even staring down a Black Shark
combat helicopter paled in comparison to facing the
desire in Gus's eyes.

A desire she longed to surrender to. If only she
could....

* * *

"Lindsay McKenna continues to leave her
distinctive mark on the romance genre with...
timeless tales about the healing powers of love."
—*Affaire de Coeur*

LINDSAY McKENNA

AN
HONORABLE
WOMAN

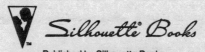

Published by Silhouette Books
America's Publisher of Contemporary Romance

 SILHOUETTE BOOKS

AN HONORABLE WOMAN

ISBN 0-373-21806-0

Copyright © 2003 by Eileen Nauman

All rights reserved. Except for use in any review, the reproduction or utilization of this work in whole or in part in any form by any electronic, mechanical or other means, now known or hereafter invented, including xerography, photocopying and recording, or in any information storage or retrieval system, is forbidden without the written permission of the editorial office, Silhouette Books, 300 East 42nd Street, New York, NY 10017 U.S.A.

All characters in this book have no existence outside the imagination of the author and have no relation whatsoever to anyone bearing the same name or names. They are not even distantly inspired by any individual known or unknown to the author, and all incidents are pure invention.

This edition published by arrangement with Harlequin Books S.A.

® and TM are trademarks of Harlequin Books S.A., used under license. Trademarks indicated with ® are registered in the United States Patent and Trademark Office, the Canadian Trade Marks Office and in other countries.

Visit Silhouette at www.eHarlequin.com

Printed in U.S.A.

For Michele Burdet of Switzerland, friend, shaman, healer and inspiration.... I cherish our friendship.

Dear Reader,

I'm proud to introduce Chief Warrant Officer Cam Anderson's story to you! For those of you who are following the Black Jaguar Squadron, the all-female helicopter team featured in my series MORGAN'S MERCENARIES: DESTINY'S WOMEN, you'll probably remember Cam from previous books. And even if you haven't met her yet, I'm sure you will love reading about her adventures, her challenges and her growth as an individual and a woman.

Cam is a combat pilot and a very good one at that. She's seen combat, had close calls, and, in her most harrowing mission, she crashed a helicopter after it was fired on and hit. She is still struggling to come to terms with this traumatic event when her commanding officer, Major Maya Stevenson, chooses her for an even more daunting mission: Maya asks Cam to become a commanding officer of a small contingent of Apache helicopters stationed in Mexico, just below the border with the U.S.

More than anything, Cam wants to impress her commanding officer—and she wants to atone for the mistakes she believes she made on her last mission. But she learns that it is one thing to be a combat helicopter pilot and completely another to be leader and manager of people—especially a squadron of male pilots, who don't want to be "bossed around" by a woman. Cam has her work cut out for her and then some! Will she make the grade? She wonders about that—and whether she should give her heart to one of those pilots, Chief Warrant Officer Gus Morales. Gus is too intriguing and charismatic to resist, and Cam finds herself in a battle to maintain her command—and keep her heart safe from being hurt again. Will she be able to salvage her honor on both fronts? Read on and find out!

Warmly,

Lindsay McKenna

Chapter 1

"Hey!" Wild Woman hissed as she stuck her head around the door of the ready room. "Have you heard yet, Cam?"

Cam halted her pacing and quit gnawing on her fingernails, which were almost nonexistent at this point. "Er, no...not yet." Turning toward the door, she watched as Jessica Merrill, U.S. Army CWO2, otherwise known as Wild Woman, entered the room, dressed in her close-fitting black flight uniform. "You got the duty?"

Cam had had flight duty for the last twenty-four hours and was waiting to be relieved by another crew.

Wrinkling her nose, Wild Woman said, "Yeah. Me and Snake are taking over from you." Hooking a thumb across her shoulder toward the door of the Quonset hut, which stood inside the massive cavern where the Black Jaguar Squadron had its base of operations, she added, "Snake'll be along any second now." Looking at her watch, she uttered darkly, "Geez, 0600 comes so early. What I'd give to have a day off and sleep in. No such thing as 'beauty sleep' around here, is there." She patted her cheek. "I'm still good-looking despite that handicap."

Chuckling, Cam nodded. Sitting down at the picnic table and picking up her cup of coffee, she said, "Yeah, I know what you mean. But you're right—we're such gorgeous girls we don't need beauty sleep."

Going to the coffee dispenser that sat on a dark green army-issue desk, Wild Woman laughed. "But isn't that why you volunteered for this new mission coming up, Cam. So you'd get to sleep in?"

"Oh, sure!" Cam snorted. Running her fingers through her shoulder-length reddish-chestnut hair, she muttered, "I'm on pins and needles. I don't think I'll get it."

"I saw Morgan Trayhern a few hours ago. He just flew in from Agua Caliente, piloted by Storm Queen." Grabbing a chipped white cup, Wild Woman poured herself some of the strong coffee. "He looked serious."

"Yeah," Cam said unhappily, "I saw him. He's with Major Stevenson and Major York, reviewing the short list of possible pilots for this mission." Shrugging, Cam watched her colleague walk confidently to the table and sit down opposite her. Jessica had short blond hair with a bright red streak dyed in it. Major Maya Stevenson, commanding officer of the BJS, allowed Wild Woman this unique expression of herself. It went well with her pilot handle, Cam thought with an inward smile. And all you needed to do was take one look at Jessica's square face and frosty blue eyes filled with feral intelligence to understand why she was one of the best Apache gunship pilots here at the squadron. She was competitive, rebellious, and never afraid to break rules and regulations over the skies of Peru or Bolivia when it came to stopping the drug trade.

"You'll get it," Wild Woman said confidently, sipping her coffee.

"I dunno," Cam muttered worriedly. She gnawed again on her index finger.

"You don't have any nails left, Cam."

Chuckling, Cam looked at her fingers, then at her friend. "You're right about that."

"You always do that when you're nervous—No Nails Tree Trimmer!" Jessica chortled.

"Tree Trimmer" was Cam's nickname. Every pilot got one after graduating from flight school. She'd earned hers by dropping the Huey helicopter she'd been flying into the jungle in Peru. Of course, at the time she was being shot at by a Kamov Black Shark helicopter, piloted by a Russian mercenary hired by a drug lord to shoot her out of the sky.

Feeling heat rush into her cheeks, Cam grinned. "I look forward to the day when I can earn a new and better handle."

Laughing huskily, Wild Woman turned her head as the creaky door to the ready room opened and closed. "Hey, Snake! My, don't you look bright-eyed and bushy-tailed, girl."

Snake glared at them as she entered the hut. Pushing her straight, dark brown hair off her shoulders, she headed for the coffee urn. "Shut up. I haven't had my java yet," she growled.

"And a dreary good morning to you, too," Cam murmured, a grin crawling across her mouth. "Depriving Snake of her coffee is like stepping on the rattles of her tail...."

"Yeah, and she bites," Jessica giggled. "Forget any hissing. This girl just sinks her fangs into you."

Cam saw that Vickey Mabrey—Snake—was dressed into her combat uniform, too. She was all set for her twenty-four-stint duty with Wild Woman. The Velcro fastening of her uniform collar was open at her throat, exposing the dark green cotton T-shirt she wore beneath. The body-fitting uniform, made of special fire-retardent materials, hugged her tall, lean figure.

"Both of you can it. Gawd, I need my coffee." And Vickey reached for the pot.

Cam grinned across the table at Wild Woman, who had a twisted, evil smile on her own face. "No one walking into this place could tell you two were the best of friends, could they?"

"Military friendships are like that—full of verve and content," Wild Woman murmured sagely, sipping her coffee.

"Humph," Snake said, pouring herself a mug of coffee.

"So, you're worried about getting this assignment, Cam? You're cut out for it, you know," Wild Woman stated.

Shrugging, she muttered, "I don't even know what the assignment *is,* so why am I sweating it?"

"Who's in the running?" Snake asked as she sauntered over and sat down at the end of the table near her friends. Stirring creamer into her coffee, she breathed in the rich scent as she lifted the cup to her lips.

"Storm Queen and Pele," Cam replied. She truly admired Pele—Lieutenant Mirella Gallardo, one of the first two women helicopter pilots in the Peruvian Army. Pele was the Hawaiian goddess of volcanoes, and Mirella had gotten the handle because of her hair-trigger temper and in-your-face attitude. Mirella was a take-no-prisoners kind of woman on the ground and in the air. She'd fought hard to become one of the first Peruvian women to fly helicopters and her competitiveness was legendary. Here at BJS, she was competent, aggressive and combative in the air—the exact qualities a gunship pilot needed in order to survive.

"Humph. You'll get it, Cam," Snake said, huddling possessively over the coffee, her long, thin fingers wrapped around the mug in a death grip.

"Yeah? Why?" Cam asked.

"Because it's your turn for something good to happen to you." A sly grin edged her full mouth. "I mean, there was nowhere to go but up after you gave that poor jungle a haircut with the runners of that Huey."

Wild Woman burst out in raucous laughter and slapped her knee. "Snake, you have deadly humor at 0600."

"Thanks, ladies," Cam growled good-naturedly. She saw a glimmer of humor dancing in Snake's narrowed green eyes. Vickey was half Navajo and half German—an unusual blend, Cam thought. She was quiet like her Indian father, and meticulous like her mother, a college professor of botany who hailed from Cologne. Snake's skin was a golden color, hinting at her mixed heritage. Cam had seen a photo of her friend's parents, and knew she favored her father physically. She had taken after him in many ways, from what Cam could tell. She was a good listener, but when she spoke, everyone stopped jabbering and paid attention.

In the air, Snake was a deadly gunship pilot. She was absolutely lethal and had no qualms about facing off with drug runners in a game of sky chicken, where whoever blinked first turned back. Snake never blinked. As she'd wisely pointed out one time, snakes don't blink at all. She was proud of her handle and lived up to it daily.

"How long have Maya and Morgan been confabbing?" Jessica asked, heading to the coffeepot for her second cup of coffee.

"At least an hour," Cam answered glumly.

"You don't even know what this mission is and you *want* it?" Snake wrinkled her nose and then shook her head. "That's why I didn't volunteer to be interviewed. I want to know going in what I'm volunteering for. Not after the fact."

Cam saw an evil grin spread across Snake's oval face. "You know the major wouldn't throw us to the wolves," she retorted. "I figured it would be fun to get out of here for a while. Three years is a long time."

"And leave us?" Wild Woman cried in a pitiful, dramatic voice as she poured more coffee into her cup. "I mean, we're *sisters!* You love us, Cam. You know you do! Hell, we've spent three years of our lives down here, hangin' out in this cave, chasin' bad guys together. We're bonded.''

"More like welded," Snake added dryly.

"Yeah, that, too. Thanks, Snake, that says it better." Wild Woman sat down and gave Cam a mock serious look. "You'd actually run out on us? Who says this new mission has any women on it? Look what Akiva got into," she exclaimed, referring to one of their colleagues. "She got chosen for that Gulf of Mexico black ops with Joe Calhoun, along with three enlisted women from BJS."

"That was a great mission," Cam said fervently. "I'd have given my right arm to take part."

"Well," Snake counseled in a soft, husky tone, "Akiva and Joe are doing well out there…now. At first it was rocky for Akiva, until she settled into her job as a C.O. Big difference, being just a pilot versus commanding officer of an operation, you know?"

"But," Wild Woman said, "she did it. She rose to the challenge."

"Do you think that because Akiva and Joe made it a success, another mission like that might be on the table?" Cam wondered.

"Don't count on it," Snake advised. "Maya isn't known to duplicate operations. She keeps things hot and lively. That way—" she grinned "—we don't grow bored around here."

"No one from personnel gave a peep about this covert mission," Jessica muttered with a frown, more to herself than to them. "I tried pumping Sergeant Prater the other day for info, but got nada. Nothing. She's buttoned up tighter than a clam about it. She works directly for Major Stevenson, so she knows what it's all about. But she ain't sharin'.''

Chuckling, Snake stated, "Prater's got more sense than you, then. She knows if she gossips about it to us, Maya will have her red head on a platter, pronto. She's smart to keep her mouth shut in front of the likes of you while you're nosin' around like a curious coyote.''

Wild Woman grinned. "Hey, I gave it the ol' college try, didn't I? I wasn't born to understand the word *no*.''

"I don't think I'll get it," Cam muttered, running her fingertips across the roughened surface of the table. "Storm Queen and Pele are both wonderful pilots.''

"You're always cutting yourself down, Cam. Don't you see yourself as equal to those two gals?" Snake demanded, her voice hardening.

Shrugging, Cam said in a painful whisper, "I guess not. I mean...after I deserted Maya out there in the jungle and left her to be captured by the druggies..." She sighed.

"Quit chewin' on that, will you?" Snake shook her head in disgust. Taking a rubber band out of the thigh pocket of her flight suit, she gathered up her straight hair and fastened it in a ponytail at the back of her head. "You made the *right* decision, Cam, not the wrong one. The Peruvian jungle is damned near impenetrable. You couldn't have carried Maya, wounded and unconscious, anywhere. You had to escape.''

"Yeah," Wild Woman interjected, "and if you hadn't gone to get help, how would we have known what really happened? It was only when Major York found you and got you back here that we knew Maya had been captured.''

''Not that Maya needed any rescuing,'' Snake chuckled darkly. ''She took care of that drug lord dude right and proper. Buried the bastard in the Canyon of Death. Yeah, that was a right fine burial ground for the likes of him.''

''Well, we got there in the nick of time,'' Wild Woman said.

Sighing, Cam slowly got up. ''I need a third cup of coffee like a hole in my head,'' she muttered unhappily, heading for the dispenser along the wall, ''but I'm in dire need today....''

''After two cups we can't scrape you off the ceiling,'' Snake complained. ''You're maxing out at three.''

''High-wire act, Cam the Tree Trimmer.''

''Funny, girls. Very funny...''

The door to the Quonset hut opened. ''Chief Anderson?''

Jumping as her name was called, Cam whirled around. Sergeant Prater, dressed in her dark green cammies, stood expectant in the doorway, a serious look on her freckled face.

''Yeah?''

''Major Stevenson wants to see you, ma'am.''

''Er, thanks...yeah, I'll be right there, Sergeant. Thank you.''

Prater smiled and nodded. ''Yes, ma'am.'' The door closed.

''Ohh,'' Wild Woman teased, ''you're gonna get this mission, I got that feelin'!''

Frowning, Cam set her empty cup on the counter. "Maybe, maybe not. Maybe the major is callin' me in to tell me Pele or Storm Queen got it, instead."

"You're such a die-hard pessimist," Snake groaned. "Gawd, gimme another cup of coffee...." Gracefully she unwound herself from the chair, a grin lurking at the corners of her mouth.

"You think?" Cam asked, heading for the door. "That I got it?"

Waving her hand, Wild Woman chortled. "Oh, honey, you're such a widget at times! My gut says yes. What does yours say, Snake?"

"That I need another cup of java."

Laughing, Cam headed out the door and waved goodbye to them. "I hope you two have a quiet shift."

"Oh, yeah, right. That's just what I want," Snake growled.

"I'm bored already," Wild Woman griped. "Don't wish that on us, Cam!"

"Okay, ladies, may the Sharks come out and hunt your butts, then. See you later! I'll let you know what happens!" Cam couldn't keep the hope out of her voice. Closing the door, she turned to her right and hurried across the black lava floor of the cave. All around her, the noise of women's voices as well as the clang of tools being used on the Apaches in the rear of the cave echoed and reechoed.

Wiping her mouth in a nervous gesture, Cam barely paid attention to the activity on the wide lip of the cave, their landing and takeoff point. At this time of morning the clouds were thick, hiding the cave entrance. The sun hadn't come up yet so the fog hadn't burned off. Hurrying across the mammoth cave complex to the two-story headquarters building on the other side, Cam felt her heart racing. Had she gotten the secret mission? Had Jenny Wright, the psychologist who worked for Perseus and who had interviewed her awhile back, chosen her to head this one up? Cam hoped so with all her heart and soul. Trying not to run, she hurried toward the steel grate stairs that wound up to the second floor of H.Q., where Major Maya Stevenson, her boss and commanding officer, had her office.

More than anything in the world, Cam wanted this mission. She *had* to prove to Maya that she was worthy, that she could be counted on not to run from a situation, as she'd run from the crash, leaving her superior behind to be captured.

Wiping her mouth again, she rapidly climbed the steps two at a time, her heavy black boots shaking the staircase in the process. She entered the door at the top, which led to a long passageway lined with open doors. The army personnel who ran the black ops base—those in charge of communications and planning—were all here. Cam hurried down the hall, nodding to various enlisted women as they came and went from their offices.

Cam headed to the last door on the right, Maya's office. The C.O. was a woman of incredible ability and leadership. Many times Cam wished she had some of the confidence and wisdom her boss had. To Cam, Maya was a role model, someone she nearly worshipped. Though she'd been born in Brazil, Maya had been adopted by an American colonel and his wife early in her life, and had grown up in the United

States. But rumor had it that Maya had a very mysterious background. Even her name suggested the mystery inherent in her birth, and pilots of the Black Jaguar Squadron were always whispering about her almost uncanny powers and abilities.

Maya had single-handedly fashioned this black ops out of nothing. She had been one of the first women to take Apache helicopter training at Fort Rucker, Alabama, getting badly burned by gender prejudice in the process. Afterward, she had contacted her father, a U.S. Army general by that time, and gotten him to help her set up the BJS base—a covert operation dedicated to stopping cocaine shipments from leaving Peru, one of the main producers of the drug. He'd agreed, and the rest was history. Now Maya was C.O. of the all-female Black Jaguar Squadron.

Cam had joined Maya when she'd graduated from the next class at Fort Rucker, volunteering to come down to the all-woman base. She'd never for a second regretted her decision.

Halting at Maya's door, which was open as usual—part of her open-door policy so that anyone who needed to could see her—Cam nervously smoothed the fabric of her black uniform. Then she knocked briefly. "Major Stevenson? You sent for me?"

Maya lifted her head from her desk, which was covered with paperwork. "Yes, come in, Cam."

Entering, Cam stood at attention. "Reporting as ordered, ma'am."

"At ease, Cam. Have a seat." Maya gestured toward a chair in front of the desk. "Oh…close the door?"

Feeling her heartbeat speed up, Cam gulped, did an

about-face and closed it. Only rarely did Maya ask that her door be closed. It meant she was going to say something that she didn't want to be overheard. Was she going to announce that Cam wasn't getting the mission? Dying inwardly, Cam kept her expression carefully neutral and sat down gingerly in the chair. Placing her hands on her thighs, she waited, holding her breath as Maya placed a bunch of signed orders into her out basket for Sergeant Prater to distribute.

Smiling warmly, Maya set her pen aside and folded her hands in front of her. "I'm sure it hasn't escaped your eyes or ears that Morgan Trayhern flew in this morning?"

Grinning a little and feeling like a kid caught with her hand in the cookie jar, Cam said, "No, ma'am, it hadn't escaped me."

"You know why he's here?"

"I think so. The new mission is on the table?"

"Very good," Maya murmured. "I've been in conference with Mr. Trayhern and Major York about it."

Cam blinked. Maya's large, emerald-green eyes glimmered with mirth. "Yes, ma'am?"

"You know," she said, pulling a few files off a teetering stack to her right and placing them in front of her, "that three of you were interviewed by Jenny Wright, the Perseus psychologist, for this mission?"

"Yes, Storm Queen and Pele were interviewed, too."

"Right." Maya slowly opened Cam's file, revealing a color photo of her stapled on the left side. "We've reviewed everything, Cam. I know none of you knew what the mission was about, and that was done on purpose. Ms. Wright knew the schematic on it, and conferred with Morgan and myself about the three of you. You were all good, strong candidates for the position.''

Heart sinking, Cam knotted her hands on her thighs. Maya was going to tell her she hadn't gotten the mission. Straightening her spine, she tried to hide her disappointment. It was so important to her to have Maya look upon her as trustworthy once more. Since that horrific crash landing, Maya had never again flown with Cam. Which was unusual, because she routinely flew missions with all her pilots from time to time.

Lifting her head, she pinned Cam with her gaze and smiled. ''We've chosen you to head up this mission, Cam. We felt you were the best qualified for it. Congratulations.'' Maya rose and extended her hand.

Blinking, Cam stared at her superior. Then she leaped to her feet and thrust out her own hand.

''Thanks, Major! Thanks so much! You have no idea what this means to me,'' she whispered, her voice raspy with sudden, unexpected tears. Cam quickly pushed them away by taking several gulping swallows. Pumping Maya's hand rapidly, she continued, ''You won't regret your decision, ma'am. I *promise* you you won't. Thanks for the chance…the opportunity… I won't fail you this time. I swear I won't.…''

Easing her hand away, Maya stood there looking at Cam. The pilot's face glowed with relief, with joy. Her green eyes swam with tears she was desperately trying to force back. Maya knew Cam needed to prove herself again.

"Listen to me, Cam," she murmured gently, "this mission is not about you proving yourself to me or anyone else. If I didn't think you had what it took in the first place, I'd have chosen someone else, so let's get over that hurdle, okay?"

Choking back her tears, which she knew were not appropriate, Cam nodded. "Yes, ma'am. I understand." Her heart was soaring. She felt giddy, almost dizzy, and so relieved. She saw respect in Maya's eyes, sincerity in her expression, and Cam was so surprised and delighted she could barely sit still in the chair. Opening and closing her hands, she whispered, "Thanks for letting me do this. It means so much to me...."

"I know it does," Maya said gently. Giving her a brief smile, she looked down at a red-and-white-striped folder labeled Top Secret. Picking it up, she handed the folder across the desk to Cam. "Here's your mission. Everything you'll need to know."

Feeling like an exuberant puppy, Cam laid the file in her lap and opened it with trembling hands. Immediately the text blurred before her eyes, and she self-consciously wiped away the tears. She didn't dare cry in front of Maya. Not now. Cam had to show her C.O. that she was up for this assignment, no matter what it entailed.

"This mission is going to be the hardest one you've ever said yes to," Maya warned in a dark tone. "Let's go to the briefing room. Morgan Trayhern is waiting to talk to you about it."

Chapter 2

"Cam, I want you to meet Morgan Trayhern. He owns Perseus, a top secret company that interfaces with the CIA and many other agencies around the world."

Cam smiled and gripped Morgan's hand. "Mr. Trayhern, this is an *honor*," she said, meeting his warm blue gaze and his smile. Morgan Trayhern was a living legend. He had been a marine captain in the closing days of the Vietnam War. Since then, he had risen to heady heights within the secret, black operations world by his success with his covert agency, which provided much-needed assistance to democratic countries all over the world. He had a knack for employing some of the best men and women from the military as mercenaries to help people in trouble. And now Cam was gripping his firm, powerful hand. She was giddy with excitement.

"It's a pleasure to meet you, Cam," Morgan said, releasing her hand. "And congratulations on being chosen for this mission. Have a seat." He gestured toward a row of chairs that faced a blank white wall.

"Yes, sir."

Maya sat next to Cam. She handed her a folder that had been sitting on the table in front of them. "You'll need this, too. Morgan? You ready?"

"Yep." Moving to one end of the table, he flipped open a laptop computer and pushed a button. The wall became a viewing screen for a slide presentation.

Cam's heart raced with excitement. She had gotten the mission! She'd been chosen! Joy warred with anxiety within her chest. More than anything, she wanted to prove that she was worthy of her C.O.'s belief and trust in her. Compressing her lips, she listened as Morgan's low, deep voice filled the small room.

"Major Stevenson has given you two files," he said. "The first is an overview of the mission. The second has photos, biographies and fitness reports of the three Apache pilots you're going to be responsible for training in interdiction in northern Mexico."

"Mexico?" Cam said, looking at Maya.

"Yeah, northern Mexico," she repeated with a smile. "Right on the border with California. Lucky you. Maybe when things iron out, you can head to San Diego and kick up your heels. Do a little partying in your spare time." Maya knew that many of the BJS pilots longed to go back to the U.S. from time to time. Living in the humid Peruvian jungle year in and year out, in constant combat mode, took a heavy toll on each of them. Maya started to enforce a thirty-day vacation for her pilots each year so they wouldn't get too homesick. Three years of duty with no down-time wasn't good.

Looking at Cam's face, lit up now with a glow of pleasure, Maya smiled. "And your home state of Oregon isn't that far from there," she added, reading her mind.

"I know!" Cam exclaimed happily. She gripped the open folder on her lap. "It's *real* close!"

"Well, first things first. Congratulations, you're going to be the commanding officer of this mission, so who knows? When things are quiet, you might put one of your other pilots—your executive officer probably—in charge, and you can take off for a weekend and visit your family in Oregon. Anything is possible once you get this mission on track."

Morgan smiled. "Major Stevenson, who is used to commanding, makes this sound easy, Cam. Leading is the hardest work you'll ever learn how to do."

"Yes, sir," Cam said, looking at him. Morgan was tall and broad-shouldered. He wore civilian clothes—charcoal-gray slacks, hiking boots, a red polo shirt. His black hair was cut military short, the silver at his temples lending his handsome face a frame for those lively blue eyes that didn't miss a thing. She smiled at him as he cocked his head and gazed at her almost as if he were looking through her. Ordinarily, Cam would have felt invaded, uncomfortable, but she didn't now. Maya had that same ability, and Cam never felt threatened by it, either. Maybe good leaders had that quality of being able to look into the heart and mind of their people in a nurturing way, to see what they were made of.

"You said 'commanding officer'?" Cam asked in surprise.

"Yes, that's you," Morgan murmured with a smile. He pressed a button on the laptop. "You may recognize this place. It's Tijuana, Mexico—a huge, sprawling city on the U.S. border, right across from San Diego. This is where you're going." He pressed the button again.

"There's a small Mexican Air Force base just beyond the southern outskirts of Tijuana. Two Apache Longbow helicopters are going to be flown in from the States for your use. Your mission, Cam, is to be C.O. for a small contingent of Mexican helicopter pilots who are just now graduating from flight school at Fort Rucker."

Her brows rose in surprise, but she tamped down her desire to ask questions.

"Two of the three pilots are Mexican nationals. The third—" Morgan pressed the button "—has dual citizenship, from the USA and Mexico. He's Chief Warrant Officer Gustavo Phillipe Morales."

Cam looked up as a color slide flashed across the wall. The man who stared back at her made her heart thump hard. About six feet tall, medium-boned and athletic, he was dressed in a dark green, one-piece army flight uniform. Looking deadly serious, he stood in front of an olive-green Apache helicopter, his helmet dangling loosely from his long, tanned fingers.

Gulping, Cam quickly perused the man's photo. There was something arresting, beckoning and frightening about him, all at the same time. His face was square, his jaw set and his mouth thinned into a hard, single line. Thick, straight brows sat over his cinnamon-colored eyes. It was his eyes, with their huge black pupils, that drew Cam the most. The eyes of a predator. But then, she reminded herself, all gunship pilots had to have that "look." If they didn't, they weren't going to cut it in combat. Morales's eyes had that gleam of a hunter looking for its prey.

Her pulse raced momentarily. His black hair was cut short, with a few rebellious straight strands dipping over his broad, unwrinkled brow. With his high cheekbones and hawklike nose, he definitely had the face of an Indian, and he reminded Cam of an Incan god she had seen carved in stone on some ancient frieze somewhere. Gustavo Morales had sharp angles and rough edges, giving Cam the impression that he'd been around the block and taken a lot of beatings, but learned from each experience. She saw confidence and pride radiating from him. Just the way Morales stood, with one hand propped on his narrow hip, his helmet in the other, spoke of his certainty about himself and his abilities.

"Warrant Morales," Morgan intoned, "is U.S. Army, Cam. Though his mother was Yaqui Indian, from northern Mexico, his father is a colonel in the U.S. Army, currently stationed in Afghanistan with a top secret contingent of Apache pilots working behind the lines to hunt down the Taliban."

"They're over there?"

Morgan nodded grimly. "Yes. But that piece of info goes nowhere."

"Of course not, sir."

"You should consider Morales as executive officer material, Cam. He's twenty-five years old, and he's been in the army for four years. He's an ace helo pilot—he grew up flying with his dad. He speaks Spanish as fluently as you do. I believe, as does Major Stevenson, that he'll be a key player in making this mission work, even though you're in charge.''

"How so, sir?''

"Let's put it delicately, Cam,'' Morgan said, giving her a droll look. "The other two officers, both lieutenants with the Mexican Air Force, are...well, for lack of a better word, somewhat biased about women having a lead role. In the Mexican military, there are no women combat pilots.''

"These two Mexican pilots are supposed to be the cream of the crop,'' Maya added. "At least, that's what their general is telling us.''

Morgan pressed the button and their pictures were projected on the wall.

"Lieutenants Antonio Zaragoza and Luis Dominguez did okay at Fort Rucker and learned to fly the Apache,'' Maya assured her.

"But,'' Morgan warned, "these men come from a country where most women are still kept barefoot and pregnant. The only way they relate to females is as mothers and lovers.''

"Yeah,'' Maya growled. "So you've got your work cut out for you, Cam. These two dudes are not going to want to accept you as C.O. or even listen to your wise counsel, no matter how much more experienced you are as a combat pilot.''

"I see....'' Cam murmured. "And Warrant Morales? He's been raised in a gender-neutral environment, where women are accepted in leadership roles?''

"Yes,'' Morgan said. "Which is one of the many

reasons Chief Morales was chosen for this duty. He isn't aware of *why* he was chosen. He'll find that out from you once you arrive at the base in Tijuana.''

''Yaqui Indians,'' Maya told her, ''have a matriarchal society, and women are considered equal to men. Morales has been steeped in a tradition where women are accepted as being just as strong, smart and effective as any male.''

''That's good,'' Cam said, relieved.

''You're going to have your hands full,'' Morgan warned her gravely. ''These are green students who have just learned the basics of day and night flying techniques. They know nothing of interdiction duties, especially in the dark. That's where you come in. We want you to build a schooling program around them, starting with day flights, and then working in night operations. We all know night flying is more dangerous, but unfortunately, the president of Mexico does *not* want Apaches flying around where people can see them. He's afraid it will scare the populace.''

''So,'' Maya said, pointing to the screen as a picture of high-desert terrain was shown, ''during the day, you're going to fly your boys into the hills along the Baja coastline and out over the Pacific. There're plenty of mountains and hills for you to play hide 'n seek in, to train them on the finer points of interdiction.''

''And then you'll train them in on night interdiction, once they've got the basics and you're confident of their skills,'' Morgan said.

''So bottom line, I'm running an advanced interdiction flight school.''

''Yes,'' Morgan said. ''You're going to create that

template. And if you're successful, we'll take on other Mexican Air Force pilots, train them at Fort Rucker and then get them flying interdiction in their own country, instead of U.S. pilots always putting their lives on the line to do it.''

"Sounds like a good plan to me," Cam said. She was in awe that they'd choose her for such a mission. Still, fear threaded through her. Could she do it? She would have to. Never had Cam wanted anything more than this. It was a plum—a huge one. And if she was successful, Maya would surely forgive her past error....

Her C.O. was watching her with an assessing expression on her face, Cam noted. "It's a wonderful opportunity," Maya said, "but I think this is going to be the roughest mission you've ever agreed to, Cam. Those Mexican pilots aren't going to sit still for your mother hen ways." She smiled slightly. "You're a nester, a nurturer by nature, Cam—you appear so warm and easygoing, even though inside there's a jaguar. You're just as competitive and cool as any of the other women pilots who fly the Apache, but you come across as soft. You can't let that happen on this mission. Those pilots see soft and they'll eat you alive."

Nodding, Cam gulped and said, "I understand."

"Down here," Maya said, "we love your mother hen ways. You're the one who makes chicken soup if one of us gets a cold or the flu. You're the one who sits down and listens when someone has a problem and needs to talk it out. You have a natural instinct for caring for others."

"Those are all good attributes in a leader," Morgan

said quietly. "But you lack the management skills, the firmness and decisiveness setting required in a leader. But you can develop those abilities."

Nodding, Cam said, "I understand, sir. I'll do my best to learn to be tough."

"Well," Maya said, cocking an eyebrow, "you won't have much time or space to do it in, Cam. I'm hoping Morales will like you, side with you and act as a natural buffer between you and those two dudes who are going to rain hell on your head every day." Her mouth quirked. "I've experienced more than my fair share of those redneck, good-ole-boy attitudes in the past. I don't look forward to you cutting your teeth on them, but under the circumstances, they are the cloth we have to work with. That's the way it is."

"I'll handle it, Maya. I swear I will."

"Oh," Morgan said, chuckling, "you'll be swearing, all right. Apache pilots aren't the tamest people to begin with. They're edgy, alert, tense and combative by nature. We're all hoping that Chief Morales will be the great leveler here between you and the others."

"Because," Maya predicted grimly, "if he isn't, it's going to be three to one—them against you—and this mission could grind to a halt in a hurry."

"I won't let it happen," Cam promised fervently. She gave them a grateful look. "I know it's going to be a challenge. But I know I can do it. Just let me have the chance…."

"You've got the chance," Morgan murmured. He flipped off the projection program and shut down the laptop. Walking to the other end of the table, he picked up an object and handed it to Cam.

"This is going to be your most precious posses-
sion, Cam. It's an iridium satellite cell phone. There
are sixteen satellites circling the globe, and this phone
is hooked up to them. You can call from anywhere
in the world and reach someone at the other end."

Cam examined the slender but heavy device.
"Okay..."

Maya got up. "The iridium is a very expensive toy,
but one you're going to need."

Cam looked up in confusion as Maya came and
stood in front of her, with Morgan at her shoulder.
"Why?"

"Because if you need help, you can call Morgan
or myself. We suspect you're going to need advice
from time to time, and with that phone you can reach
us."

"Good leaders ask for help when they get their
backs to the wall," Morgan told her. "Good leaders
are forged in the fires of hell, they aren't born. You've
not had the privilege of college level management
courses, Cam. We're throwing you into this mission
without any background education. Being a good pilot is one thing. Being a leader is a whole other ball
game."

Nodding, Cam murmured, "I realize that from talking to Akiva."

Maya smiled. "Yes, Akiva became C.O. of a covert black ops base on the Gulf of Mexico, and she
found out about it the hard way, too."

"She did it, though," Cam said firmly. "And so
will I." She held up the phone and said, "I'll be
calling often."

Grinning, Morgan patted Cam's shoulder. "Excellent. That's what we want to hear. No one knows everything. If I don't miss my guess, Morales will be your ace in the hole. Use his knowledge and listen to him, too. Take what he says under consideration.''

''Cam's a good listener. She always has been,'' Maya murmured.

''We're throwing you to the wolves,'' Morgan said worriedly. ''You're a helluva good Apache pilot, Cam. You're the best. The Black Jaguar Squadron has more time in grade in drug interdiction efforts than any other aviation group in history. That's why you're being chosen to run this mission—because of your three years of hard-earned experience.''

''She's still alive. That says it all.''

Cam grinned up at Maya. ''Yes, ma'am, you taught us well.''

''Take that training up north, Cam, and use it to help educate these pilots.''

''I will,'' she promised, a catch in her voice.

''I only hope,'' Morgan said, ''that when you meet these macho Mexican pilots, they don't think you're breakfast, to be eaten alive.''

Rising, Cam grinned. ''Mr. Trayhern, I may *look* like a cream puff, but in here—'' she pointed to her heart ''—I'm a black jaguar. They just don't know it yet.''

Chapter 3

"I can't believe they're sending a *woman* to teach us," Lieutenant Antonio Zaragoza muttered, his long legs stretched out in front of the door to the barracks room where they waited for their C.O. to arrive.

Gus Morales, who stood at the window, peering through the venetian blinds, glanced over his shoulder at his schoolmate, who sulked like a petulant child. Zaragoza was five foot nine inches tall, only average height for a helo pilot. He made up for his lack of stature by being arrogant and brazen. Lifting his mouth in the ghost of a smile, Gus said, "I think it's ironic."

Lieutenant Luis Dominguez, who sat at the table smoking a cigarette, twisted to look in Morales's direction. "I think it stinks." He flipped ashes into the ashtray in front of him.

Chuckling, Gus looked at the two Mexican Air

Force pilots, who, like him, were dressed in dark green, single-piece flight uniforms. Each of them had the Mexican flag sewn onto his right shoulder. On his own uniform, Gus had the American flag, reflecting the fact that he was in the U.S. Army.

"They want us to fail," Zaragoza said flatly, his black brows dipping, his arms wrapped across his chest in defiance. Staring down at his highly polished black flight boots, which blocked the entranceway, he glowered. "Women have nothing to teach men!"

"*Sí*," Luis agreed. "Their place is in bed, with us."

"Yes, they are good for pleasure," Antonio stated darkly. "But not as Apache instructor pilots, teaching us the finer points of drug flight interdiction."

"Where I come from," Gus told them lightly, a cockeyed grin on his face, "women are not only teachers, but equals. I guess you two need to square away your attitudes on that one. Otherwise, you won't learn a thing from Chief Anderson."

Snorting vehemently, Luis took a deep drag of his cigarette, then blew the smoke out—an eloquent, if silent, reply.

Gus turned and looked out the window again. He and the others were on the second floor of the barracks, waiting for their new commanding officer, C.R. Anderson. They'd been informed she was an Apache gunship pilot who had been on duty in Peru for three years, flying drug interdiction on a black ops combat mission. That's all they knew. He was curious. And anxious to learn what she knew. At Fort Rucker, they were given basic Apache training, but time did not allow for them to learn the finer points of certain types of missions, such as drug interdiction.

Outside, the air base was quiet. It was small in comparison to other Mexican military bases. Gus saw two dark green Boeing Apache Longbow helicopters, their blades tethered, sitting in the revetment area, waiting like they were. Hungry to get in the air again, to feel the power and surge of the world's most lethal and deadly gunship, Gus shifted position. He was eager to get this show on the road.

"I don't see why our *presidente* would allow us to be taught by a mere woman," Antonio drawled in frustration. "This is mano a mano—hand to hand fighting in the air. No woman can fly a combat helicopter."

"Women in the U.S. Navy and Air Force fly fighter jets all the time," Gus reminded him. "And they're just as good, some of them better, than their male counterparts. I don't see the difference."

Luis glared at him. "You wouldn't. You're still tied to your mamacita's apron strings, amigo." He chuckled indulgently.

Gus allowed the insult to slide off his broad shoulders. He knew both pilots well enough from their time at Fort Rucker. Both used to bluster and fluff their feathers like bantam roosters when the flight instructors at Fort Rucker challenged them on their lazy attitudes toward flying. In Gus's opinion, neither one really had the competitiveness needed, that primal urge, to hunt down sky predators. Both pilots came from rich families. Zaragoza came from new money, his father being quite a phenomenon in the computer world. Dominguez's father, from old money, was mayor of Placido, a suburb of Mexico City.

His colleagues' condescending attitude throughout flight school had been amazing to Gus. And instead of making them buckle down and do the work, the U.S. Army instructors had let these two pilots slide, not pushing them to work to their potential. Morales figured it had to do with politics and the fact that they were "foreign exchange" pilots that they didn't get their chops busted like the rest of the class did.

Looking down at his watch, he saw that it was nearly 1400, or 2:00 p.m. Chief Anderson was due to arrive at their newly designated H.Q.—this small room on the second floor of the only barracks at the base—momentarily. None of them knew how she would arrive. Smiling to himself, Gus wondered obliquely if she'd ride in on an Apache in a thunderous display of her power and skill. Probably not. The president of Mexico didn't want the Apaches seen by the local people, for fear it would frighten them. The helos were lethal looking monsters, for sure, decked out with an awesome array of weapons that included rockets, a cannon and missiles.

His mind wandered back to C.R. Anderson. What did she look like? How old was she? If she'd been flying drug interdiction in an Apache for three years, and was a CWO2, she was most likely around twenty-five or twenty-six, like himself. Was she married? Did she have children? What was her husband like? What events in her life had shaped her, to make her what she was today?

Gus laughed at himself, and at his curiosity, which often got him into trouble. He enjoyed people, enjoyed figuring out how and why they worked the way they did. He glanced at his cohorts, who thought they were the best Apache pilots in the world—despite the fact that they'd just graduated from school, at the bottom of their class with barely passing grades. Gus thought the instructors must have padded their grades to pass them, so as not to embarrass the Mexican military. It would have been better if two far more hungry, less rich applicants had been selected. Hunger made a person want to prove himself in the eyes of his peers. These two had everything money could buy and wore their considerable egos like royal coats to make up for what they didn't have internally.

Sooner or later, Gus felt, they would be exposed. During training, neither had had that competitive zeal that characterized the other Apache gunship students. When he sat in the seat of an Apache, he felt like a hungry jaguar on the prowl looking for his quarry. That was the way it should be. Gus found himself wondering if Chief Anderson was the same.

The door to the rear of the barracks, just down the hall, opened and closed.

Gus looked at his watch. He gazed at the other two pilots, who lifted their heads to listen. "Fourteen hundred hours, guys. That's her. Our new C.O., Chief Anderson."

"Humph," Luis snorted, "no woman is *ever* on time."

"Not the ones you know," Gus said, barely able to hold back a smile. He pinned his gaze on the olive-green-painted door. Any second now she would come through it.

"It's just a soldier entering the barracks," Antonio said in a bored tone, waving his hand languidly.

The door opened.

Gus immediately came to attention, his arms at his side—standard procedure when a C.O. entered. He saw with shock that neither of his fellow pilots moved.

Cam Anderson stood in the doorway. The first thing she saw was a thick, choking cloud of cigarette smoke. The second thing that struck her was the malevolent stares of the two pilots sitting before her. Heart pounding, she kept her face carefully arranged. Determined to learn how to be a good leader, Cam had decided to let Maya Stevenson, her C.O., be her role model. Maya never looked harried, pressed or anxious. She walked with a confident, quiet and commanding presence that automatically demanded respect. She never raised her voice, but no one mistook that as a sign that she didn't mean exactly what she said. At all costs, Cam was going to try to be like Maya and not melt into her usual warm, motherly self.

Her gaze snapped from the pilot whose legs barred her way to the one smoking at the table, his dark brown eyes alive with distaste—for her. Lastly, Cam looked across the room. The man standing at attention at the window wore an American flag on the right sleeve of his flight uniform. That was Chief Morales. He knew that when a C.O. entered, one came to attention until told otherwise.

Realizing with a sinking heart that her career as a leader could be over right now depending on how she handled this insubordination by the Mexican pilots, Cam allowed the anger she felt to flow through her.

"Lieutenant—" she peered down at the pilot whose feet barred her path "—Zaragoza. I know the Mexican military has different protocols, but I do believe one of them requires that you stand at attention when your commanding officer enters the room. Get off your butt and on your feet, mister. Right now."

Gus choked back a laugh as Zaragoza's head snapped toward the woman. Gus saw the firm, quiet look on her oval face. Even though her thick, shoulder-length chestnut red hair gave her the look of an angel, he saw the devil in her narrowed green eyes which were now focused like a laser on the hapless pilot.

"Get up, Lieutenant. And if you can't make it to your feet, then crawl out of here and get out of my sight forever. Because that tells me you really aren't serious about training for drug interdiction."

Cam swallowed hard. She'd never been so brazen before, but her career depended upon it. Would Maya have said the same thing? Would she have handled this situation differently? Cam wavered inwardly, but refused to show her fear and indecision.

Zaragoza slowly retracted his legs and stood up in a semblance of attention, his eyes ahead, staring at the light green wall opposite.

Cam fixed her gaze on the second pilot, who was grinning down at the table, cigarette in hand. He had a lean, narrow face, short black hair, thick brows and a smirk across his full lips.

"And you...Lieutenant—" she peered at the leather patch sewn above the left pocket of his flight suit "—Dominguez. This is a nonsmoking zone. It will always be a nonsmoking zone, from here on out. Put out the butt, mister, and come to attention.''

Lazily, Luis smashed out his cigarette in the glass ashtray. The smirk never left his features as he pushed back the chair and got to his feet.

They thought this was a game, Cam realized with a sinking feeling. The only pilot here who had shown respect was the U.S. Army chief.

''With your permission, ma'am,'' Gus said, ''I'll open the window to let in fresh air?''

''Good idea, Chief Morales. At ease.'' Cam looked at the two Mexican pilots. ''Sit down at the table, gentlemen. We have business to take care of.''

Turning, Gus drew up the venetian blind and forced open the heavily painted window sash. He saw that Chief Anderson had left the door open on purpose, to create enough of a draft to get the heavy smoke out of the room. Walking to the green metal table, he sat at her right elbow.

Cam forced herself not to appear nervous. She told herself to slow down, to take her time. Never mind that she had jet lag, or that she hadn't slept in the last twenty-four hours because she was so anxious about this assignment. Never mind that two of the pilots obviously resented her and were barely giving her the respect the situation demanded. Opening her briefcase, she set several folders and a notepad on the table.

She noticed that Chief Morales took a pad from the right pocket of his flight suit and pulled out a pen from his left breast pocket. The other two pilots sat back, arms crossed, watching her with obvious distaste. Cam swallowed hard. Her throat felt dry, as if it was going to close up. She had to continue this charade and make them think she was in charge.

Taking a pen from her own flight suit pocket, Cam opened the top file. "First order of business is to ask each of you about your flight experience," she told them.

"You've got our personnel jacket," Luis drawled, his voice condescending. "Haven't you read it?"

Antonio snickered.

Cam glared at them. "Lieutenant Dominguez, tell me the extent of your flight experience with helicopters."

Shrugging nonchalantly, he said in a bored tone, "I joined the Mexican Air Force because it is a tradition in my family. I went through flight school and was assigned to helicopters."

"How many hours have you flown?"

"Two hundred."

Cam turned to the other pilot. "And you, mister?"

Chuckling, Zaragoza said, "Only two hundred hours, Luis?" He shook his head mockingly.

"Forget him," Cam ordered tightly. "I'm interested in your hours, mister."

"Four hundred." Antonio nearly spat the words.

"And how did you earn them?" Cam asked, jotting down the information on her yellow legal pad.

"I started flying helos when I was seventeen years old."

"And why did you join the Mexican Air Force?"

Glowering at her, Antonio said, "Not that it's any of your business, *señorita* or *señora,* but I *like* to fly."

"Mister, you will address me as either Chief Anderson or ma'am. Got it?"

"Yes."

"Yes, what?"

Antonio's jaw clenched. He held Cam's narrowed gaze.

"If you can't say it, mister, get out of this room and don't bother coming back."

His eyes flared with surprise. "You cannot threaten me—"

Cam leaned forward, her elbows on the table. "It's not a threat, mister. It's a *promise*. Now, you make up your mind here and now. Either go by strict military protocol from this moment forward or get up and get out of here. *Comprende?*"

Anger surged through Luis. How dare this slut of a woman make such a threat to him? "This—this is an insult! Do you know who I am?"

Cam gave him an icy smile. "Yeah, a pilot in a helluva lotta trouble with me and his superiors if he doesn't square away right now."

Silence fell in the room. Luis slanted a glance toward Gus, who was sitting there relaxed, hands on the table. He had a poker face, but Luis could see the laughter in his cinnamon-colored eyes. He knew Morales was laughing at him. That stung even more. Nostrils flaring, he jerked his gaze back to the woman who sat across from him.

"Your call," Cam told him quietly. "Do it right or get the hell out of my sight, Mr. Dominguez. I don't think your father will be very proud to learn that you can't carry out simple military protocol, do you?"

Cam's heart was thundering in her chest. She knew this was high-stakes poker. And she knew she held the cards to Luis's career. If, indeed, he was in the Mexican Air Force to fulfill a family obligation, the last thing he would want was a dark blot on the family record by being thrown out of the U.S. Army's Apache program—by a woman, no less. That would be an insult he would never live down, and she knew it. Cam was prepared to do just that, however. She'd get rid of any pilot who didn't want to play by strict military rules.

Grinding his teeth, Luis looked for help from his friend, Antonio. The unhappy grimace on his friend's face, the anger banked in his dark eyes, indicated he felt similarly. Yet he obviously didn't want to be kicked out of the program, either.

"You do not have that authority over me!" Luis snarled.

Cam reached down into her briefcase, located another file and opened it before her. Lifting out some papers, she turned them around so that Luis could read the top.

"I'm sure you recognize this, Mr. Dominguez. It's a set of orders. All I have to do to reassign you is fill in this blank—" she pointed to the page "—and sign my name down here, at the bottom. Now, I'll be more than happy to do that for you. There's a lot of good pilots who didn't get this mission, and who want it a lot more than you do, apparently. So which is it? You want me to fill you out a new set of orders, sending you back to your superior? Or do you want to stay with us? Your call, mister. Just make it in a hurry, because I don't have time to play games here."

"You cannot do this!" Luis shouted, balling his hands into fists beneath the table.

"Try me. I'd love to sign you off, mister. I don't need sulky little boys on my team. I need mature men who are ready to be responsible, who are hungry to fly and who want to go after the real bad guys. You want to target someone in your gun sights, you aim at them, not me. Is that understood?"

Wiping his wrinkled brow, Luis cast a desperate glance toward Antonio. His friend stared straight ahead and refused to look at him. Jerking a look at Morales, Luis saw the same hint of laughter in the warrant's eyes. He thought this was funny! Angrily, Luis swung his gaze back to the C.O.

"I'm staying."

"No, mister, you will say 'Chief Anderson, I'd like to stay with the team. Please?'"

Breathing hard, Luis repeated the words through gritted teeth. He watched with relief as Anderson put the order back in the file and the file back in the briefcase.

"Very good, Mr. Dominguez. Thank you for the information on your flight background."

Cam turned to the last pilot. Her heart speeded up, but not out of fear. It was something else—some other feeling that emerged so quickly under the tense circumstances that Cam couldn't name it. As she looked into his warm, cinnamon-colored eyes and saw the slightest hint of a smile on his full, well-shaped mouth, she struggled to keep her voice low and firm. "Chief Morales?"

"Ma'am, I was born in a helicopter."

She looked at him and blinked once. "Excuse me?"

Gus grinned and opened his hands. "My mother

was in labor with me. She's Yaqui Indian, from northern Mexico. She was visiting her family when she went into labor with me. My father, who is a U.S. Army helicopter pilot, had flown her to the desolate area where her parents lived, and flew her out again when her water broke. He was hoping to get to Nogales, and then across the border into Texas, to get her to the hospital on time.''

Cam smiled. ''Don't tell me! You were actually born *in* the helo?''

He liked her smile. There wasn't anything not to like about their new C.O., Gus decided. That pale sprinkling of freckles across her broad cheekbones, the way her hair glinted with red-gold highlights beneath the washed-out fluorescent light above them... Chief Anderson suddenly looked a lot less threatening than she had earlier.

''Yes, ma'am. By the time my father landed the helo on the hospital roof, she'd given birth to me.'' Gus's smile widened. ''The attendants who came out were kinda surprised.''

''That's a great story, Chief Morales. So, did the helicopter ride stay in your blood?'' Cam liked the way his eyes crinkled and dimples flashed as he smiled fully.

''Yes, ma'am, it did. My father flew civilian helicopters for the Civil Air Patrol in his free time. I got my helo license when I was thirteen years old, when my legs were long enough to reach the pedals.''

''I see,'' Cam said, trying not to sound impressed. But she was. The natural warmth and openness of Morales compared to the other two pilots was like night and day. Cam realized instantly that he didn't have a problem with his C.O. being a woman, as the other two did. Jotting down the info, she asked lightly, "And I suppose you have over a thousand hours built up in helos?"

"Yes, ma'am. I got fifteen hundred in civilian types. When I joined the army air program, I acquired six hundred more hours."

"And in the Apache?"

He shrugged. "Not enough."

Cam grinned. "Don't worry, you're going to be getting plenty of hours shortly. We'll make up for it."

"Sounds good to me."

"Hours in the Apache?"

"A hundred and fifty."

Cam knew that the school gave each student seventy hours of flight time. She frowned and looked at Morales's personnel jacket. "Where did you get eighty more?"

"Oh…" Gus opened his hands and had the good grace to flush beneath her sharp gaze. "Well, I volunteered for a special class on drug interdiction tactics *before* I went through Apache school."

Frowning, Cam studied him. "How is that possible, Chief?"

Slightly embarrassed, Gus said, "My father's influence, if you want the truth, ma'am. He's head of an Apache squadron. He wanted me to learn the drill. At the time, I was flying another type of helo. Within his squadron, he had set up a unique program of flight interdiction tactics, so he wrote orders for me to attend it."

"I see family nepotism at work," Cam murmured. "Well…that's good."

"Yes, ma'am. I loved it."

"And that's what got you into Apache school, officially?" Cam knew there were hundreds of applicants for each seat in the training program, and it was the most highly prized aviation school in the army. Morales had the good grace to look humble when he owned up to the nepotism that had gotten him that far.

"I got in because I passed all the tests and qualifications," he told her seriously. "Not because of my father."

"I understand, Chief." Cam brightened and sat back. She looked at all three pilots. "We're officially a squadron, according to the U.S. Army, as well as a black ops branch of the Mexican Air Force. We're Black Jaguar Squadron 2, a spinoff, as it were, of my squadron down in Peru." Cam pulled three patches from her briefcase and carefully laid them out on the table.

"This is our squadron patch, gentlemen. As you can see, it is square, with a red and blue border around it. In the center is a black jaguar with gold eyes on a white background, and our squadron name is embroidered at the bottom in gold." Cam pointed to the patches. "You're going to earn them the hard way— through a lot of work and elbow grease, consistent one hundred and ten percent effort on your part. I have it in my power as C.O. to release you from the obligation to learn drug flight interdiction at any time, if you fail to jump over the bar I hold up for you. Where I come from, you earn every hour you spend in the seat of an Apache. It's not a given that you deserve to sit there."

Gus saw Anderson's expression grow even more serious as she perused the three of them, her hands folded on the table. On the right shoulder of her uniform he saw the identical patch, on the other shoulder an American flag.

"If you thought Apache school was tough, just wait. This is where we separate the women from the girls..." Cam smiled slightly "...or in this case, the men from the boys. If you've got what it takes, at the end of an eight-week period you'll be awarded this patch. If not, I'll be calling you in, writing you up a new set of orders and you're out of here. Do you understand?"

"Yes ma'am," the men murmured in a subdued chorus.

"Good," Cam said, relief flowing through her. She gathered up the patches and placed them back in her briefcase. "Now, I need an X.O.—executive officer." She looked at Morales. "You're it, Chief Morales."

"Me?" Gus hooked a thumb toward his chest, surprised. He saw a hint of approval in Chief Anderson's green eyes.

"Why not you? You've got more hours in helos. You've had advanced drug flight interdiction training. From this moment on, you're my X.O., which means you get a lot more duty and a lot less free time to party in Tijuana. Are you up for it, Chief Morales?"

Straightening in his chair, Gus took a deep breath. If he carried out his duties well, he just might go from a CWO2 to another pay grade. He could barely conceal his excitement. "Yes, ma'am, I'll take it. Thank you. I hope I won't let you down."

Cam smiled thinly. "The only way you fail, Chief,

is by not trying.'' She looked at the other two pilots, whose sulky expressions indicated their current mood.

"Okay, let's roll,'' she told them. ''Get on your feet, gentlemen, and let's go out and meet our ladies.''

Chapter 4

Gus could hardly wait to get his turn in the Apache with Chief Anderson. The rest of the day was spent studying special manuals of flight interdiction operations back in their tiny H.Q. office while she took each of them for an introductory flight. Gus was still champing at the bit when he saw Luis Dominguez come back from his hour-long stint. The Mexican was looking disgusted. His brow was beaded with sweat and the underarms of his flight uniform were dark with perspiration. Chief Anderson escorted him to the office and ordered Zaragoza to come with her next.

The moment Dominguez was alone with Gus, he started bitching. "That woman is loco! Crazy!"

"Why?" Gus asked, placing his hand across his manual to keep his place. Luis's face was dark with frustration. He started to reach for the pack of cigarettes he kept in the left thigh pocket of his flight suit and then thought better of it, remembering the orders that this area was now off-limits to smoking. Cursing, he glared around the simple but clean facility.

"She put me through a flight test of maneuvers I've never done before!" he fumed, crossing his arms and glaring down at his unopened flight manual.

"Isn't that what the introductory flight's about? To find out what areas we're weak or strong in?" Gus asked Luis mildly.

"Bah! The witch had me trying to do things I wasn't taught in school. I failed miserably. She sat in the back seat with that clipboard across her knees, rating me on every damn movement I made in the Apache."

"Did she say you failed?"

Luis blew out a long breath. "She let me know every time I did something wrong! I heard her voice in my helmet every minute of that damned flight!"

Gus shrugged. "School doesn't fully prepare us for what we have to do out here, Luis. No matter what squadron we got sent to, we'd have a lot to learn. It's called advance training, amigo."

"Oh," Luis sneered, lifting his upper lip, his canine teeth showing, "and I suppose you're looking forward to getting graded on every flight maneuver out there?"

"It's inevitable. It's part of our learning curve. How can Chief Anderson develop a proper training program for us if she's not familiar with our abilities and skills?"

Getting up, Luis shoved the chair away in disgust. Pacing the room, he growled, "I can hardly wait until she flies with all three of us. It will be like the Spanish

Inquisition. She'll peel off our hides, one at a time. It's shaming. It's cruel. At least the inspector pilots back at Fort Rucker did it on a one-to-one basis. She'll enjoy shaming us.''

Grinning, Gus said, ''Luis, you never had this reaction to any of your instructors at Fort Rucker.''

''None of them were women, that's why!'' Standing, he glared out the window and tapped his boot on the floor.

Gus smiled to himself. He knew Chief Anderson was going to put him through his paces and then some. However, he wasn't worried, because he felt intuitively that she would be fair.

''This wasn't a flight test to see if you get to stay or not,'' Gus reminded him. ''If you screwed up out there, look at it this way—you have only one way to go. Up.''

''Bah! I need a smoke.'' With a snort, Luis headed out the door and down the hall to the back door.

Sitting there, Gus closed his eyes and pictured Anderson in his mind. She was tall and womanly, curved deliciously in all the right places even though she wore that drab and loose-fitting flight uniform. He liked her face, liked the sprinkling of freckles that made her look younger than she probably was. Her face was oval, with huge green eyes that he could easily read, although Gus wasn't sure she realized how much her emotions were revealed in them. Oh, Anderson tried to keep a poker face, but Gus felt he had an edge because he could see her feelings clearly in those evergreen eyes of hers.

He liked the fact that although she worked in a man's world, she kept her reddish-colored hair long, wearing it parted in the middle. He liked the way it curled slightly around her attractive face. He longed to ask her personal questions. Maybe he'd get the chance on the flight, but he didn't think so. She was all-business.

Gently closing the manual, after marking his place with a piece of paper, Gus got to his feet. Glancing at his watch, he realized it would be another forty minutes before Chief Anderson came back and asked him to sit in that cockpit and fly the Apache. A thrill raced through him. He loved flying that helicopter. And he sensed that Anderson was one helluva pilot at the controls of that combat machine. Gus could barely rein in his eagerness to learn the finer techniques of flying from her.

After pouring himself another cup of coffee, he stood at the window and pondered another reaction he was having to Anderson. She was a woman. Not just any woman, but a very unique one in the highly skilled role of combat helicopter pilot. That excited him. Enthralled him. Made him very curious about her. Who was she really? Where had she been born? What had happened to her as she was growing up to push her into this line of work? Was flying a passion with her or just a job?

So many questions and no answers. At least, not yet, he thought, grinning a little as he lifted the cup to his lips.

As he stood there eyeing the small, sun-baked military airfield and the many red roofs in the distance that showed where the sprawling city of Tijuana began, Gus felt a twinge in his heart. Frowning, he wondered where it had come from. Unsure, he turned and went back to his manual. The more he read, the more he would be prepared for what Chief Anderson would put him through. He didn't want to fail her. He wanted to at least scrape by with a shred of her respect for him intact. After all, she'd chosen him as X.O., and he didn't want to start off by having her questioning her choice.

Cam's heart wouldn't settle down as Chief Morales flawlessly took the Apache off the ground and rose to an altitude of five thousand feet, heading in the direction of San Diego.

The shaking and shuddering of the Apache always soothed her fractiousness when she felt uptight or nervous. Now, as she sat in the piggyback seat above and behind the pilot's cockpit, with the late afternoon sun shining through the Plexiglas and the cooling air-conditioning sweeping around her, Cam smiled for the first time. She settled the clipboard on her lap, the pen in her gloved hand shaking with the vibration of the aircraft.

"Memorize this route, Chief," she told him over the cabin intercom, moving the mike a little closer to her lips. Pulling down the dark green visor that shielded the upper half of her face from the invasive sunlight, Cam kept her attention on the two HUDS—heads-up displays—in front of her.

"The U.S. and Mexico have authorized us to use one specific air corridor along the border for takeoffs and landings during our training phase. Because the president of Mexico doesn't want the civilian population to get overly concerned about military gunships in the vicinity, we have to fly in restricted airspace."

"I understand, Ms. Anderson," he replied.

"It was in your new flight manual."

"Yes, ma'am, it was, and I'd already read that part of it."

Cam chuckled. "You're probably the only one who's cracked the manual."

Gus grinned. He liked the feel of the Apache around him. She was a deadly machine—board ugly, but dangerous and efficient. His right hand on the cyclic between his legs, his left hand around the collective, he said, "I'll bet they're both looking at it in detail now."

How badly Cam wanted to break down the all-business facade with Morales. She liked his easygoing nature. Earlier, when he'd walked around the gunship as part of the ground check, she'd seen his eye for detail. He missed nothing. How friendly a C.O. could be with her X.O. was something Cam hadn't a clue about. Was an executive officer like a best friend? Someone she could confide in? Or should she trust her X.O. only up to a certain point and try to keep an emotional distance from him? Cam wished she could talk to Maya about this. And she would, tonight, after she went to her barracks room. In the meantime, she would simply enjoy Gus's warm, low laugh, which sent tingles through her for no explainable reason.

"Once you hit the San Diego vector at Imperial Beach, make a ninety degree left turn and head out to sea for fifteen miles, Chief Morales."

Below her, Cam saw the sagebrush-covered hills of Mexico disappear as they moved into U.S. airspace. She pressed a button in the cockpit, which sent out an automatic signal to the radar scanners that swept the border area, showing who they were. Cam had no wish to be intercepted as a possible unfriendly aircraft.

Below them the dry hills were covered with twelve-lane freeways and housing estates. San Diego was a beautiful large city on the Pacific Coast. Ahead she could see the graceful sweep of the Coronado Bridge, connecting the island of the same name, with its naval air station, to the city.

Morales, so far, had a light, silken touch with the Apache. When he made the requested turn out toward the deep blue, sparkling ocean, Cam smiled.

"Your hours are showing, Chief," she murmured, marking down a grade on her sheet regarding his flight skills.

"Oh?" Gus watched the light green of the ocean turn to a marine blue, indicating deeper water, as they flew quickly away from the coast. The western sun was shining straight into his eyes and he was glad for his visor.

"You have a nice touch with her."

"I love this woman."

Chuckling, Cam said, "You see the Apache as a 'she'?"

"Always did. Always will."

Luis and Antonio didn't. To them, it was merely a machine to be wrestled around in the air. "That's good," she stated.

"Every helicopter has its own personality. I'm sure you've noticed that?"

Pleased that he'd speak with her as an equal, Cam

said, "Oh, yes. We have names for each of our ladies down at the squadron."

"Any hangar queens?" These were helicopters that broke down frequently and spent more time in the hangar than flying on missions.

Laughing, Cam said, "No. The Apache has a pretty low breakdown record. No hangar queens, thank goodness. The way we push them, they've stood up when they shouldn't have over the years even in high humidity. An Apache's a tough machine."

"I'd like to know more about your squadron, any time you have a free moment to fill me in."

Hearing the excitement in his voice, Cam said dryly, "Chief, it's a black ops, so I can't say much about it."

"That's what I thought. Well, you can't blame me for asking, can you?"

"No. Nice try. Okay, once you hit the five-mile mark, I want you to turn ninety degrees south."

"Yes, ma'am." On the mark, he brought the Apache over in a quick, banking turn. From this elevation, he could still see the rim of land to his left and the mighty Pacific spreading out to the south and west.

"Good. You're going to fly southward exactly twenty miles. We're going to parallel the Baja Peninsula, as you well know. At the twenty-mile mark, you will execute another ninety degree left turn, moving due east. That will take us into our authorized military flight test area."

"That's all mountains and hills, with very little population," Gus said.

"That's right, Chief. Our playground for the next eight weeks."

"I used to hike in those mountains," Gus said.

"Really?" Cam was hungry to know something about Morales on a personal level. "How old were you?"

"I told you my mom is Yaqui Indian?"

"Right, you did." With his golden skin and the hint of a tilt at the corners of his large eyes, Morales reminded her of a lean, golden jaguar. There was a strength to him as well—quiet, powerful and yet steady. Cam could feel it. There was something so solid and grounded about him that it made her want to trust him. The man was terribly good-looking, in her opinion. One moment he'd appear serious and mature, and the next he'd give her that unexpected, little-boy grin of delight. She liked him more than she should, Cam realized.

"My father was an attaché to the U.S. Ambassador to Mexico when I was a kid, and he used to take me over here to go hiking. My dad is a great outdoorsman to this day."

"A hunter?"

"No, a hiker."

"Did your mom go along?"

"No. My dad has a great love of the land, and he would show me animal tracks and interesting plants. We'd take a camera along and shoot the birds and animals we saw. I have scrapbooks at home filled with pictures we took."

"Better to shoot them with a camera than a gun," Cam said.

"Right on."

"And yet you're an Apache pilot. A combat pilot who will have to pull the trigger someday, and possibly kill someone. How does that set with you, Chief Morales?"

Making the turn at the twenty-mile mark, Gus pushed the Apache toward the brown-and-green looming mountains in the distance. "I don't know. All my targets have been wooden, with no human involvement."

It was a good answer.

Cam got down to business. "All right, Chief, I'm going to give you a series of flight maneuvers. When I give the orders, I want them executed immediately. Understand?"

"Yes, ma'am." Gus felt his heart speed up a little. Below, the ocean was an aquamarine color, indicating it was becoming shallow. Up ahead rose mountains that were anywhere from two to six thousand feet in height. The bumpy foothills in front of them were lined with green valleys filled with brush and short trees; the sloping sides were dotted with sagebrush and cactus. Beyond them the tops of the mountains were bare and brown.

Gus tightened his hands around the controls as he anticipated the series of flight commands Chief Anderson would put him through.

"Climb to twenty thousand."

Instantly, Gus followed her orders. The engines howled. The Apache strained. Nose up, the helicopter clawed for the blue sky, which was dotted with white cottony clouds. The gravity pushed Gus back in the pilot's seat. It was always a good feeling to him. This was what he loved best—flying this powerful, responsive machine.

The moment he hit the targeted altitude, he heard Anderson snap, ''I want an inside loop.''

Gus was surprised, but didn't hesitate. Immediately he sent the aircraft nose down in a sharp descent toward the green-and-brown earth. The Apache was the only helicopter in the world that could do an inside loop. Because gravity would drain the fuel from the lines on other machines, none but the Apache could attempt this maneuver. Boeing engineers had figured out how to keep the fuel pumping to an Apache's engines to keep it from dropping out of the sky.

Cam was pinned back in her seat as gravity built during the loop maneuver. She felt the sureness and confidence in Morales's handling of the Apache as he executed the required moves. They had eaten up ten thousand feet of airspace in the process, and now, as he brought the shrieking Apache into the lower part of the loop, gravity tried to pull them to the earth.

Cam had had to take the controls from the two other pilots at this point because they were awkward and lacked the confidence to get the screaming helicopter up and out of the dive. Morales, she knew, would finish the loop without her intervention.

As Gus brought the Apache back to its original altitude, he felt a thrill of joy arc through him, and he laughed. It was a sound of triumph. When he heard Chief Anderson laugh with him, his heart opened with an incredible sense of happiness. She understood his joy. Knew how he loved riding this fearless machine, which could do nearly anything that was asked of it.

''That's incredible!'' he said, emotion in his voice.

"Vertical dive to ten thousand."

"Yes, ma'am!" And he plunged the Apache straight downward, the rotors thumping hard and sending battering waves of vibration through his body.

Pleasure surged through Cam as, for the next twenty minutes, she put Morales through his paces. He was nearly flawless in his command of the Apache. It was a relief to her. At least one of the three pilots on her team had the goods to do interdiction work. Concerned about the other two, Cam wasn't sure what to do. Putting that worry aside, she ordered Morales back out to sea to follow their designated corridor back to the air base.

Over the Pacific, Gus began to relax. He knew he'd done well on the flight test. "Are you sorry yet that you asked me to be your X.O.?"

Cam lifted her head and stared down out of her cockpit. Below, she could see the green helmet Morales wore, but not his face. "Not at all."

"Then," he suggested, "when we're alone, could we be on a more friendly footing with one another? Could you call me Gus?"

Cam smiled slightly. "So long as the other pilots don't overhear us, that's fine. You can call me Cam."

"Cam? Now, that's an interesting name."

"Short for Camelia. My mother had three daughters, and she named us after her favorite flowers—camelias, iris and dahlias."

"Very nice," Gus murmured. "I'm an only child—an army brat. My mother had me and said that's it. One kid born in a helo and no more dramatics." He chuckled indulgently. Below, the dark blue of the Pacific blazed with gold highlights as the sun sank closer to the western horizon.

"So, you were a handful, eh?"

Shrugging, Gus swept his gaze from the instruments to the ocean below, then to the sky above. It was a habit and a necessary part of flying. "I was a good kid."

"You seem like you would have been."

"Oh?" He was very curious about how Cam saw him.

Laughing a little, she said, "You strike me as someone who is very serious about work, but also knows how to play and be a big kid at times, too."

"Very perceptive," he murmured. "But that's why you're the C.O. You have this radar vision to see straight through your personnel and know what and who they are."

"Oh, don't give me that kind of credit," Cam protested, frowning. "This is my first time at it. I'm learning as I go. The hunt and peck method, with a lot of mistakes along the way."

"I'd say you're doing real good so far."

Mouth flexing, Cam looked up, enjoying the view of the sparkling ocean beneath them. With Gus, she could relax. He made it easy for her to banter with him. "Well," she muttered, "I'm not so sure of that. At least not yet."

"I'd say you've done a credible job of handling those two jay birds."

Smiling, Cam said, "Thanks."

"They threw the kitchen sink at you. I was shocked. I watched you deal with their insubordination and turn it against them. I know a lot of C.O.'s who would have strung them up on court-martial charges. You did it differently than a man would, but I think your way may give them a chance to grow instead of being canned. You were patient and firm with them. You let them know what their choices were, and then left them to hang themselves if that's what they wanted to do. I found your method very instructive."

Savoring his praise, Cam felt more relief flow through her. Folding her gloved hands on the board in her lap, she muttered, "I wasn't expecting that kind of reception, to tell you the truth."

"Yeah," Gus said. "I wasn't, either. Those two do a lot of bluffing, but this time they were serious." He smiled and sheepishly admitted, "I wanted to speak up and defend you."

"I'm glad you didn't. It would have eroded my authority."

Gus chuckled. "I still have some old officer-and-gentleman habits ingrained in me from my dad. Women are still goddesses to be worshipped on a pedestal, not hung out to dry."

Unable to help herself, Cam laughed with him. "You're good for my soul, Gus. Thanks for being here."

"Believe me, it's my pleasure."

The sincerity in his baritone voice moved through Cam like a lover's caress. She sat there assimilating the sensation. She'd heard the huskiness, the emotion, behind his words. Knowing that Gus meant them, Cam felt a little more confident in how she'd handled the two rebellious pilots.

"What, exactly, am I to do to help you as X.O.?"

Gus asked. He saw they had five miles to go before he initiated the turn to fly over San Diego. He wished he could slow time down, but knew he couldn't. The only thing missing in this private and personal conversation was being able to see Cam's facial expressions, her reactions to what he said. Some of it he could hear in her soft, low voice.

"Not protect me when I'm toe-to-toe with either of those pilots in future, that's for sure."

He heard the derisive tone in her voice. Frowning, Gus murmured, "They shouldn't have gone after you like that. They did it because they don't respect women in general, not just you."

"They're not used to working around military women," Cam agreed quietly.

"Part of it is the Mexican culture," Gus said.

"I know. I was warned of it before I took this mission."

Brightening, Gus made the turn. San Diego spread out for miles along the coastline, and the windows of the tall skyscrapers in the downtown area glimmered golden, reflecting the setting sun. "Well," he drawled "at least one of your team isn't prejudiced against women."

"You. I think it's because you're part Indian. My C.O. comes from Indian and Brazilian heritage, and she's from a matriarchal culture like yourself. That's probably why."

Nodding, Gus paid strict attention to flight protocol at this point. "My mother drilled into me at an early age that women are just as strong, smart and capable as men. She was right." He really didn't want this flight to end, because he was enjoying talking to Cam so much. Making the next turn, they began heading over the border toward Tijuana.

Moistening her lips, which were dry due to the desert environment, Cam gazed down at the landscape. Tijuana was a major border city, a city of haves and have-nots. The poor lived up on the hillsides, sometimes in shacks made of cardboard, with pieces of corrugated tin for roofs. It was a heart-wrenching sight to her. No one should live in that kind of poverty.

As Gus brought the Apache in for a perfect three-wheel landing, Cam felt sad. He had been the only positive part of her day. She gritted her teeth, girding herself for her next duty, which was to talk individually to each pilot about what she saw as his weaknesses and strengths. The task was not going to be fun at all.

Cam missed the camaraderie of her sisters, as well as her fellow pilots at the BJS base in Peru. Akiva had been right; when one assumed a leadership role, the fun of being a pilot went out the window—pronto. Having no one to talk to on a personal level weighed heavily on Cam.

She gazed out the windshield as the rotors stopped turning. Below, a U.S. Army crew tethered the rotors and the chief of the ground crew gave the signal that it was safe to open their individual cockpit covers. Until Mexican Army crews could be trained to take over these jobs, the U.S. Army would supply ground crews to Mexico.

Pushing up the canopy, Cam unharnessed herself, trying to tuck all her fears away. Somehow she had to look confident and authoritative, as if she knew what she was doing when she talked to Antonio and Luis. It wasn't going to be pleasant.

On the ground, she saw Gus take off his helmet. He quickly ran his long fingers through his short, thick black hair, taming it back into place. When she looked at him, he grinned at her like an excited little boy. In that moment, all her consternation dissolved beneath the warmth and joy in his eyes as he held her gaze. Taking off her own helmet, Cam set it on the fuselage of the Apache as the ground crew rapidly worked around them. She had her hair in a ponytail, and reaching up, she loosened it so that it flowed down around her face and shoulders once again.

Unexpected hunger sizzled through Gus as Cam's hair flowed like a chestnut cape around her proud shoulders. The sunlight caressed her as she picked up her helmet and tucked it beneath her left elbow, then picked up her clipboard. The breeze lifted some strands, highlighting the gold-red tones. She was incredibly beautiful to him in that moment. The world seemed to stop turning for Gus as Cam looked up at him from only a few feet away. The voices of the ground crew, the calls of the seagulls wheeling above them, the noise of a diesel fuel truck coming toward them, all dissolved. He was aware only of her. That oval face dotted with girlish freckles, those thoughtful but worried green eyes of hers and her very soft, parted lips all conspired against him.

As their gazes locked and held for an instant, Gus felt the armor he'd placed around his heart crack. He literally felt and heard it, and the sensation was startling. Frightening. Euphoric. He stood there staring at her, and really looked at Cam for the first time, man to woman.

Swallowing hard, he forced himself to tear his gaze from hers a second later. But not before he saw her cheeks turn a distinct rose color. Had he seen her eyes change? Had they really become a velvet green with flecks of sunlight in them as she'd stared back at him? Trying to shake off the sensation, because it wasn't appropriate under the circumstances, Gus turned away. But he remembered her eyes. They were like dark, placid green pools he'd seen in the jungles of the Yucatan peninsula that he'd visited with his parents as they taught him about his ancient Mayan heritage. If she met her, his mother would whisper that Cam had ''jaguar eyes.'' Eyes that now held Gus frozen, a captive—but what an eager one he was! To his consternation and shock, he realized that he could have fallen helplessly into Cam's gaze, a willing prisoner.

Turning, he fell into step with her as they headed back to the barracks. Cam kept a casual distance between them, and glancing at her out of the corner of his eye, Gus wondered if she'd felt anything toward him in that crazy moment out of time. Her cheeks were still a high pink color, and she was looking down at the ground, her brows drawn downward. Realizing abruptly that she probably hadn't, Gus found himself in an unexpected quandary.

He liked Cam. Liked everything about her, probably more than he should, given their professional relationship. Wiping his mouth with the back of his hand, he took off his flight gloves and jammed them into the left pocket of his flight suit. Within moments they would be at the two-story barracks, climbing the outside wooden stairs to the second floor, where their H.Q. was located. Time. He needed some quiet time to think about what had just occurred. Tonight, when he went to his assigned cubical on the first floor, and the lights were out, he'd feel his way through it all. Maybe then he'd get some answers.

Chapter 5

Exhausted, Cam walked down to her small room on the first floor of the barracks—her "home" until she could find an apartment near the base. Darkness had fallen. After spending so much energy talking individually to the two arrogant Mexican pilots, she was emotionally whipped. Gus had been a dream in comparison. He'd hung on every word of her critique of his flight performance, asked good questions on how to become better the next time around. Gus was her only bright spot in the whole day.

Heart heavy, Cam realized she wasn't even hungry. It was 1900 and she knew she should eat, but she was too upset. Being a leader was harder than she'd ever envisioned. Gaining a new respect for her own C.O., Major Stevenson, Cam unlocked the door to her room. Stepping in, she turned on the overhead light. Earlier in the day, when she'd arrived at the base via commercial airline, she'd thrown her two pieces of luggage into the room, shed her civilian clothes and quickly donned the dark green flight suit worn by U.S. Army aviators.

Looking around as she quietly closed the door, Cam decided that even though this was a spare room, it was posh in comparison to her digs at the cave in Peru where the squadron was based. Here she had a double bed, a wooden dresser with a mirror, and two large metal lockers to store her few clothes in. A television, DVD player and radio were all unexpected bonuses to her. At BJS, no one had these things, though one building on the other side of the mountain—the mining operation that was a front for their black ops—had a satellite dish where off-duty personnel could go watch television and find out what was happening in the rest of the world. It was a treat to have time to do that.

Cam's new room had a small desk and a phone, and she'd brought her Mac titanium G4 laptop, which she'd use to communicate with her colleagues. Next to it she placed the very expensive iridium satellite phone.

Cam reached for the Velcro closing at the top of her flight suit and tugged it open. Pulling out the white silk scarf she always wore around her neck in order to stop the uniform from chafing her skin as she scanned the skies, Cam sat down. She needed someone to talk to. Someone whose advice could help her get through this messy situation. Picking up the satellite phone, she dialed a number.

"Stevenson here."

"Maya? This is Cam. I hope it's not too late?"

Chuckling, Maya said, "I figured I'd hear from you. And late? When I'm known to stay up half the night and then crash for a few hours on the bunk in my office? I don't think so."

"It's great to hear a friendly voice," Cam said, meaning it. She gripped the phone anxiously.

"So, you hit a brick wall with your pilots?"

Sighing, she nodded. "Yeah, two out of the three are challenges. Only one, Chief Gus Morales, is the material we're looking for."

"So, give me the down and dirty on all of them. Let's talk."

Relieved, Cam quickly related the day's events. Her heart was beating hard in her chest because she didn't want to disappoint Maya. She didn't want her to think she wasn't up to the job before her. Right now, Cam felt like a loser.

"Let me do some more background snooping on Dominguez and Zaragoza, okay? If they're that bad, why the hell did the army allow them to pass? That's my first question. Secondly, I know that the Mexican military have been putting only two students per rotation through Apache school. Why should these two get it, instead of guys who really want the training?"

Rubbing her aching head, Cam muttered, "I don't know. There's nothing in their personnel jackets to indicate why."

Chuckling darkly, Maya said, "Personnel jackets are sanitized versions of reality, and tell you little. Don't worry, I'll get to Morgan and have him do some looking into the *real* records at the flight school at Fort Rucker, to find out what you need to know."

"I feel inept, Maya."

Laughing, she said, "Welcome to the real world of being a leader. Crappy, isn't it?"

"No kidding. I sure have a new respect for you...for what you must go through every day down there, while all we do is climb into the cockpit and fly."

"Well, Cam, you pilots put your lives on the line. I don't. I fly a desk most of the time. I take other slings and arrows—glares, silent name-calling and outbursts of anger from time to time with my people, but that's not often. And you're in another league on this. With an all-woman squadron down here, we have a natural tendency toward teamwork and helping one another. Whereas with men, at least most macho ones, there's nothing but rivalry. Some guys just don't like to work together. They like to show off—strut their stuff and show you what they know as an individual, not a team member."

Laughing softly, Cam nodded. "Well, the one bright spot, like I said, is Gus Morales. He's a dream, really."

"Yeah?"

Cam filled her in on the Mexican-American pilot.

"He was a good choice as X.O.," Maya affirmed.

"Maya, I'm going to ask a stupid question."

"No question is stupid, Cam. Only the one that goes unasked. What is it?"

Relieved that Maya didn't mind holding her hand as she learned how to become a leader, Cam felt the courage to go on. She shifted in the chair and crossed her legs.

"I see the closeness and confidence you have with Dallas Klein, your X.O.—the confidence you have in her. I was wondering…well, do I want to create that same situation with Gus?"

Chuckling, Maya said, "X.O.'s are people, Cam. Sometimes you get lucky, like I did with Lieutenant Klein, who became an immediate friend. She's someone I can blow off steam to, cry in front of, talk and laugh with. And whatever I say to her stays with her. She knows how to keep a confidence. She's not a gossiper. As a leader, you can't cry in front of your people. You have to look confident, strong and sure of yourself even if your gut feels like jelly and you're questioning yourself every step of the way. The right X.O. can give you a safe harbor to vent your anger and frustration, share your humor over dumb things, mistakes, talk about your personnel, and in general, help you run the command. You want an X.O. who is perceptive, who can give you feedback and who isn't afraid of you just because you're the boss. You don't want a boot licker."

"Gus isn't that."

"Good. Is he reliable, you think?"

"In my gut, he's like Dallas, I feel."

"Trustworthy?"

"Yes, but I haven't had time to really verify that. It's just an instinct thing."

"Well," Maya drawled, humor in her husky tone, "you know how much we work on gut instinct around here. And you know how accurate it is. Often, it saves our lives when a Black Shark is lurking around and our Apache is unable to pick up its identification signal. The only thing keeping us from getting blasted out of the sky sometimes is our intuition.

If Morales feels right to you, feels like he's trustworthy, I'm sure he is, whether he's proved it yet or not."

"You're right," Cam murmured. "You'd like him, Maya. He's enthusiastic, he's smart and he catches on fast."

"Well, at least one of the three is a winner, Cam. What you have to do as a leader is figure out how to bring these other two dudes not only into line, but also up to scratch with their air skills."

"I'm going to work out a mission plan when I get off the phone with you. I'd like to discuss it with you tomorrow night, if that's okay with you?"

"Sure."

"You don't mind?"

"Heck no! I'd be worried if you weren't calling me, Cam. Good leaders aren't born, they're made one grueling day at a time."

"Gosh, that's true," Cam whispered, wrinkling her brow. "I've got to learn not to get emotionally involved when dealing with those two pilots."

"That's right. They'll teach you what I call the Zen-like art of detachment," Maya chuckled. "You've got to change your attitude, Cam. Down here at BJS, everyone likes everyone else. We all get along. We're one big team. We're like a bunch of sisters out on this wild and crazy adventure together. From what you've said, Zaragoza and Dominguez want to set you up to fail, to embarrass you, to show your faults instead of reflecting on their own skills and weaknesses. It's a game, and you've got to learn the game in a hurry and turn it back on them."

"I have to be tough in ways I never wanted to be,

Maya. The only way I got through today was to act like our Inspector Pilots back at Fort Rucker.''

''Yeah—lean, mean mother machines,'' she said derisively.

''And *mother* wasn't used as a nice word, either,'' Cam said, smiling a little.

''Right on. So be a mean mother. Don't give an inch. And don't let them know they've taken a pound of flesh out of you. Keep them off balance. That means you have to be thinking way ahead of them. You have to know them so well, their individual personalities, that you know what their action or reaction is going to be before they initiate a response.''

''I think I need four years of psychology, Maya, to do that.''

Laughing, Maya said, ''Nah, real life will teach you in about three months' time.''

''I'm supposed to turn these pilots into interdiction specialists in two months,'' Cam said, anxiety tingeing her tone. ''And I don't know if I can do it or not.''

''Listen, just set up your mission plan, then get back to me tomorrow night and we'll talk. Give these two a week with that plan and see what happens. If they don't improve, if they continue to fight your authority, then other, more drastic measures will need to be invoked.''

''Okay,'' Cam said, wondering if Maya might yank her out of the C.O. spot as one ''drastic measure to be invoked,'' and put someone else who was better and tougher in the slot instead. That was all she could see happening, but she didn't say that. Worried that Maya would think her a poor leader if she couldn't turn these two pilots around, Cam compressed her lips and withheld her worst fears from her.

"Get some sleep, Cam. And remember to eat, okay? Food is fuel. It keeps you sharp."

Smiling wryly, she said, "Okay, mother hen, I will."

"G'night, Tree Trimmer. Hang in there…"

Clicking off the button on the iridium phone, Cam set it gently back on the wooden desk. Her stomach growled, but she still wasn't hungry. Looking around, she felt as if the cubicle was closing in on her.

"Get moving, Anderson," she told herself grimly, and stood up. She planned to take a quick shower to wash off the smelly sweat of fear she'd garnered today, and change into civilian clothes. Heading down to the end of the hall, where some vending machines were located, she'd grab a quick snack and take it outside. Cam loved the outdoors and missed it acutely. Maybe munching on potato chips under the stars would help her.

There was a quarter moon shining brightly in the night sky as Cam stepped out of the barracks and away from the floodlights surrounding it. Every window in the barracks was lit up as well as the inhabitants, both enlisted soldiers and officers relaxed after a long day's work. It was a noisy place, Cam realized, at this time of night. Lights would be doused at 2100 hours, and then things would quiet down. Until then the place was a cacophony of sound that had bled through her door as she jotted her mission ideas down on paper. She was glad to be outside now, dressed like a civilian in her jeans, pink tank top and a light denim jacket with flowers embroidered on it. In her hand, she had a small package of potato chips.

Though the barracks were surrounded by asphalt, earlier in the day Cam had spotted what appeared to be a picnic area with tables, benches and several barbecue grills under a grove of trees about a quarter mile to the west. She felt lighter with every step as she headed there now, into the darkness. In the distance, she could see the dark shapes of the trees silhouetted against the moonlit sky.

Cam released a long, painful sigh as the night embraced her. Oh, to be hidden again! Out of the glaring spotlight of real life, with all those responsibilities bearing down on her. As she stepped off the edge of the asphalt and onto the sandy earth, her ears picked up the faint sound of guitar music.

Stopping to listen, Cam realized the sound was coming from the grove. Hesitating, she wondered who was there. Was it one of the pilots? The last thing she wanted to do right now was come face-to-face with Zaragoza or Dominguez.

Standing there uncertainly, Cam felt her heart give a tug. Then her gut told her to move on to the grove. Curious, she followed the sound. The guitar music was soft and unobtrusive, sounding friendly and welcoming in the dark. It was such an unusual sound to hear on a military base. Music and military. They both started with an *M*, but that was all they had in common, Cam decided, a crazy smile coming to her lips.

As she approached the trees, she halted. Her night vision was excellent, and with the quarter moon's luminescence, she could make out several wooden pic-

nic tables with benches scattered around the large
grove. At a central one, a dark figure was sitting on
the table, his feet resting on the seat as he hunched
over his guitar.

Her heart jumped as she recognized the man's profile. It was Gus Morales! Standing quietly, Cam felt
tension begin to bleed out of her as she allowed the
soft, haunting strains of the music to envelop and heal
her. He played wonderfully, and she was once again
surprised by his talents. Not only was he an excellent
pilot who had a natural feel for the Apache, but those
same long, lean fingers could stroke a guitar and make
it sing beautifully as well.

Something pushed her to move toward him as he
ended the song, and her pulse bounded unsteadily as
she did. She saw him lift his head and gaze through
the darkness at her. Cam was feeling euphoric. Hopeful. He was a friend, not an enemy, she reasoned. That
had to be why she felt so at ease around him. Gus
had been like a safe harbor during the hurricane that
had swept around her all day.

"Hi, Cam. Come and join me?" Gus said, lifting
his hand and gesturing for her to come and sit at the
table with him.

Smiling hesitantly, she halted in front of him.
"That was beautiful, whatever you were playing."
She met his gleaming eyes, which were dappled with
moonlight. Her entire body responded boldly to his
look. The feeling made her happier than she'd been
in a long time, but at the same time she was scared
to death.

"Thanks. That was a healing song from my
mother's people," Gus murmured, as he studied her

in the darkness. He liked what he saw. The pale tank top she wore outlined her upper body to perfection beneath her denim jacket. Her jeans were loose, and yet, as he quickly perused her figure, he decided she was beautifully built for her five-foot-nine-inch frame. She was medium boned, and probably weighed around a hundred and fifty pounds. Gus liked women who had some meat on their bones, not the skinny sticks whose pictures were plastered on magazine covers.

Gazing up into her eyes, he saw her shyness. "Have you eaten yet?"

Cam lifted the unopened bag of potato chips. "Dinner."

"Ah, I see." Gus pointed to a box on the picnic table. "I went into town earlier, to a great little Mexican restaurant, and bought some chicken enchiladas. There's more than enough for both of us. Would you like a couple?"

She felt his gaze scan her, as if he could read her feelings and her mind. "How did you know I hadn't eaten anything?"

Chuckling, Gus quietly strummed the guitar, gazing down at it. "The whiplashing you took today would wreck my appetite as well. Come on, sit down. Share my enchiladas with me." He lifted his head and grinned, his teeth pale against his shadowed face. "You could probably stand a little quiet company with someone who isn't interested in disemboweling you because you're a woman."

At first unsettled by his perception, Cam wavered. And then she recalled Maya's sage words of advice and moved to the table, sitting down near the white box of food. "How did you know?" she asked, putting her feet on the rough-hewn seat.

"Know what?"

"That I was tied in knots? Was I that transparent today?"

Gus put the guitar aside and picked up the box. "Want the truth?" he asked, opening the container and handing her one of the wrapped enchiladas. Their fingers touched briefly, and he saw her eyes go soft once again at the contact. "No, you weren't." He opened the crinkly paper and placed his own fragrant enchilada on his lap. Watching out of the corner of his eye, he saw Cam delicately unwrap hers and carefully pick it up. She was so graceful. Her fingers were long and artistic looking. Pilot's hands.

"Speaking as your X.O.—" Gus gave her a humorous side glance as he bit into the enchilada "—I thought you carried the day well."

Munching on the delicious chicken dish, which had been well spiced, yet wasn't hot enough to numb her mouth, Cam nodded. Just sitting quietly with Gus was healing her. She didn't know why, but right now, Cam needed that safe haven he was automatically providing.

Gus handed her a white paper napkin from the box. "You've got sauce on the right corner of your mouth...." He fought the urge to lean over and wipe it off himself. He hadn't realized how beautiful Cam's mouth really was until now. Now that she was relaxed, he discovered that her mouth was really full and marvelously shaped—for kissing. For loving. Those thoughts hit him hard, and he felt his stomach clench for just a moment.

In the moonlight, her thick, slightly curled hair looked like a cloak about her graceful neck and proud shoulders. Gus squelched the urge to run his fingers in exploration through those strands, which gleamed in the watery moonlight. Her looks invited touching. That was disconcerting.

Cam took the napkin from him and quickly wiped away the offending sauce. She saw his mouth twist in a slight smile. The shadows emphasized the strength of Gus's face, from his broad, unlined forehead and large, alert eyes, to the high cheekbones and hawklike nose he'd inherited from his Indian ancestors. And then there was his strong, full mouth… She felt incredibly drawn to Gus. Still, she checked her emotional response, quickly stuffing it back inside her.

"I'm glad you picked me as your X.O.," Gus confided as he continued to enjoy his enchilada.

"Why? It's a tough job with little thanks." Cam wiped her mouth after the next bite. The food tasted good. More than good. She suddenly discovered she was famished.

"You know my dad runs an Apache squadron?"

"Yes, that's what you said earlier."

"He's over in Afghanistan right now on a covert ops."

Hearing the concern in his voice, Cam said, "You wish you were with him?"

"Yeah, I do, but the army isn't going to put a son and father together in the same squadron."

"No, they won't."

"Besides, I don't have the degree of training I need

to do that kind of work. I'm still a baby learning the building blocks.'' Gus chuckled indulgently.

"I like your attitude,'' Cam said sincerely. She caught and held his glance and gave him a slight, one-cornered smile. "You'll do well in the future with it.''

"I don't like the other choice,'' he stated, then chuckled sardonically. "The attitude Luis and Antonio wear like a bad friend isn't my style.''

Cam groaned. She hesitated before taking another bite.

Gus saw her face turn dark with worry. "Sorry,'' he murmured, "let's talk about happier, more positive things.'' Instantly, he saw her expression change from consternation and pain to one of hope. How readable Cam was! But then, Gus realized that she was allowing him to see her emotional side right now, and not that C.O.'s poker face she'd put on earlier today.

"I was sayin' that my dad runs an Apache squadron. When I was in my late teens, I remember him getting his first assignment as X.O. for a helo squad. He was always the type of father who would sit down with you and tell you the good and bad, the ins and outs of his day. I used to sit with him at the dinner table, over dessert my mom had made, and he'd share with us all this stuff that went on in the squadron.'' Gus gave her a measured look. "I learned what being an X.O. meant, through his eyes and experience, and that's what I wanted to share with you. I think I can be a good assistant to you, Cam. At least, I'll try.''

Heat moved into her cheeks as his husky voice reached her, an invisible, supporting caress. "It's good to hear that. You probably have a lot more ed-

ucation on being an X.O. than I do on being a C.O.,
if you want the truth.''

Gus heard the pain, the self-doubt in her voice.
''You were a pilot in the BJS before you came here,
right?''

''Yes. *Just* a pilot. I didn't have any management
training for leadership stuff like this….'' She waved
her hand toward the brightly lit barracks in the distance.

''You got thrown to the wolves then,'' Gus murmured in concern. ''I don't know that I could do half
as good a job as you did on your first day as C.O.
You held your own against two men who were really
challenging your authority.'' He gave her a slight nod.
''You handled them well. I would have decked
them.''

Words of praise were exactly what Cam needed.
''Coming from you, that's music to my ears.
Thanks.''

Gus wiped his hands then his mouth, and stuffed
the used napkin back into the empty food carton.
''Speaking of music…'' He grinned at her as he
picked up his guitar and settled it like a lover against
his body, strumming the strings quietly. Gradually,
the music began to ease the worry he saw in Cam's
darkened eyes.

Sighing, Cam finished her enchilada and tidied up.
Then she folded her arms and sat there, allowing the
melodic notes to wash her clean of all her angst. Closing her eyes, she absorbed the heat and energy of Gus,
sitting so close to her. His quiet demeanor, his insight,
seemed like a huge gift to Cam, for she desperately
needed what he offered as a man and as a friend. For

the next ten minutes Gus played, and she allowed herself to become lost in the sounds as his fingers stroked the strings and brought them to life.

When he finally stopped playing, Gus turned and looked at Cam. She was sitting there with her elbows on her knees, her profile sharp and clean, outlined in moonlight. Her mouth, once grim, was now parted and relaxed. The wrinkles in her brow were gone. Her eyes were closed, and he noticed how thick and long her lashes were against her freckled cheeks.

In that moment, Gus had the powerful urge to put his guitar down, place his arms around Cam and draw her close, in an embrace that would protect her. Soothe her. Let her know that someone respected her, supported her and liked her. Frowning, Gus looked away. He couldn't "like" Cam. Telling himself that over and over again, Gus resolved to keep her at arm's length. She was so soft, so womanly, a powerful package in combination with her pilot's confidence and courage. But then women who lived on the ragged edge of life and death always drew his interest.

Giving himself an internal shake, Gus sternly warned himself that he'd already lost the woman he loved because of her dangerous career. He couldn't stand to do that again; his heart simply couldn't take that kind of blow. No, somehow, he had to stop his blind, stupid heart from longing for Cam. It had to be all-business between them. Only business.

Chapter 6

It wasn't working, Cam thought as she sat, hand pressed against her head, elbows resting on her desk, with the flight scores she was studying blurring in front of her eyes. For a week she'd been running a flight training program to bring Luis and Antonio into line. The statistics spoke for themselves: Gus had made a seventy percent improvement, while the other two pilots, who were purposely dragging their feet, had gained only ten and twenty percent, respectively.

It was nearly midnight, but lifting her head, Cam picked up the iridium phone, which she kept on the desk. Her heart was heavy and she felt like an utter failure. Sensing Maya would still be up even at this late hour, she punched in her number.

"Stevenson here."

"Maya, it's Cam. Am I calling too late?"

"Oh...no, that's fine. You sound down. I've been

checking in on you all week and haven't been feeling very good about it. You okay? What's goin' on?''

Tears flooded Cam's eyes. Just the way Maya spoke, in that warm, concerned tone, broke through her reserve. That was one of the many things Cam loved about her superior. Maya was tough, but fair. She was a steady guiding hand that Cam could always count on. The fact that Maya had been ''checking on her'' was part of the mystery surrounding this legendary woman. Cam knew what most of her colleagues knew of their illustrious leader: that she was a member of the fabled Jaguar Clan, a secret organization steeped in mystical tradition. Many times in the past, Cam could swear Maya had read her mind, because she'd speak about what Cam was thinking before Cam had uttered a word.

Tonight, Cam was glad that Maya had that ESP or whatever it was. Sitting back in the chair, she blinked rapidly to clear her eyes of tears. ''Maya, I'm feeling like a failure, but before you say anything, let me also say I have a fall-back plan that I created in case this first plan didn't work.''

''Good!'' Maya exclaimed warmly. ''A leader always has plan B in case plan A goes to hell in a handbasket.'' She chuckled. ''So, I've got a fresh cup of coffee in front of me and I'm sitting here at my desk, which is miraculously cleared of all paper, and I'm all-ears. What's goin' down?''

Laughing a little, her voice strained, Cam looked at her own desk. It was a mess, piled high with work. Some of it was done, much of it not. ''I'll cut to the chase.'' She knew Maya wanted the bottom line. As a C.O., she didn't have time for preambles. ''My original plan, which was to fly with each of the pilots two hours a day, and put them through advanced flight training, hasn't worked. It worked with one of the three pilots."

"Morales, right?"

"Yes."

"Good. At least you have one who's handling his end of the deal. The other two dogging it?"

Cam hated to admit it. "Yes."

"Okay, you're outnumbered, so what do you do?"

Cam knew Maya wasn't going to give her any easy answers. The way she taught was by asking people hard questions, and letting them search their own experience and intelligence and come up with a fix.

"You aren't going to like it. And neither will Morgan."

"Plan B, right?"

"That's a roger."

"I'm listenin'."

Taking in a deep breath, Cam launched into her other idea. "I need a third Apache. And I need two women from the squadron, specifically Wild Woman and Snake. I can't divide my time among three pilots, especially when two of them are playing around and not getting serious about their commitment to this mission. I need enough Apaches to set up a game plan, so that I've got an IP—inspector pilot—with each of the students. That way, it forces the two Mexican pilots to put up or shut up. I'd like to be able to tell Dominguez and Zaragoza that if they don't start crunching the percentages and improving, they'll be washed out and two new pilots will replace them."

Cam frowned and went on. "Gus Morales is wonderful, Maya. He's learning, he's hungry and he's committed. But the other two hate me because I'm a woman telling them what to do.''

''And they're acting like petulant teenagers rebelling just because you are a woman.''

''You got it.''

''That's your plan?''

She gave a sharp, sad laugh. ''Yeah. I know it's not a good one. I know that asking you to send two of your top pilots on TDY—temporary duty—up here, leaves you shorthanded. You run on the lean side with pilots at the best of times, I know. I've been beating my brains trying to come up with another solution, Maya. But I haven't found one. There's no one I can pull from Fort Rucker to stand in their stead. I need pilots with interdiction experience to pull this plan off.''

''Tell me more about what would happen if you got that third Apache and two of my pilots.''

Heartened, Cam launched into her plans for the next five weeks of training based upon having an extra bird and two IPs to help her bring it about. At the end of her explanation, she fell silent and waited for Maya's reaction. The phone was quiet for a long time. Cam began to sweat in earnest.

''Of course, the other option here,'' she added quietly, ''is to pull me as C.O. and get someone else up here that you feel is better qualified, or who can force these two pilots to perform up to expectations. It could be me, Maya. A personality conflict. I've pulled every rabbit I know out of my hat, and nothing is working. Right now, as it stands, I'll never make that projected deadline to get these three pilots up to interdiction duty standards.''

"A good leader assesses all possibilities," Maya told her gently. "And yes, you have to look at yourself. You have to ask yourself what part do I play in this problem? How can I change myself? Is it my attitude hurting the people that work under me? You've asked those questions."

"Yeah," Cam said bitterly, "I have, and I see I come up wanting, but I don't know how to fix it."

"Sometimes a leader has to accept that there are going to be personality conflicts. The key is to try to dissolve them, to try to move on and motivate that individual, anyway. And sometimes," Maya said, "there's nothin' you can do. That person or group of people are gonna hate you just because."

"The core of this problem is gender prejudice."

"Right. And you can't change your gender, can you?"

Chuckling, Cam shook her head. "No, and I wouldn't want to, either."

"Okay, so you've assessed yourself and come up with the root of the problem. And it's not something you can fix. So, that leaves you out of the equation. You don't have to change. You don't have to quit your command."

Relief spread through Cam. "When I talk to you, Maya, everything seems so simple and clear."

Laughing, Maya said, "With experience, leading gets easier, not harder. Okay, as to your two boys? I called Morgan a day after we first talked a week ago, and here's the scoop on them. They had the lowest grades in their class in Apache school. Morgan made some phone calls to Fort Rucker and talked to one IP there who admitted privately to him, off the record, that he was pressured into giving Dominguez a passing grade simply because this was a political hot potato.''

"Political?"

"Yeah," Maya growled. "Dominguez is the son of old money in Mexico. His father is allied closely with the president of Mexico, and is looking to run for mayor of Mexico City in two years. Pressure was put on the IP because the father doesn't want his record besmirched by a son who is a playboy and isn't really serious about much of anything. I had Morgan check into Dominguez's past, and this guy behaves like a fourteen-year-old most of the time. He's consistently shown a lack of responsibility and maturity no matter where he's gone."

"And Zaragoza?"

"New money, father is very rich and has spoiled Antonio completely. He floats through life with the same attitudes as his wealthy friend."

"They're a pair," Cam said unhappily.

"Right, so here's the bottom line. You're stuck with them, and so is the army and the Mexican Air Force. They're screw-ups, to put it bluntly, and no one wants to handle them because they have power, money and political influence behind them. These two good ole boys know it, too, so that's why they're not getting serious with you."

"And I can't get rid of them?" Cam's voice rose in consternation. It would be hell on earth to keep these two in her command.

"Listen, you get some bad apples in every squadron, almost always. When it comes down to biting the bullet, you have to find something that will force these two pilots to *want* to do what you demand of them.''

''But,'' Cam said helplessly, opening her hand in frustration, ''if they can skate through Apache school, get their grades changed, and they still don't care, what can I do to *make* them care?''

Maya chuckled. ''What do they value, Cam?''

She snorted. ''Oh, they can hardly wait to get out of here at night. They hit the party spots in Tijuana, dance and drink and woo the *señoritas* until dawn. When I see them the next morning at muster, they're hungover, their eyes are bloodshot and they look like death itself because of lack of sleep.''

''Okay, so you order them to stay on the base. They don't get any liberty unless they produce. And they must produce up to the bar—standards you've set— with a minimum passing percentage.''

Nodding, Cam said, ''Okay…'' She could imagine how angry they'd be over her ordering them to stay on base twenty-four hours a day. ''What else?''

''Well, what else do they value?''

''Dancing, drinking, smoking their cigarettes…''

''Enforce a non-smoking rule. No smoking until off base.'' She chuckled darkly. ''You and I both know that smokers have to satisfy their addiction. If you cut them off, they're really going to scream. But let them.''

''None of this will work unless they think they can be held to it,'' Cam protested.

''What are you prepared to do if you find them smoking on base?''

Shrugging, Cam said, "I don't know...."

"Have them wash the Apaches—inside and out. Or have them run five miles with fifty pound packs on their back. Put Morales out there to make sure they do it. He's your X.O. He gets to do the dirty work."

"And what about banning them from partying?"

"Well," Maya said, "if they are stupid enough to go off base when you've ordered them to stay, then that's a major offense, and they can be thrown out of the military. It's called going AWOL. I don't feel they're willing to test the combined might of the U.S. Army and the Mexican Air Force on that one. And if they do, then you have them dead to rights and you can, at that point, get rid of them."

"I see...."

"Yeah, always think about what someone isn't willing to give up. That is where you work with them, Cam. That's the ground you plow."

"Okay...I can do that."

"As to the other thing," Maya said, murmuring more to herself than to Cam. "I'll contact Morgan and see about gettin' you a third Apache. Your plan makes a lot of sense."

"But you can't really afford to lose Snake and Wild Woman...." Cam said worriedly. There were no extra pilots to pick up the slack at Maya's squadron if the two left, even for six weeks.

"There you go, mother hen," Maya teased. "The problem is getting the army to let loose of one of their Apache Longbows for six weeks. I can get the women you want up there, no problem."

"But—"

"Look at it this way," Maya told her. "Dane and

I will step in and make up the difference while they are gone, so it won't be a problem.''

Disheartened, Cam sat there in silence. That meant Maya and her husband, Dane, would not only be handling their immense responsibilities at the squadron, they'd take on twenty-four-hour flight duty as well. That was an awful strain and Cam knew it.

"I thought you'd say that.''

"That's the way the cookie crumbles, Cam. Sometimes you bite the bullet and just do it. No one said life was always easy, did they?''

"No,'' Cam grumped, "just damned unfair.''

"The way I see it, your two rich boys need a boot in the butt. You've selected two of the best pilots to ensure they're going to be living in hell from now on, once they get up there and start working with them.''

"Yeah,'' Cam laughed, "Snake and Wild Woman won't take any crap from either one of them.''

"That's right, they'll be in their faces. And what you need to do is stand out of the way. So does your X.O. You let the ladies handle their immature charges. You back them and support them and keep the two Mexican pilots on a real short leash. No liberty unless they produce. No smoking unless on liberty. These two boys are gonna find out in a helluva hurry that playtime is over and it's nose to the grindstone time instead.''

"I'm feeling better, Maya…thanks so much! I know what kind of effort you're putting into this to help me.''

"Listen, that's what this is all about—teamwork and support. You have a mission to complete. You're going to need help we didn't think of at first, because of the players you're stuck with and can't get rid of. So, in essence, we're callin' in the cavalry—Snake, Wild Woman and a third Apache. I'll get it done for you, so don't worry. You need to tell your X.O. what's going to happen, though. He needs to know and then support you a hundred percent when the crap hits the fan.''

"I know Gus will," Cam said. "He's supported me from the beginning.''

Maya laughed lightly. "Do you realize that every time you mention that dude's name, your voice goes soft and mushy, Anderson? You like him or what?''

Shocked, Cam sat up straight. Her heart pounded briefly as she considered her C.O.'s words. "What? Er…no. Why…no, of course not. I mean, he's a likable guy, Maya. Real easygoing compared to the other two jerks. But like him?''

"Whoa!" Maya chortled. "Rein in your horse, lady, I was just wonderin' out loud, was all. Your energy changes when you talk about him. Your voice changes.''

"Well," Cam sputtered, "probably because he's my only safe port in this storm!''

"I see. Okay, gimme a couple of days to put plan B in motion for you. I'll give you a call at midnight, your time, in forty-eight hours.''

"Thanks, Maya…as usual, you're magical, the way you pull rabbits out of hats to save my butt.''

"Your butt's worth protectin', Cam. Relax. You're doin' things right and to the best of your abilities. No one can ask more of you. Now, I'd be hunting down my X.O. and lettin' him know ASAP about plan B. I actually feel sorry for Zaragoza and Dominguez. You need to decide which one gets assigned to Snake and which to Wild Woman.'' She chuckled darkly. ''I wish I could be there to see their faces when my women pilots get into *their* faces. It oughta be a Kodak moment.''

Laughter spilled from Cam's lips. She loved the black humor that was so much a part of BJS. ''Maya, if I didn't know any better, I'd say you were going to enjoy this.''

''Damn straight. I don't put up with crap like that from a green pilot, man or woman. They're in the military and they're damn well gonna respond accordingly or else.''

Relief flooded Cam and she rested her elbow on her knee, the phone in her hand. ''Maya, thanks. I don't know what I'd do without you.''

''Same here, Cam. We miss you down here. Our mother hen is gone. The women miss your nurturing, the chicken soup, the chocolate chip cookies you bake for them when they have pilot duty.'' She chuckled. ''Get some sleep, Tree Trimmer. Tomorrow's another day. A better one, I promise.''

Gus sat with Cam in the darkness of the grove on the picnic table that had become their ritual meeting place. He had his guitar in hand, his arm resting over it as he listened to plan B. Overhead, the stars were bright in the blackness of the night.

He liked Cam's husky, soft voice. He liked the way she used her hands to gesture as she spoke. Did she realize how beautiful her hands were? ''Flight hands'' was what they called them in the military. Good pilots had a certain look in their eyes, and hands that were long, graceful and lean—all hallmarks of a good flyer. She was certainly that—and more—but Gus refused to go there no matter what the cost to him personally.

He liked to bring dessert out to the grove and share it with Cam during their nightly chats. It was the only time she seemed to have free to discuss his X.O. duties. If Cam wasn't flying six hours a day and trying to bring the two Mexican pilots up to par in flight skills, she was at her office plowing through a mountain of paperwork. Some of it Gus had been able to talk her out of, and do himself. Little by little, they were learning what a C.O. and X.O. did to help one another and balance the workload.

Looking down at the opened box of chocolate chip cookies he'd bought in town Gus saw that half of them were gone. He looked up at Cam, sitting two feet away from him on the table, waving a fifth cookie in her hand as she talked. Smiling to himself, he felt his heart growing warm as he studied her profile.

''So, that's what is gonna happen,'' she told Gus, turning and looking at him. She watched as he picked up another cookie and bit into it. ''What do you think?''

Raising one eyebrow, he murmured, ''I'd invoke the loss of privileges after the third Apache and the two IPs arrive. I wouldn't try it now.''

Nodding, Cam said, ''Okay.''

''That way, you're hitting those two with maximum firepower all at once. What you're trying to do is jolt them out of the cozy little world they've established here under your command. When you have three IPs around, they're less likely to buck you, I think. It's a matter of numbers. It's a matter of overwhelming them with equal or greater firepower.'' He grinned.

''That sounds right,'' Cam murmured. ''Good advice.''

Heart thudding as Gus gave her that wicked little-boy smile, Cam eagerly drank in the look in his darkened eyes. Oh, how she looked forward to these nightly talks. Of course, Cam said it was business—serious business—and he'd agreed. However, tonight of all nights, Gus had brought her her favorite cookies. She'd casually mentioned it a week ago, when their talk had strayed into the personal realm, and he'd asked her what her favorite dessert was.

Finishing the cookie, Gus wiped his hand on his jeans and then stroked a few chords on the guitar. The music filled the grove and he saw Cam's face relax. When the little things he did for her made her happy, his heart soared. He knew the pressures Cam was under. Yet she had a quiet strength, a steely quality that wasn't revealed outwardly. Cam had a kind-looking face, but she was tough when she had to be. Maybe there was a difference in how a woman commanded, Gus mused. It was an interesting fishbowl experiment, as far as he was concerned. He knew a man could sometimes be aggressive and in-your-face as a C.O. But Cam's quiet firmness worked for him. Not on his two cohorts, however.

Strumming the guitar more loudly, Gus played another melody. Cam smiled and his heart melted. Her eyes grew dreamy, as she sat with her arms wrapped around herself, elbows on her thighs. Smiling back, Gus lost himself in the tune.

For ten minutes he played, and Cam was able to

surrender to the gentle, healing melodies that Gus coaxed from his old, beat-up guitar. For the first time today, Cam utterly relaxed. It was him, she decided— Gus was quiet, yet so perceptive of her needs. It was as if he could read her mind and see inside her heart. Cam had never met a man who had that ability or effect on her.

When he ended the tune, she turned to him. "That was beautiful. What was it?"

"It's a lullaby of the Yaqui people," he murmured, his fingers brushing the guitar lovingly. "My mother used to sing it to me. I grew up listening to it."

"It's lovely. I'm glad you bring your guitar out here when we meet."

"Yeah?" Gus grinned a little. Her eyes lightened.

"Yeah. It makes a good ending to a tough day." And Cam frowned.

"Well," he murmured, "your bad days are comin' to an end. Your C.O. said the Apache will be here tomorrow and so will the two IPs. Then those bad days will land on Zaragoza and Dominguez." Chuckling, Gus added, "And it couldn't happen to two nicer dudes, in my opinion."

Heartened, Cam gave him a weak smile. "I'm glad your dad taught you about the life of an X.O. I'm almost jealous. I wish I had better skills, more education in management."

Reaching out unthinkingly, Gus slid his hand over her slumped shoulder. His fingers grazed her denim jacket and he felt the strength of her beneath the rough material. The look in her soulful eyes at his unexpected touch affected him deeply. For a moment, just a brief moment, Cam had leaned into his hand, as if starved for a human touch. A little care. It was then that Gus realized—too late—that his gesture was personal and intimate. Certainly not military.

Unhappy with himself, Gus pulled his hand away and muttered, "You're making the best of a bad situation, Cam. I think you're doing a good job."

Skin tingling where Gus had briefly and unexpectedly touched her, Cam stared at his profile. His mouth was set in an unhappy line; his dark brows were knitted. She had never expected him to touch her—ever. But he had. And that instant had been a wonderful, healing gift. His hand had slid across her shoulder in such a gentle, caressing gesture that Cam had automatically, without thinking, leaned closer, starved for his touch. Really starved for him to embrace her and hold her.

The whole brief moment was so shocking to Cam that she straightened up, her hands clenched on her thighs. Somewhere in her colliding thoughts, she realized a huge part of her had wanted desperately to walk into his arms and be held. Gus gave her that— a sense of safety and protection in a world where she felt continually exposed and vulnerable, especially in the presence of the other two pilots. With Gus around, Cam relaxed. She felt safe with him. They always laughed and joked in the cockpit, even though they were in training. It was fun. Being alone with *him* was something she looked forward to daily.

Swallowing hard, Cam whispered, "I think we'd better go. I gotta get up early tomorrow…." And she slid off the table and dusted off the rear of her jeans. Cam saw the sober look on Gus's face. He seemed unhappy about his action toward her. She tried not to take it personally, but she did anyway.

Her heart cried out in protest as they began the trek back to the barracks. Cam made sure there was plenty of space between her and Gus as they walked so there'd be no possibility of their hands brushing.

Floundering around for a safe topic, because she felt so awkward and unsure of herself, Cam said, "You must have a wonderful woman waiting for you stateside, right?"

Moving the guitar strap to his left shoulder so that the instrument was between them, Gus felt his heart contract. He slowed for a moment, then resumed his usual stride. "No," he said, more abruptly than he'd meant to. "There's no one." He looked over at her, his face in shadows. "What about you? You said the BJS is primarily all women, with a few support men. Is there someone special down there waiting for you to come back?"

Cam shook her head. "No..." She chewed on her lip. "I...I don't have a good track record with men. I swore off them for a while because of it. The last three years have been wonderful in some ways without men in my life."

"Yeah, relationships are hard," Gus muttered. Then why did his heart soar when he heard Cam admit she had no man in her life?

"And right now," Cam added, her voice growing strong with conviction, "I'm more focused on my career than a personal life."

"Makes two of us," Gus said fervently, meaning it. Or did he?

Chapter 7

Gus knew things were going to explode the moment the two BJS women pilots confidently sauntered into their small classroom the next morning. Gus and the two pilots were sitting at their respective desks, facing a green chalkboard, where Cam stood, briefing them on the day's flight mission. Only he had been taking serious notes on the upcoming maneuvers. Luis and Antonio, upon hearing the door open behind them, turned. Gus, who was sitting on one side of the room, his desk positioned so he could see them all, lifted his head.

The two women pilots who walked in were in typical U.S. Army flight uniforms. What wasn't typical was the blond woman; she had a red streak dyed in her hair. The other one, taller and leaner, followed her in like a cat on a prowl for its quarry. Shifting his gaze, Gus saw Cam smile slightly at them in welcome. By the gleam in her eyes Gus knew she was glad to see her sisters from her old base in Peru.

"Come in," Cam invited them, "and stand up here. Let me make the introductions."

Gus saw the mischievous glint in both pilots' eyes as they walked toward the front of the room. They each wore the patch of the Black Jaguar Squadron on their left shoulder and an American flag on the right. The black leather patch above their left breast pocket had their pilot handle or nickname, their real name and their rank.

As Wild Woman, the shorter of the two, started to walk past Zaragoza, he gave a low wolf whistle of appreciation.

Instantly, she turned around. The expression on her face changed from one of innocence to a snarling grimace. She grabbed the collar of Antonio's flight suit, pinned him against the chair and put her face an inch from his own, their noses nearly touching.

"What do you think you are doing, mister?" she snarled. "Whistling for your dog? Funny, I don't see any dogs in here. I see a stupid jerk, though. Right in front of me. Now, you wanna do that again?" Her lips curled back from her clenched teeth.

Zaragoza croaked. He jerked his hands into the air, not daring to touch the hissing woman pilot.

Gus squelched his laughter. Antonio was sliding down in his seat, trying to escape the gringo woman's unexpected response. *Serves him right.*

"Well?" Wild Woman barked. "You got a dog in this room, mister?"

"Uh…no. No, *señorita*—"

"What?" Wild Woman practically roared into his

face, her hand tightening on his collar and jerking it savagely. "I don't see any *señoritas* in this room, either. What's the appropriate military response, mister?"

Antonio choked and coughed, his eyes growing huge. Waving his hands spastically in surrender, he tried to move, but was pinned. "I, uh…*Sí*, ma'am."

Releasing him and giving him a look of utter disgust, Wild Woman growled, "That's better, mister. You do any more whistling and I'll rip your lips off your face. *Comprende?*"

Shocked, Zaragoza tried to sit up and straighten his flight suit. "Uh…yes, *sí*, ma'am, *sí*…" he mumbled, highly embarrassed.

Luis, who sat beside his friend watching the whole thing with widened eyes stayed very still. Gus thought he might be in shock. The two women pilots continued their nonchalant walk to the front of the room as if nothing had happened.

They came to attention, saluted Cam and did everything militarily correct, under the circumstances. Gus silently applauded them. Nothing like showing the "boys" in the room what was expected of them. Cam returned the salute.

"About-face," she ordered the two women pilots, "and stand at parade rest."

Instantly, the two concurred, performing the move crisply, in unison. They stood in front of the room, to Cam's right, hands behind their backs, their booted feet slightly apart, chins high and shoulders thrown back with pride. Gus thought they were magnificent looking. He saw rock-solid confidence in every inch of their unsmiling faces, especially in their eyes, which reminded him of alert eagles, poised and ready to strike. The caliber of these women blew him away. Gus understood from talking with Cam earlier that they all had three years of wartime combat flying under their belt. Whoever had trained them had done so to a blade's fine edge. They looked intimidating. Dangerous. Moving his gaze to the two male pilots, he slid his hand across his mouth to hide his burgeoning smile.

Zaragoza was completely shaken. He'd thought he'd get away with a wolf whistle. The last thing he'd expected was for the blonde to turn and confront him on his undesired male behavior. Now he sat stiffly at his desk, hands fluttering nervously around his collar, constantly readjusting it. His skin, normally a golden-tan, was rosy and flushed.

Luis Dominguez wasn't smiling. He was scowling, and Gus could see him measuring up the two pilots who had just come in. Though Gus wasn't sure about what Luis was thinking, he wasn't about to whistle, that was for certain.

Cam smiled benignly at the three male pilots. "Gentlemen, I want to introduce the rest of our squadron." Lifting her hand toward the woman nearest to her, she said, "Chief Warrant Officer 2 Jessica Merrill. We call her Wild Woman." Cam kept her face serious as she nailed the still-shaken Antonio with a look that spoke volumes. He'd just had a taste of her wild, unpredictable side.

"And to her right is Chief Warrant Officer 2 Vickey Mabrey. Her handle is Snake." Cam went on to quietly introduce the three student pilots. Then she went to her lectern and picked up a set of papers.

Holding them out to Gus, her X.O., who stood up and approached her, she said, "Mr. Morales, please pass out this new set of orders to everyone?"

Gus nodded. "Yes, ma'am." And he turned and handed a set each to Luis and Antonio. Returning to his seat, he sat down with his own copy in hand. He knew what they contained, because he'd typed them up earlier that morning.

Cam passed sets to Wild Woman and Snake. "All right, let's go over them together, because these orders are in force as of right now."

Gus watched covertly as Cam read the pages in a low, authoritative tone. He saw first shock, and then rage in Luis's and Antonio's eyes as they found out they were ordered to stay on base—permanently—until their flight scores improved to eighty percent. Right now, their marks hovered in the thirty to forty percentile range. When Cam told them they couldn't smoke until they were off base, their mouths dropped open.

"But...but—" Luis stammered, starting to get out of his chair.

"Sit down, mister," Snake snarled at him. "Where I come from, you sit and raise your hand. Do it."

Stunned by the tall, dark-haired pilot's order, Luis sat. Immediately. Shock was clearly written on his face. It took him a moment, but he hesitantly raised his hand.

"Mr. Dominguez?" Cam said. "You had a question?"

"Uh...*sí*, ma'am."

"And what might that be?" Cam kept any satisfaction out of her tone. She silently thanked her sister pilots for their aggressive, intimidating stance. Though Cam hadn't known exactly what to expect from them, Wild Woman's and Snake's behavior seemed appropriate under the circumstances. Never had Cam been so glad to see them as now. Already, just having them here was tilting the balance in the room to her favor. Now there were three women pilots, all skilled, and two petulant male students who clearly realized things were changing.

Luis wiped his sweaty brow. "Ma'am, no smoking?"

"Oh, of course, Mr. Dominguez, you can smoke. Once your flight marks hit eighty percent, you can smoke in your room or outside the barracks."

Gulping, he cast a wild look of appeal in Gus's direction.

Gus shrugged eloquently, his body language clear: he couldn't get the orders changed.

"But—but—"

"No buts, Mr. Dominguez," Cam said smoothly. "You perform in the cockpit, you get to smoke. If you choose not to try and become more skilled in flight interdiction, then I guess you've chosen to stop smoking for the time you are with this mission." She smiled faintly. "Of course, you can choose to leave this mission at any time." She picked up a set of papers from her lectern. "The necessary forms are right here. All you have to do is ask for a transfer and I'll be happy to give it to you. All any of you need to do is ask." Cam couldn't help it; she gloated. A good leader probably didn't do that, but she couldn't stop herself right now.

Cam knew that neither pilot would take that option.

It would shame them to their families, and being first-born sons, much was expected of them. They were supposed to excel, not run away from something. No, she knew they'd tough it out, but down deep inside her she prayed they'd jump at the chance to leave.

Both pilots stared at her as if she were Cerberus, the three-headed dog from Greek mythology who protected the gates to hell.

"No takers?" Cam asked them sweetly, raising an eyebrow. "No?" She put the orders down on the lectern. "Very well. Then this means, gentlemen, that I need to assign you an IP for the duration of this mission."

"Ms. Merrill?"

"Yes, ma'am?"

"I'd like you to teach Mr. Zaragoza the finer points of interdiction in the cockpit of the Apache."

Wild Woman smiled, gazed at Antonio, who had another shocked look on his face, and said with great pleasure, "Yes, ma'am!"

"Excellent," Cam murmured. "And Ms. Mabrey?"

"Yes, ma'am?"

"You're to take Mr. Dominguez under your wing and teach him the more refined aspects of interdiction in the air."

Snake didn't smile. She rarely did. Giving Dominguez a glare that spoke volumes, she saw the Mexican pilot, whose ego was larger than the Empire State Building, begin to deflate. "My pleasure, ma'am. We'll make it happen." Her mouth twisted into a smirk. "Or else…"

"Excellent," Cam murmured, pleased. She saw

Dominguez go white as a proverbial sheet. And she saw the rage in his eyes, but he had the good sense to keep his mouth shut. With Wild Woman physically intimidating Antonio, she knew Luis didn't want Snake descending upon him. And she knew Vickey was fully capable of doing it, too. These women didn't put up with gender prejudice one iota, especially in the military world.

Luis raised his hand.

"Yes, Mr. Dominguez?"

"Er...ma'am...how is it we cannot leave the base? We have left every night so far."

Cam opened her hands and gave him a stern look. "You've made choices that aren't appropriate for good military training, so something had to be done about it, Mr. Dominguez. When you demonstrate to me, on a daily basis, that your flight training can maintain an eighty percent, then you will be authorized liberty for that night. Your curfew is 2200."

"Twenty-two hundred hours?" Luis yelped.

"Mister," Snake hissed, "you want me to come over there and rearrange that mouth of yours? Your response to our commanding officer is 'ma'am.' Got it?"

Gulping, Luis nodded jerkily. His gaze was pinned on Snake, who had taken one step toward him, her entire body suddenly tense, her hands tightened into fists at her side. The look on her face made it clear she shouldn't be messed with. Luis had no desire to have this woman, who was at least six foot tall, come over and do something to him similar to what Antonio had just experienced.

"*Sí*, ma'am. Yes, ma'am."

Snake gave him a narrow-eyed look. "That's better, mister." And she snapped crisply back into parade-rest position.

Luis sent Cam a desperate glance. "Ma'am, you cannot do this to me. To us!"

"Of course I can, Mr. Dominguez. It's my responsibility to see that you three pilots meet our expectations. If you do, you get rewards. If you don't..." Cam shrugged eloquently and opened her hands "...well, then it's your choice, and your own fault. These women are IPs in the Apache Longbow. They've got three years of daily combat experience in South America chasing down bad guys who are trying to haul cocaine out of the country where they're stationed. I assure you that if you set your minds and hearts to learning from them, in five weeks time you will become excellent at interdiction."

Disheartened, Luis sank back into his seat.

"Mr. Morales, please hand out today's mission folder to everyone? Chiefs? If you'll have a seat." And Cam motioned for her sister pilots to sit down at the desks at the rear of the room. Both of them came to attention and then quickly took their seats.

While Gus distributed the mission plan, the room practically vibrated with tension. Luis and Antonio were clearly in shock over everything that had just transpired. Gus was glad for more reasons than one that Cam was going to be his IP. As he handed out the mission flight plan and training techniques to be flown, he tried not to admit to the secret personal pleasure he felt at being in her company. The emotional wounds of his past ate at him hourly when he was around Cam now, and it was getting to him.

* * *

"Very good, Gus!" Cam said over the intercom of the Apache he was flying. As they flew over the mountainous training area at four thousand feet, she wrote down his final grade for today's flight on the clipboard on her lap: a ninety percent. Sitting in the upper cockpit, she glanced down proudly at his helmeted head and saw his hand resting confidently on the collective between his legs.

"You get to go on liberty tonight," she said, laughing.

"That's great to hear," he said, joining her laughter. Although he'd been focused on his own training, he wondered how the other two pilots were faring. Not well, most likely, but they weren't in radio contact. At least he wasn't. He was sure Cam was, as C.O. From time to time this afternoon he'd seen the other two Apaches in the distance over the mountains, but that was all.

"Well," Gus said, turning the Apache back to the usual restricted flight corridor that would take them fifteen miles out over the Pacific Ocean, "if I get liberty tonight, do you want to meet me in the grove around 2100?" His heart beat a little harder in his chest. God help him, but he really enjoyed spending time with Cam. Her soft, low voice was always nurturing to him. Even when he made mistakes and she corrected him, she did it gently. She was such a dichotomy. Gus knew that, in the air, she could be an aggressive combat pilot, and yet with him that aggression was never apparent, just the nurturing teacher who shared her delight with him when he performed flawlessly.

"Sure," she answered promptly.

Feeling relief, Gus smiled as he urged the Apache to the required five-thousand-foot altitude. Below, the Pacific was a smooth, dark blue color, with rolling waves sparkling in the setting sun. "Business, of course," he assured her. "I think we've got a lot to talk about tonight, C.O. to X.O."

Cam finished her remarks on his flight test for the day and slipped the pen back into the pocket on her left sleeve. "Of course," she murmured, "all business." Sliding the clipboard into a pocket on the left side of her seat, she sighed.

"I'm going to have a meeting with Snake and Wild Woman at 1800." She glanced at her watch; that was an hour from now. The mission they'd flown today was four grueling hours of nonstop training. Cam knew the two Mexican pilots were probably feeling like limp dishrags at this point. Or they should be if they cared. Only time would tell, after they landed and she got together with her sister pilots to be briefed on their flights.

"Okay. You want me to sit in?"

"Absolutely."

"And then chow?"

Chuckling, Cam said, "You're never far away from that chow hall, are you?"

Gus grinned and studied his HUDs carefully for other aircraft, authorized or not. "I'm a chow hound, for sure. Guilty as charged. Are you going to go eat there tonight after the briefing?"

"Yeah," Cam said, relaxing in her seat and enjoying the ride, "I probably will."

Gus couldn't help but get excited. Cam was like an

addiction to him emotionally. He went to bed dreaming about her. When he woke up in the morning, he'd hurry through his routine to get to the chow hall because he knew she always ate breakfast. From then on, he was with her most of the day. Usually, Cam didn't eat at the chow hall at night. Understanding that she was stressed out about Luis and Antonio, Gus ate alone. Now that the new IPs were here, she was going to be able to relax and enjoy an evening meal. That made him happy.

"Maybe you want some personal time with your friends at the chow hall, though?"

Cam was finding Gus very astute about relationships. It was one more plus in his column. "Yes...I'd like that. At least tonight, Gus. Can I meet you at the grove later?"

"Sure, no problem. I imagine you'll have a lot to catch up on with them."

"Yes," Cam murmured, "I do."

"You really miss your squadron, don't you?"

"Is it that obvious?"

Chuckling, Gus said, "Maybe just to me, because I've been around you a lot more than the other two."

"They're like a second family," Cam explained, flexing her gloved hands. The sunlight was strong and bright in the cockpit. She was glad for the constant air-conditioning that kept the space cool.

"Judging from the looks in their eyes, they were glad to see you, too."

Cam smiled wistfully. "Down at BJS, I'm the squadron mother hen. I take care of them when they're sick. I make chicken soup and bring it to the barracks for them."

"You're a good listener," Gus murmured. "I like talking with you. Sharing. I always feel like you're there for me, a hundred percent. You aren't just there in body, but in heart, mind and spirit, too."

Warmth flooded her face, and Cam knew she was blushing. "Snake calls me Big Mama in the Sky."

Gus grinned. "Nice. Yeah, that fits you, Cam. Anyone with an ounce of intelligence can see you care. You nurture others, you don't take a pound of flesh out of them."

"Well," Cam answered dryly, "that depends upon the person I'm dealing with. You *want* to learn flight tactics. Luis and Antonio didn't, so I don't think Snake or Wild Woman are going to be very nurturing or pleasant to them."

Gus laughed heartily. "No, I don't think there's any mothering coming their way right now. Just hell on earth. But they've sown the seeds, so now they'll reap the harvest."

"Yep, where we come from, we call it rubber band karma. You put it out there, and that's what's gonna come snapping back at you in an instant."

"Well, I'm grateful to you for passing on what you know to me. I've learned more from you this week alone than I did in the ten weeks of Apache flight school. You're hard, demanding, but you teach like no one I've ever encountered."

"Are you bucking for a hundred percent on your grade?" Cam teased, privately pleased at his praise. It was nice to get some feedback.

Chuckling indulgently, Gus swung the Apache toward San Diego and followed the invisible flight corridor over the sprawling city. "No, ma'am, I'm not.

It's just that I feel you need to know how good you
are at what you do. If you ever questioned volunteering for this assignment, you should stop that.''

"With the other IPs and a third Apache, I think we
can get this mission accomplished,'' Cam said. She
saw the graceful arc of the Coronado Bridge on her
left. Rush hour was upon them, and there were
thousands of cars moving slowly across the bridge,
bumper to bumper. She was glad to be in the Apache,
above it all.

"Well, let's see how Luis and Antonio took to their
lessons today,'' she murmured in a droll tone.

"Yeah,'' Gus said merrily. "I can hardly wait for
the briefing.''

The truth be known, he was really looking forward
to meeting Cam tonight, as he always did, in that
darkened grove. It was their quiet time together,
something Gus hungered for and counted on. Did
she? As he made a right turn for the downwind leg
of their flight corridor, over the Mexican border once
more, Gus wondered if Cam liked him at all. In his
heart, he wanted her to. In his mind, when he remembered his tragic past, he knew he shouldn't dare
dream of loving Cam.

Chapter 8

"Who the hell gave these two dudes pilot licenses?" Snake growled as she dropped her report on the green metal table in front of Cam in the briefing room.

Gus sat with Cam behind the table. The room was barely big enough for a dozen people. Snake was visibly agitated, her green eyes angry slits as she came and sat down opposite him.

"Yeah," Wild Woman muttered as she shut the door and handed Cam her report on Dominguez. "Snake and I are in agreement—the only thing they should have licenses to drive are tricycles. That or go to Disneyland. Take your pick."

Squelching a laugh, because he knew it wasn't appropriate, Gus said nothing as Wild Woman pulled out a metal chair and sat down. Blowing out a sigh of obvious exasperation, she ran her fingers through her blond hair, which was flattened from wearing her flight helmet.

"Hold on...." Cam murmured, quickly paging through the grades on each mission priority that the pilots had had to fly that day.

"I need a drink," Snake said, looking around. "A double." To her dismay, she saw there wasn't even coffee available.

Chuckling, Wild Woman put her hand on Vickey's shoulder and patted it. "Don't let those two macho egos drive you to alcohol. They aren't worth it, believe me."

"Ain't that the truth?" Vickey said, scowling darkly.

"Here," Cam said to Gus, and handed him Zaragoza's graded report, "read this."

Nodding, Gus took the flight report. He was familiar with this type of report because during school he'd been graded every single day on every single flight. After he'd landed, the IP would go over what he'd done right and wrong, and give him a final grade. Gus hated the schooling and he hated the grading. He always walked away from the cockpit with sweat staining the underarms of his flight suit. It was a tense time, and he had a lot of sympathy for Antonio and Luis. But then, he reminded himself, they had chosen to do things their way and not the army's way. They had literally skated through Apache school because they were foreign nationals, and no one wanted to flunk them out even if they deserved to fail. Such was politics, he guessed.

His gaze fell to the bottom line of the evaluation: twenty-five percent. Quirking his mouth, Gus set the report aside and glanced over at Wild Woman, who was sitting back, her arms crossed, legs spread out beneath the table, studying him.

"Stunning figures, aren't they?" she said.

"Very," Gus agreed. He saw Wild Woman assessing him, not sure at this point if he was friend or foe. He wondered if it was because he was male. Gus wasn't sure. He knew these women were a tight group, and he felt like an outsider right now.

"The other one," Cam said dryly, and handed him Luis Dominguez's report.

Gus quickly paged through it. Cam waited, her hands folded, while he skimmed it. Dropping to the bottom line, he saw that Snake had given him eighteen percent as a final grade.

"Well," he said, putting the second report down, "they didn't do very well."

"That is an understatement," Snake muttered defiantly. She shook her head.

Cam nodded and pursed her lips. She remembered her training at their secret base in Peru, and how Maya would bring all the pilots together afterward to talk about their flight. A part of her wanted to bring Antonio and Luis in, but right now her gut said not to. Unfolding her hands, she looked at her sister pilots.

"Give us the scoop. Wild Woman? Tell us what went wrong up there with Zaragoza."

Rolling her eyes, Wild Woman sat up. "He peed his pants."

Gus looked at her. "Excuse me?"

"I pulled a twin engine failure on him at five thousand feet, and he freaked out. He couldn't remember how to set the Apache up for anything. In flight school, we always got single and double engine failure tests. Everyone has to know how to set the bird up so it can make an emergency landing without power. This is preliminary, basic training, so I followed your protocols, Cam. He blanked out. I was the one who had to do the recovery.'' She shook her head. ''On the ground, when he left the Apache, the seat of his pants were dark and wet. I figured out the rest.''

Cam gave Gus a glance that spoke volumes. On their first day together, she'd tested him on single and double engine failure, and he'd done everything right and recovered without stress.

Gus gave her an unhappy look. ''Is there more to this, Gus?'' she asked him.

''Yeah, there is.'' He looked across the table at the two scowling women. ''I went through Apache school with them.''

''Oh,'' Snake muttered, ''so you know these dudes intimately.''

''Unfortunately, I do. In school, they didn't haul their weight. They thought it was playtime, not serious work. They kept passing the flight tests and I couldn't figure out why at the time.''

''And,'' Cam told them grimly, ''we found out from Maya that there were serious politics being played to get these two boys through the school no matter how badly they flew. There are indications that IPs signed off their flights with a passing grade when they shouldn't have.''

Groaning, Snake got to her feet. She scratched her head and paced the length of the room, then stopped.

"Okay, so what I'm gathering is we've got two so-called 'pilots' who really aren't anywhere near up to grade. They skated by because of the smoke and mirrors, right?"

"Right," Cam agreed quietly. She saw Wild Woman's blue eyes widen.

"Then how the hell do they expect *you* to have this drug interdiction mission up and running in four weeks?" Her voice was high and off-key with anger.

"Bingo," Cam agreed. "That's why I called you two in. I needed help."

"Help?" Snake asked, frustrated. "How about kicking these two jerks out of the cockpit and going back to the school and getting two people who *did* pass?" She pointed to Gus. "He passed. And he's doing a good job, according to you. So why not find two more Mexican pilots who are hungry, who are damn good pilots, and trade them off for these two playboys?"

"It's not that easy," Gus told her.

Snake glared at him. "I'll tell you something, Chief. Our C.O. down at the base would kick these two guys out in the blink of an eye. She wouldn't stand for this kind of ineptness in the cockpit. They'll get someone killed up there real fast, and it isn't gonna be me in the back seat getting it because they're sloughing off and don't know what the hell they're doing. No. Not on my watch."

"I agree," Gus said. "But Cam's been saddled with them. This mission is more than just what it seems on the surface. It's political, too."

"Yes," Cam agreed, growing grim and giving Vickey a sober look. The pilot sat down.

"I'm caught between a rock and a hard place," Cam told Jessica and Vickey. "The only way I can get rid of them is to force them into signing those papers that say they agree to be reassigned elsewhere."

"And if you know anything about Hispanic men," Gus added, giving Cam a glance, "they have machismo and ego to burn. My personal opinion is that now that Cam and you have put them up against the wall, they'll try to come around because they won't opt for the second choice."

"Which is to look bad, look like the failures they are," Snake muttered, rolling her eyes. "Dude, this sucks."

Cam sat back in the chair, her hands on her thighs. "Yeah, it does. I didn't realize what I was stepping into."

"Dominguez threw up in his cockpit," Snake said. "I made him stay out there and clean it up himself. I wasn't about to let the ground crew clean up after he barfed."

"Good!" Cam exclaimed. "What maneuver did it?"

"Inside loop," Snake growled. "He couldn't do it. I had to take the controls and get the bird out of it. He was barfing all over the place and complaining he has a 'delicate stomach.'"

Jessica laughed and looked at her friend. "You gotta be kidding me!"

Snake gave her a dirty look. "I'm glad our cockpits are separate. I'd hate to have had to smell that awful odor for three hours."

Cam wrinkled her nose. "You mean you didn't land right away?"

All the women chuckled. Everyone who flew experienced nausea and at times threw up. But they kept on flying.

"No," Snake said, "because the dumb idiot forgot to put his barf bag in the thigh pocket of his flight suit. If he'd had it with him, he coulda used it and things wouldn't have ended up so bad. So—" she grinned wolfishly "—he suffered the consequences of not making sure he had the appropriate gear during preflight. Oh, well…"

"I'll bet next time he will," Gus said.

"That's my bet, too," Snake agreed, her mouth pulling into a sour smile. "You only forget once in our business."

"Well," Cam said, "that's the least of our problems, as I see it."

"Yeah," Wild Woman griped, "how do you get these two dudes to qualify for legit flight status? They can't possibly learn interdiction at this point. Isn't there something you can do, Cam? Can't you *force* the Mexican government to give us two *qualified* pilots?"

Shaking her head, she murmured, "No, I can't."

"Okay," Snake said, "then we'll force these dudes to quit by making them work so hard they'll want to leave here screamin'."

"That's the plan," Cam said. "I have no other options. That's what I saw before you came." She gave Gus a slight smile. "If we had two more pilots like Chief Morales, we'd be on easy street, but that's not what we got handed."

"Okay," Wild Woman said, rising and giving Snake an evil look as she stretched her hand toward Gus. "You got our flight mission for tomorrow?"

"Yes," Gus said, and handed it to them.

"Good. C'mon, Snake, let's go into TJ, have some tequila and lime straight up, plot, plan and figure out how to chase these two tricycle pilots outta here so we can get two good replacements on this mission."

Gus saw Cam smile as the two women left. There was relief in her wide, beautiful eyes. She deserved to have help, under the circumstances. When the door shut and the room grew quiet, he slowly rose to his feet.

"Want to have chow with me?"

Looking up, Cam smiled. His face was strong and chiseled. There was nothing not to like about Gus. "Yeah, I'd like that, X.O."

Grinning, Gus said, "I kinda like this new position. I'm privy to all the dirt that's goin' around in the squadron."

Laughing, Cam stood and gathered up the reports. She would transmit them to Maya and Morgan later as proof that the two playboy pilots were as bad as she had originally described them. Over time, she hoped the mounting evidence in each day's flight would, perhaps, force Morgan Trayhern to do something about it.

"Yeah, well, I'd rather *not* have dirt to sweep under the rug of our squadron, if the truth be known."

Opening the door, Gus smiled down at her as she hefted the dark brown briefcase in her left hand. "I know. There's nothing like a well-oiled, well-run squadron. My dad has that touch. He's a great manager of people.''

"I'm learning how to be," Cam said goodnaturedly as she stepped out into the hall. A number of crews were coming in for the night, making the place noisy. Looking up and down the corridor, she saw nothing of Zaragoza and Dominguez. They were probably in their rooms on the first floor, nursing their wounded egos after today's humiliating flights.

Heart lifting with joy, she walked with Gus at her side. This was the first time she'd be with him at the chow hall. It was something Cam was looking forward to. "Does this mean we won't have our nightly meeting out in the grove?" she asked, because she really looked forward to that quiet, uninterrupted time with him.

"Heck, no. That's still on the table, if you want it to be?" Gus searched her wide, forest-green eyes, which shone with gold flecks in their depths. Cam was happy, he realized. And that made him feel good.

"Great," Cam sighed. "It's a special time and I look forward to it, Gus."

The strumming of the guitar made Cam want to melt into Gus's arms. It was nearly midnight, and the stars shone brightly, like glittering pinpoints overhead among the black branches of the trees. Tonight Gus had brought her fresh baked cookies once again. She'd learned that he'd found a Mexican woman not far from the base who could bake them so long as he supplied the ingredients. Somehow—Cam didn't know when—Gus had made a trip across the border to San Diego, to go to a grocery store and buy the items needed. His thoughtfulness was never ending, in her opinion. The bag of chocolate chip cookies sat between them. She sat on the rough picnic table, her feet on the bench below.

As he finished one of his many songs, Cam smiled over at him. "I really love your music."

"Thank my mother. Maybe mothers humming lullabies to their children from birth on put songs like these in musicians' memory." Gus gazed back at Cam, absorbing her soft, dreamy smile. Tonight her hair was newly washed and hung in chestnut folds around her face and shoulders. She wore a pale green tank top, her denim jacket and a pair of dark green cotton slacks. In his eyes, she looked like a lovely young woman, certainly not an Apache gunship pilot.

"I think you got the best of both worlds growing up," she murmured.

Running his fingers across the smooth surface of his guitar, Gus nodded. "Tell me about your growing up years, Cam. You said your mother named you and your two sisters after flowers?"

Munching on a cookie, she said, "Yes. I'm the oldest. Iris is twenty-four and Dahlia, whom we call Dal, is twenty."

"And are they in the military?"

She shook her head and wiped her fingers on her slacks. "No. Just me."

"So how did you get interested then, in the army? And flying combat helicopters?"

"My dad, who runs an automotive shop, was a helicopter mechanic when he was young and in the army. I guess he passed it on to me." She gave Gus a humorous look. "When I was little, my dad used to let me come to the garage, and he'd show me how car engines worked. By the time I was ten, I was changing oil and spark plugs and adjusting carburetors.''

''That's where you got your interest in mechanics,'' Gus said with a nod. In the moonlight, her profile was clean and soft. ''So, where did you get the passion, the assertiveness a combat pilot needs, I wonder?''

''My dad was a super athlete, Gus. He's a quiet kind of guy and you'd never realize he had the heart of a lion inside him. He's intense and focused when he works on a car engine. In high school, he was track champion, and went on to the nationals. He could have gone on to the Olympics, but he suffered a knee injury that took him out of competition.''

Nodding, Gus said, ''But like his daughter, he never quit.''

''No…my dad's not a quitter. Ever.''

''And your mother? What do you have of her in you?'' Gus saw her lips curve softly.

''Oh….my mom.'' Cam's voice dropped as she spoke. ''Well, she's a schoolteacher in a middle school. She's a biologist. Actually, a microbiologist. That's what her degree is in. She loves to teach kids about nature, about the life that surrounds them.''

''So that's why you all were named after flowers. I see.'' Gus grinned as Cam smiled at him. How close they were. And how much he wanted to touch those full lips. An ache grew in him, keen and sharp. Would Cam let him kiss her? Gus wasn't sure. But he wanted to, despite the loss he'd endured that had nearly destroyed him.

"Yes, she used to tease us fondly and call us her 'blooming idiots.' She meant it lovingly, because she really supported us in doing whatever our heart, our passion, led us to do."

"And you wanted to reach for the sky?"

"Yes," Cam murmured, taking another cookie. "I love flying. No one else in our family flies now, but my parents think I got the bird blood from my grandfather on my father's side. He was a pilot during the Korean War. He flew P-51 Mustangs, and he was an ace."

"Impressive."

"What about you? What moved you to fly? Your dad?"

"Yes." Gus strummed the guitar gently, the sounds vibrating softly around them. "I admired him. I still do. He's been my best teacher. My role model. I want him to be proud of me."

"I don't know how he couldn't be," Cam said sincerely. She liked the slight smile that curved Gus's mouth. A bolt of heat went through her as she studied those lips. She wanted to taste that mouth of his with her own. Would Gus be as strong and cherishing as she suspected? Sharing something more with Gus was too much to expect, Cam tried to tell herself, especially with her bad past history with men. She knew her idealistic side, the dreamer, wanted someone exactly like him, but that in reality dreams like hers never came true.

"My dad said I was like an eagle," he chuckled. "My mother, who as I told you is Yaqui Indian, said I had the earth in my blood. The blood of the Jaguar."

"Jaguar? That's really something. I wonder if

you're a member of the Jaguar clan in South America like Maya is?''

''My mother never mentioned that. She said I had a jaguar spirit guide but I've never seen it.''

''Looks like the eagle won out?''

Shrugging, he said, ''I guess so....''

''You don't sound so sure.''

Gus strummed the guitar again. He liked the vibration of the wood against his body, and the sound of the chords. ''Maybe I'm both. I'm not sure of that yet. I thought I was, but...well, life changes you sometimes.''

She heard pain in his voice and saw his hooded eyes darken. ''Something bad happened.'' It was a statement. Cam knew what she'd sensed was true because she felt an enormous sadness cloaking Gus.

Looking over, his hand stilling the strings of the guitar, he searched Cam's luminescent eyes, which radiated concern for him. His heart almost burst with a shaft of pain. Without thinking, he spilled his trauma to her.

''I fell in love with a woman three years ago,'' he began quietly. ''Sandy Grove was an aerobatic pilot of international caliber. In some ways, she was like you, Cam. She had that quiet confidence, that gutsiness that didn't always show until she was in her plane, doing the tricks. She was superconfident, a good person who lived life with a passion, right at the edge.'' Frowning, Gus looked down at his boots. ''I fell in love with her. She was an incredibly heart-centered person, so full of life. Unafraid to grab it and go for it.''

Cam frowned as she heard the sadness in his tone.

Gus straightened up and looked at her. "Sandy died two years ago in a flight accident. She was creating a new maneuver for an air show over in France when the wing of her plane tore off...."

"I'm so sorry," Cam whispered, and without thinking, she reached out and gripped his left arm for a moment. "So sorry. I can tell you loved her with your heart and soul."

Mouth quirking, Gus said, "Yeah, loving a woman in a dangerous profession isn't a wise idea." He felt her hand, the firmness of it, the gentleness of her touch on his arm, and his flesh tingled wildly. Seeing the tears in Cam's eyes, he felt like crying himself. In that moment, he wanted to pull her close and bury himself in her warm, comforting arms. But he couldn't. He didn't dare. As beautiful, caring, brave and wonderful as Cam was to him, Gus was too scared to reach out to her.

His words sank deeply into Cam's pounding heart. Gus had loved a woman in a dangerous profession.... Searching his shadowed face, caught in the mire of grief and longing she saw in his eyes, Cam sat there, confused. She couldn't understand the look of longing in his eyes as he held her gaze. Was that desire emanating toward her? Releasing his arm and shaking herself internally, Cam fiercely told herself no, that was impossible. His grief-stricken statement about never loving another woman in a dangerous job included her, no doubt. For she was an Apache gunship combat pilot. Her life could be snuffed out at any minute, Cam knew. And so did Gus.

She sat there, feeling a sharp pang of anguish in her heart.

Chapter 9

Cam was in her office at 0530 the next morning, working on the mountains of paperwork she had to process. Now she understood what Maya and her X.O. Dallas Klein, went through. No wonder they looked forward to getting away from their offices! Giving the piles of paper a glum look, including her Out basket, stuffed full of things that Gus would have to handle, Cam stopped working for a moment.

Gus's words came back to haunt her—again. He wouldn't or couldn't fall in love with another woman who was in a dangerous profession. That meant her. Frowning, Cam tightened her fingers around her pen. So why was she so bummed out about it? Gus had never said he loved her. Maybe because she was so lonely for male companionship, she had misinterpreted his looks and all too brief touches as meaning more than they really did. Cam had committed that crime before, in other relationships, and had gotten badly burned. Why, when she knew better, was she allowing herself to get emotionally involved with Gus, then? She sat back and digested all these revelations.

She hadn't slept well last night. The mission was weighing heavily on her. Cam was unsure what kind of knee-jerk reactions the two Mexican pilots would have to being firmly boundaried and forced to work. She wondered if it would really turn them around. Her personal life was an unexpected part of this mishmash as well. That was disconcerting. Never in a hundred years had Cam even *thought* of the possibility of being drawn to another man.

There was a knock on her door. Who could that be? Cam looked at her watch. No one was due for another twenty minutes.

"Enter," she said in a loud, firm voice.

Snake stuck her head around the opened door. "Got a sec, Cam?"

"Hi, Snake. Sure," she said, gesturing for her to come in. "Yeah, always. Just shut the door. I don't want any pilots eavesdropping as we chat." She grinned widely.

Snake laughed and quietly shut the door behind her. She was dressed in her one-piece olive green flight suit, her helmet tucked beneath her left arm.

"Gettin' to see you without the students around is proving to be a major chore," Snake said, setting the helmet on the edge of Cam's desk.

"Yeah, no kidding. I miss our easy talks in the chow hall back at the cave."

"Or in the hall. Or in the cockpit," Snake griped

good-naturedly. She took her shoulder-length, straight brown hair and expertly wrapped it up into a chignon at the base of her neck as she usually did before she put on her helmet, to keep her hair from getting in the way.

"I know," Cam sighed. She sat back in the chair and smiled up at her friend. "How are you doing in this mess? I haven't really gotten to talk with you one-on-one since you arrived."

Hitching a hip on the edge of Cam's desk, Vickey nodded and pursed her full lips. "I know. I was talkin' to Wild Woman last night." Her mouth curved in a feral smile. "We went carousin' around TJ last night in that rental car we got at the civilian airport where we landed. Some dude told us Club Flamingo was a good place to drink and dance."

"Was it?" Cam asked, smiling more widely. She was glad to see that they could cut loose and enjoy themselves despite the stresses they were under here.

"You'd better believe it." Vickey waved her right hand as if she'd touched something that burned her. "I gotta tell you, doin' the tango with these Latino dudes who know what they're doin' is awesome!" She laughed heartily.

Joining her laughter, Cam said, "Kinda nice to have guys around, isn't it?"

"Well," Snake growled, "*Some* guys. Not those two nose-outta-joint student pilots we have to play kindergarten in the sky with. But yeah, the guys we hooked up with last night were terrific." Vickey rubbed her hands together in anticipation. "We're gonna meet them there tonight for some more rousin' rounds of dancing."

"No hangover?" Cam inquired politely. She saw Snake's smile grow.

"Ah, maybe a touch. You know, we don't do much drinkin' and dancin' back at BJS. It's not the same. Here…" Vickey waved her arm "…you got a real city, close to the good ole U.S. of A., and it's like being back home, almost."

Hearing the homesickness in Vickey's tone, Cam lost her smile. "Yeah, it's been a long time since any of us have seen home."

Becoming more serious, Vickey tilted her head and gave Cam an intense look. "Maya is now giving us thirty days a year starting this year. That's as good as it gets."

"I know. I'm not blaming anyone," Cam murmured. "But we've been putting in three unrelenting, drug-busting years down there and it's getting old for all of us."

"Maya included," Vickey agreed. "I think we're all pining for 'home' one way or another."

Nodding, Cam said, "I don't know how Maya is going to overcome that. We can't stay down there forever, flying combat without a change of tour. I know the army's pressuring her right now to get more male pilots rotated down there to give us relief."

"Yeah," Vickey chortled, "and I heard that Maya's telling them to get her more *women* Apache pilots down there, instead."

Cam chuckled. "Good for her. Women work well together."

"Yeah, we do," she agreed. Moving her long, graceful hand down the right thigh of her uniform to smooth out the wrinkles, Vickey continued, "I dropped by to see how *you* were doin'. Wild Woman and I can see you're in over your head with this rotten situation. Talk about bein' handed crap.'' She shook her head, scowling.

"A bag of worms, for sure," Cam agreed. She laced her fingers across her stomach and leaned back in the chair. "But it's not all bad, Vic. I have Gus, and he's been a great help and support."

"Ah, Gus…" She gave Cam an evil grin.

"What's *that* look for?"

"Don't you know? Geez, Cam, both of us saw it the moment we walked into your briefing."

Frowning, Cam muttered, "Saw *what?*"

Snake rolled her eyes. "Are you blind, deaf and dumb, girl? Or just pretending with me?"

"I don't know what you're talking about. Wanna spell it out to this dummy?" Cam said with a laugh. Her friend's face glowed with humor, and Cam liked the dancing, elfin expression in Vickey's dark green eyes. Usually Snake was very quiet and said little to anyone. She was a Scorpio, and fit that zodiac profile well, in Cam's opinion. Normally, she was a highly private person, an introvert, and never said what was on her mind unless someone pried it out of her. Today she seemed just the opposite. It must have been the tango and tequila last night, Cam surmised, with an inward smile.

"You really don't see it, do you?"

"I must not. Wanna come clean and tell me what you two divas see that I don't?"

Grinning, Vickey leaned across the desk and in a hushed, dramatic voice whispered, "Gus Morales. That's who, dummy!"

Blinking, Cam said, "Gus? What about him?"

Sitting up, Vickey shook her head. "You really deserve the name Tree Trimmer, Cam. You got sawdust for brains on this one. And generally you're sharp as the razor edge of a sword."

Seeing the smirk on her friend's face, Cam sat up. When Snake wriggled her eyebrows, which was something she did when she was up to no good, Cam got it. "Oh!"

"Yeah, no kidding. Oh. Now you see where we're going with this little collective observation of ours."

Heat swept up Cam's neck and into her cheeks, and she avoided Vickey's prying look.

"Now you're blushin', Tree Trimmer. That confirms what we thought."

"You two," Cam managed to choke out in defense, "have nothing better to do than—"

Holding up her hands, Vickey slid off the corner of the desk and grinned hugely, flashing her even white teeth.

"Whoa, girl, whoa! I'm just tellin' you what Wild Woman and I see goin' on. Gus *likes you*. Don't you know that? We thought you did, but I can see you don't. The guy has *eyes* for you, Cam. He's like a puppy mooning over you every time he thinks no one's noticing." Snake gave an evil laugh. "But we don't miss a thing, Wild Woman and I. These dudes don't realize how sharp and alert we really are. Combat-honed alertness makes us look at every teeny, tiny detail."

Groaning, Cam sat back and covered her eyes with her hand while Vickey chortled delightedly.

"You like him, Cam?"

Hearing the serious tone in Vickey's voice once more, Cam removed her hand from her eyes and looked across the desk at her friend. She had her helmet beneath her left arm once again and was standing there expectantly, a warm look on her face. Vickey could be a merciless tease at times, which was typical of her Scorpio nature, but in the end, Cam knew, she cared deeply for the friendship that had built between them over the years down at BJS.

"Where do I begin on this one?" Cam muttered, more to herself than to Snake.

"So there *is* something? Wild Woman thought so. I said no, that you're too busy runnin' this squadron to have a personal life right now. Looks like I was wrong and I owe her a hot fudge sundae. That was our bet, and that's why I came to see you before the fireworks began again today—to see if Wild Woman was right. Damn, I shouldn't bet with her. I always lose."

"You owe her the hot fudge sundae, Snake," Cam said unhappily.

"Why so glum? The dude has got some things goin' for him." She grinned suddenly and then looked at her watch. It was time to go. "Hey, you have our seal of approval on him, if you're interested. We think he's a cool dude. Gotta rock 'n roll. See you later...."

Waving her hand, Cam regretted that they'd run out of this precious, private time with one another. "It's a long story, Snake. Yeah, later..."

Snake hesitated at the open door and turned back. "Well, when you want a night outta this evolving nightmare, come and tango with us and these hot Latino dudes over at Club Flamingo. Maybe then we can talk more?''

Right now, Cam didn't feel like partying. She was beginning to understand in earnest the difference between being a pilot and being a C.O. "No, dancing isn't my thing. But you two go ahead and enjoy yourselves. You certainly deserve a diversion from Luis and Antonio, that's for sure."

Snorting, Vickey said, "Ain't *that* the truth! I've never seen such sniveling, immature Apache pilots in my life. The army ought to be ashamed for even passing Dominguez. I guess Wild Woman is about ready to pitch her student out through the front cockpit Plexiglas." The front Plexiglas on an Apache was hardened to the point where it could take a direct hit from a twenty millimeter cannon and not crack.

Cam nodded. "Stay on 'em. Don't give them any breathing room at all," she growled. "They're either gonna shape up or ship out."

"Ha! I hope it's the latter," Snake crowed. "We're doin' our best to crowd these two ego-bustin' rich boys and break 'em down so we can cobble them back together and make real pilots out of 'em. But I don't know that they're gonna break, Cam."

"I don't, either, Vic. Just stay on them. Keep up the pressure."

"Well," Snake said with satisfaction, "last night Dominguez was nearly in tears, his hands shaking because he hadn't gotten to smoke at all. He's going into real nicotine deprivation today, I'm sure, and he's gonna be a grouchy bear in the cockpit because of it. He probably spent half his night trying to buy cigs off the people here in the barracks after you had Gus go confiscate his stash in his quarters.''

''Well, if any of us catch him smoking, he knows he's out of here—permanently.''

''Yeah, he knows that. But he's a sneaky bastard. My gut tells me he'll manipulate others, pay lots of pesos to some poor enlisted guy to provide 'em.''

''If he does that, then it's one more mark against him. He has no morals and doesn't respect the military system.''

''Like we didn't know that already. Hey, I gotta turn and burn. Have to walk my prize student around the lady out there.''

Nodding, Cam lifted her hand. ''Yeah, okay. Five hours of flight ought to reduce these two to puddles by this afternoon.''

Chuckling, Vickey said, ''I sure hope so. Have those transfer orders ready to be signed when we get back.''

After Snake left, Cam felt lonely. How much she missed the chatter between herself and her sister pilots! Talking with Gus was always a high, but after last night's admission from him, Cam felt as if ice water had been thrown on her. Telling herself that honesty was always the best policy, she decided to tuck away her feelings and work with Gus on a less personal level because that's what he wanted. Besides, Cam told herself sternly, her experience in male relationships was less than stellar. So why would she want to put herself through that kind of horrendous pain and humiliation again? She didn't. Not ever.

Sighing, Cam grabbed another report and began to fill it out. Gus was due to drop by in thirty minutes,

and they'd begin their mission flight for today. Just
thinking about it made her inexplicably happy.

"Well done, Gus," Cam said into the mike positioned near her lips. She scribbled intently on the clipboard resting on her thighs. The shaking and shuddering of the Apache surrounded her like a lover's
caress. It also played hell on her ability to write leg-
ibly.

"Thanks," he called out. "Want me to head back
to base now?"

"Yeah," Cam murmured, finishing up the totals on
each of his flight demand columns for the day. Sunlight poured into the cockpit, making her squint. It
was 1300—1:00 p.m.—and they'd just put in five
grueling hours of maneuvers over their stay-and-play
area in the mountains south of Tijuana. From time to
time Cam had eavesdropped on Wild Woman's and
Snake's communications with their students. Things
weren't going well at all, it seemed. But to give the
two male pilots credit, they were trying today, so that
was a hopeful sign. Emotionally, Cam had to gird
herself for facing Luis and Antonio when they got
back to the base. Things were coming to a head and
she knew it. Would they stay or leave? Did they have
the strength to gut it out? She wasn't sure.

Gus looked around, as he'd been trained to, from
left to right, and then down to the two HUDs on the
instrument panel in front of him. Feeling euphoric, he
knew he'd excelled at the demanding flight tests, and
he grinned.

"Has anyone ever told you how good a teacher you
are? I think you missed your calling. They should

have had the smarts to pull you back to Fort Rucker, to be an IP and teach students the ropes there.''

With a laugh, Cam said, ''The only thing they ever wanted to do with the first all-woman Apache Training class was get them through and out of there, Gus. Out of sight, out of mind was the army's motto.''

''But you've shown them that they were wrong about women pilots in a combat gunship,'' he argued.

''Yeah, that was three, nearly four years ago now,'' Cam murmured. How she looked forward to talking with Gus personally. It was one of the few rewards of her day.

''Your stats speak for themselves,'' Gus said. ''I was talking with Wild Woman and Snake yesterday and they told me a lot about BJS. I'm really impressed. Major Stevenson is way ahead of her time, a real visionary.''

''And the army doesn't like visionaries, believe me,'' Cam growled. ''She was a woman with an idea. A good one. If her father, an army general, hadn't been there to make sure it got instituted, Maya's dream of BJS would have gone unnoticed.''

''Sometimes,'' Gus said as he eased the Apache into a banking turn toward the blue of the Pacific, ''it's not what you know, but who you know.''

''Unfortunately. That's one of my many gripes with the army. Creativity and ingenuity aren't always welcomed with open arms. If you don't happen to be male, or of the proper rank, and have no political strings to pull, you aren't going to be listened to.''

''You'll be ignored,'' Gus agreed. The ocean glittered beneath them, with sunlight dappling its rough surface. White, cottony clouds surrounded them. A front was coming through today, and the winds were a lot stronger from the west. The turbulence had been rougher than normal, and it had taken all of Gus's skills to do as well as he had on the flight tests. When the weather worked against a pilot, it was harder to fly at specific altitudes and aim electronic "missiles" at stationary targets on the ground and accurately hit them. But he had. Gus felt proud of his abilities. He liked showing Cam that he had the right stuff to be an Apache pilot like her. Any pilot who had seen combat was usually set upon a pedestal and worshipped by the others. For a pilot, experience counted for everything. Gus held all three women pilots in high esteem. They had not only gutted it out for three years in combat mode, they had survived. And there was a lot he could learn from them, he knew.

As the Apache bounced and bobbled, hitting an invisible air pocket at five thousand feet, Gus steadied the machine with his feet and hands. The Baja coast grew small behind them as he flew the required five miles out to sea.

"Hey, on a personal topic, how would you like to leave this coming Saturday night open for something special?" His heart beat a little harder in his chest as he asked the question. He was afraid Cam would say no. Hand tightening momentarily around the cyclic, Gus held his breath as he waited for her response.

Lifting her head from her work, Cam said, "What?"

"Saturday. You know, that's two days away? I thought…well, we always meet every night in the grove, on the picnic table for an hour or two. I thought that I'd like to take you someplace else."

Cam felt a frisson of fear. And then joy. She tried to ignore both feelings. "Not a date." Remembering Gus's words, she wanted to be clear about this request and have no illusions about it. Still, she wished it *would* be a date.

"Er…why, no. Business. Just like always," he mumbled. "You know how we sit on the picnic table and talk over the day's events? C.O. to X.O.?"

"Yeah…" Cam's hand stilled over the clipboard, her pen poised. His stubbornness made her feel sad. Still, it was a chance to be with Gus, and Cam wasn't going to cut him out of her life. Somehow she was going to have to learn how to turn desire for him into friendship. That was a tall order and something she'd never attempted before.

A trickle of sweat ran down Gus's left temple. He had the wild urge to push it away. Setting the collective, he did just that, shoving his index finger up beneath the dark green visor that protected his eyes from the harsh sunlight. He tried to gage Cam's tone of voice because he wasn't sure she was happy with the idea.

"I know a sweet little spot in Puerto Nuevo. In fact, I can point it out to you on the way home today. One of the bays where Mexican trawlers come in and sell their goods, Puerto Nuevo is known for its lobster. I know a great restaurant there, Café Flor, which has the best seafood in town. It's small but it's clean. I'd like to buy you dinner."

Cam loved lobster. In fact, after being at BJS for so long, she'd almost forgotten how much she loved seafood. It was rare to get anything but local trout from the Urubamba River in their chow hall.

With a slight grin, she asked, "How did you know I love seafood?"

Gus heard the joy in her tone. It made him suddenly feel lighter. Happier. "Just a hunch. Besides," he replied, "as X.O., I need to take care of my C.O. You need a break. I heard from Wild Woman and Snake that they're having a high old time at Club Flamingo in TJ. They, at least, are getting away from this heavy energy and drama Luis and Antonio stir up. I think you should, too."

"I see. A little R and R—rest and relaxation?"

"Sure," Gus coaxed enthusiastically. "I have my car. I drove it down here from Fort Rucker, so we got wheels. Interested?"

Was she? Cam pursed her lips and stared at his helmeted head below her. The thumping of the blades soothed some of her fear.

"Just business. Right?"

"I promise," Gus told her fervently. "Just pretend we're in the grove, that it's dark and we're on our picnic table, and I'm strumming on my guitar from time to time as we talk over the day's events. Okay?"

Thrilled and yet wary, Cam said, "Okay…"

"Great! I can hardly wait. You'll love Puerto Nuevo. You'll love the lobster."

There was that word *love,* Cam thought darkly. Placing her gloved hands over the clipboard, she looked out the cockpit window, unsure of how to feel. Still, as she sat there mulling it over in her heart, a thread of happiness wound through her. Suddenly she felt like a teenage girl who had just been asked to the prom by the boy she had a wild crush on.

Chapter 10

"Maybe this isn't a business comment," Gus told Cam in a low, intimate tone as they sat at the white-linen-draped table at Café Flor, "but you look beautiful."

Cam looked down at the pale lavender tank top she wore with a ballerina-length, silk skirt of the same color. Around her shoulders was a silk shawl in a deep plum. She touched the amethyst pendant at her throat and smiled. "Thanks...."

"It's a far cry from seeing you in that shapeless flight suit," he mused as he picked up his glass filled with a pale chardonay wine. In the background, several men played guitars in one corner of the busy restaurant. "Here's to R and R, Ms. Anderson."

Cam lifted her glass and gave Gus a shy smile. "We clean up pretty good, don't we?" she murmured, gently touching her glass to his. Gus looked devastatingly handsome in his navy blue blazer with brass buttons, white silk shirt, paisley tie and tan slacks. He'd shaved earlier, and Cam realized the pains he'd taken getting ready for tonight. His black hair gleamed beneath the low lights overhead.

Cam tried to stay detached, to keep her heart at bay. It had been too easy to be lulled by Gus's quiet voice as he chatted about the day's events on the drive down to Puerto Nuevo. She'd bitten her lower lip many times during that forty-five minute drive in his red sports car, to stop herself from asking him personal questions instead of staying on track with business only.

"Here's to R and R," she agreed throatily, and took a sip of the white wine.

A Mexican waiter, dressed in a long white apron, black slacks and a starched long-sleeved shirt with a black bow tie, came over and handed them menus with an elegant flourish.

Cam thanked him in Spanish and so did Gus. The man beamed with pleasure. When Cam had entered the second-floor restaurant, with its huge windows facing the Pacific, she'd noticed most of the patrons were from the States. Most spoke English only. The gleam in their waiter's eyes told her he was grateful that they spoke his language. It was a way of honoring where they were, Cam felt.

"Well," she told Gus wryly, glancing over the tall menu, "I really don't think I have to look at this thing. I want lobster with all the trimmings."

Chuckling, he nodded and put the menu aside. "We do lobster down here a little differently than the folks in New England," he cautioned. "It comes with soft corn tortillas on the side, rice and hearty black beans.'' He smiled. ''Plus a knockout salsa you can dip your lobster into.''

''No drawn butter?''

''Sure, if you want. Aren't you adventurous, though?'' he teased, watching her eyes grow warm with humor. ''Ever had lobster tail dipped in a dynamite salsa that makes you want to smack your lips because it tastes like heaven itself?'' Placing his elbows on the table, he clasped his hands together and rested his chin on them as he studied Cam's softly glowing face. The lighting was perfect, he decided. Her thick chestnut hair was in a French braid, with strands loose across her brow. It made her look very different—younger, perhaps. Her usual C.O. mask was gone. The change in her was breathtaking and Gus hadn't realized until just now what a chameleon Cam could be.

''Oh, I'm adventurous, all right,'' Cam said, her lips lifting wryly as she placed her menu on top of his.

''So that's what drew you to fly a combat aircraft?'' Gus wondered out loud. He hoped she thought that was a business topic. When her brows lifted and she laughed, his heart expanded.

''Yes. Underneath this—'' she pointed to herself and the outfit she was wearing ''—I'm competitive and have a deep patriotic streak in me. My parents raised us to know that we have freedom today because of the people who gave their lives, their time in the military, to make it so. I see this as paying my country back for the privilege of living in it.''

''Never mind that you've spent nearly four years

out of it," he said, unclasping his hands and sipping his wine.

Shrugging, Cam said, "What is duty? Where do we rank what's important to us, Gus? How do we pay our share of dues for what we have?" She gazed through the windows at the cobblestone street below, saw how each stone had been lovingly laid by hand to create the roadway along the sea. The village was poor but bustling. The people who lived in Puerto Nuevo relied heavily on their American neighbors to come down, eat and put money into their coffers. Not that anyone was rich here.

"When I look out there," Cam told him in a hushed tone, "and see little kids five or six years old barefoot, their noses running, their hair needing to be combed, or adults wearing worn, tattered clothes, I know how lucky we are. It breaks my heart that we can't bring all countries up to our standards." She looked over at him. "And in Peru, it's the same thing. I don't take what we have in the U.S.A. as a given. We have to earn it and keep earning it."

Nodding, Gus said, "I understand."

"You would. You said you visited your mother's people in Mexico as a child?"

"As often as I could," Gus said. "My father was being shipped around the world as an army pilot. I grew up mostly in the Far East and Europe, because of his assignments. My mother, bless her, was a real trooper. She taught herself German. And then, when we went to Japan, she learned Japanese. She has an amazing ear for languages and she likes learning how to fit into different societies."

"It shows in you," Cam said, giving Gus a slight

smile. She warmed at the look in his darkened eyes, which smoldered with an undefined emotion. Cam tried to resist that look, but Gus was too close, too appealing, and she felt irresistibly drawn to him.

"Thank you. I think the best thing that happened to me as a kid was having the opportunity to kick around the world and learn about other cultures. I never regretted that."

"And what did you think of your mother's people when you went down there and saw where she'd grown up? How did it compare to those other cultures?"

Gus sat back and gave her a lazy smile. "I like your perceptiveness, Cam. You ask the right questions."

Picking up her wineglass, she murmured, "We are what we are today because of where we came from. Our roots. I'm curious how the Indian side of you integrates with the American side."

Grinning, Gus sipped his wine and then set the glass back on the linen tablecloth. "My mother lives in a magical world. My father lives in a black-and-white, hard-core-reality world."

Tilting her head, Cam said, "Interesting. So now you've really got my curiosity going. How do you mate magic with reality?"

"My mother has often told me that I live with one foot in her people's world of magic and transformation, and the other foot in my father's world of fact. I grew up listening to stories of her people that have been passed down through generations. And my dad, when he could, would read to me at night. I grew up with stories of endless possibilities. I think that gave me the ability to see the world a little differently, or at least more broadly, than other people do.''

Cam was caught in a spell by his deep, quiet voice, mesmerized by Gus's ability to convey his thoughts. Understanding clearly that that was a gift of his— verbal communication—she simply absorbed his words into her heart and listened.

"Give me an example?"

Opening his hand, Gus said, "Okay. This game with Luis and Antonio. I see them on several levels at once. In one way, I see them as struggling through life because of the choices they've made along the way. On another level, a more symbolic one, which is how my mother sees the world and how she taught me to see it, they are men wrestling with authority. They are learning about authority. The question is,'' Gus murmured, ''what will they do with the lesson?''

"So, you see life as lessons?"

"I see people as teachers coming into our life, to show us something. We're to learn from them."

"That's your mother's contribution?"

"Yes, and it's a good one."

"And that's why you didn't have a knee-jerk reaction to having a woman commander?"

"Yes." Gus smiled slightly. "By seeing you as my teacher, I left open all possibilities. I didn't try to catalog you, define you or put you into some convenient, labeled box as Luis and Antonio tried to do."

Nodding, Cam murmured, "I like that idea. That people are our teachers."

"That's not to say all teachers are going to give us happy experiences," he noted with a grin. "Pain makes us learn, too, unfortunately."

"But," Cam said, sipping her wine, "if you go into the situation with an attitude that you're going to be taught something, then you can decide whether to learn it right away or repeat it again and again until you do get it. Am I on the right track?"

"Bingo," Gus exclaimed. "You're fast on the uptake."

"In our business you'd better be or you're dead."

Laughing softly, Gus nodded. "No doubt about it." How beautiful Cam looked in that moment, sitting there in her feminine dress, her face glowing with interest and that strength and confidence shining in her eyes. Only a person who had powerful experiences and lived to tell about them had that look.

"Was it hard on you, going through Apache training with Luis and Antonio?" Cam asked.

"Not really. Oh, we were the only three Latinos in the class, so we got judged, right or wrong, by that label." Grimacing, Gus said, "But they pretended I didn't exist, and that was fine with me. When they started sloughing off and not working to get passing grades, I really wanted to be separated from them in every way. I didn't want the rest of the class or the IPs to think all Hispanics were lazy like they were."

"And so you worked twice as hard to show everyone that wasn't so?"

"Yes."

"I saw your flight scores from school," Cam said, "when I was going over your personnel jacket. You graduated at the top of your class, with a ninety-five percentile. That's pretty impressive."

"I worked my butt off to prove that we weren't all like the two spoiled rich boys," he muttered defiantly.

"I'm sure you succeeded," Cam said. "I graduated with a seventy-eight. Of course, the head instructor was completely against our all-women class, and downgraded all of us. I passed. That's all I cared about."

"More prejudice," Gus murmured, shaking his head.

"Yeah," Cam sighed, "it's everywhere. You're fighting for people to respect Hispanics and their abilities, and I'm fighting a gender war." She gave him a twisted smile. "Two peas in the same pod?"

"I kinda like being in the same pod with you," Gus said, looking into her eyes. Noticing that the band was playing a soft, slow tune, he said, "Want to dance?" and he rose and held out his hand.

Seeing the startled look on Cam's face, Gus knew this wasn't in the playbook they'd agreed to. Asking Cam to dance was not "business." But he couldn't help himself. She was beautiful, radiant, desirable, and that smile of hers was driving him crazy. How many nights had he lain awake wondering what it would be like to have Cam in his arms? How she would feel?

Holding her startled gaze, Gus gave her his best boyish smile. "All women know how to dance," he challenged.

Grinning broadly, Cam said, "Oh? Is that another one of those stereotypical labels?"

"Yeah, I guess it is." He kept his hand stretched toward her.

Cam lifted her chin and gazed up at him, and he could see that she was in a quandary. Was it because she really didn't like him as much as he did her? That was a crushing thought, and Gus pushed it away. A feeling that she did want to know him better warred with his other sense about Cam. She seemed, at times, to seesaw back and forth with him, as if she wondered how much intimacy was the right amount. Maybe she was unsure because she was still learning how to be a C.O. Still, his heart told him that no, she wanted him just as much as he wanted her.

Gulping, Cam saw that Gus wasn't going to take no for an answer. Several other couples had moved out on the polished wood floor. "Okay...but I haven't danced in a long time..." she murmured.

Moving around the table, Gus pulled out her chair, then removed the shawl from her proud shoulders and draped it over the back. The small, teardrop-shaped amethyst pendant at the hollow of her throat gleamed in the low light as she turned toward him.

"I promise not to step on your feet," he assured her, taking her by the hand and leading her onto the floor.

His hand was strong and warm. Cam tried to ignore the quiet strength he emanated as he turned and drew her confidently into his arms. She was tense, expecting him to grab her and press her against him. He didn't. Looking down at her, Gus held her at a comfortable distance, one hand placed lightly at the small of her back, the other grasping her hand.

Moving with Gus was like moonlight slipping over the surface of the dark, calm Pacific, Cam discovered. She looked up into his hooded eyes and drowned in them. She felt lost and yet secure. Scared, but happy. Wanting to run and wanting to stay. So many feelings coursed through her as they moved fluidly to the slow guitar music. Inhaling his male scent, Cam enjoyed his closeness.

"Not bad for someone who hasn't been on a dance floor for a long time," he teased, leaning down near her ear and whispering the words.

His moist, warm breath brushed her cheek, and Cam closed her eyes. Gus's voice vibrated through her, embracing her with its husky, intimate tone. Heart expanding euphorically, Cam felt her defenses crumbling quickly as she swayed in his strong, guiding arms.

"You make it easy for me to look like I know what I'm doing," she said as she opened her eyes. He was smiling down at her and warmth sheeted through her. Feeling him squeeze her hand briefly, she squeezed his back. It was a bold move. The look in his eyes grew smoky, and Cam knew he desired her. The thought was enticing. Scary.

Seeing the momentary panic in her green gaze, Gus decided to give Cam the distance she needed. "Well," he said lightly, straightening up again, "you do the same for me up in the air. You teach me some pretty complex flight maneuvers and make it easy for me to learn from you."

"Maybe we're both good teachers to one another?" Cam's heart wouldn't settle down. The desire she'd seen for an instant in Gus's eyes was gone, and her panic was abating to a degree. Still, he was so incredibly masculine that she found herself wanting to lean up and kiss that cockeyed smile she'd come to love so much. At the craziest moments, Gus would give her that rakish smile and her heart would melt, and all the tension she was feeling would flow out of her. He was part little boy and part man. She'd never encountered anyone like him in her life.

"Certainly."

"That just goes to prove your mother's world view."

"Yes, it does. But you're a teacher I like, and I want you to teach me everything you know, Cam."

Hearing the sincerity in his voice as Gus brought her around in a circle, she closed her eyes again. Oh, if only that were true! All the mistakes she'd made in the past with men were still haunting her. What had they taught her? Bitterly, Cam opened her eyes and stared past Gus's broad shoulder. They had taught her that she consistently made bad choices. That she wasn't seeing the men or herself properly. Turning her head, Cam looked wonderingly up at Gus. He looked down and held her gaze.

"I see so much in your eyes, Cam. What are you thinking so hard about? I can practically feel it."

How easy it was to talk to Gus. For the first time in her life, Cam found that revealing her inner self to a man could be painless. "I was thinking about my past. My mistakes. My poor judgment."

"Oh?" he murmured, keeping his voice light as he moved her smoothly across the floor.

Compressing her lips, Cam said, "I've never talked about this to anyone. I'm really ashamed, Gus...."

Squeezing her hand gently, he said, "I can't ever conceive of you doing something you'd be ashamed of." Yet he could see the war in her eyes, the way her brow wrinkled. Wanting to hold her, caress her and take away that pain he saw in Cam's eyes was nearly his undoing. Still, he continued to lead her across the dance floor in rhythm with the guitar music. Right now, he could see that she wanted to entrust him with some awful secret that she was grieving over. Was this C.O. to X.O., woman to man? Unsure, he cocked his head and leaned close to her ear to say, "I'm here. I'll listen...."

"This is going to sound silly," Cam told him.

"Nothing you say will ever be silly."

Cam stared at his Adam's apple. Finding the courage, she whispered, "You talk about people being your teachers, Gus. I've been thinking a lot about that, seeing everything from that more macrocosmic perspective. I've been thinking about people who have come in and out of my life. What did they teach me? What did I learn?" Cam frowned. "Or did I? Sometimes I wonder if I even knew *what* I was being taught. I look at some situations, especially with guys..." She shrugged painfully.

Gus held his breath. Cam was obviously revealing something that was incredibly painful to her. Nearly losing the beat of the music, he forced himself to concentrate, worried that she'd stop.

"Well," Cam muttered defiantly, "I just wonder what the heck my three very bad wrecks of relationships taught me. Three men. I crashed and burned with every one of them."

Gently, Gus squeezed her hand. "Why do you blame yourself and not them?"

It was a fair question, and Cam had no logical answer. Feeling the warm strength of his hand as he squeezed hers reassuringly, she shrugged. "I don't know, Gus.... I guess I have a lot more thinking to do about it all...."

"Relationships are a two-way street," he agreed. "I found that out growing up and watching my parents in their marriage. It isn't easy. It's painful sometimes, and what I realized more than anything was that there had to be respect between the two people involved. If there wasn't, the relationship gets railroaded and becomes a power play for one individual, disempowerment for the other. The marriage becomes a war game, with winners and losers. In a good relationship, people look at one another like team members. What do they bring to the collective table? What are their innate strengths? Their weaknesses?" Gus gazed down at Cam's troubled expression. "In a good partnership, the people are a team, and the team operates from their strengths, not their weaknesses."

Wrinkling her nose, Cam muttered, "I fall into the first category. The relationship wars."

"I think we all do," Gus said, listening to the music begin to fade away at the end of a song. He slowed his steps until they stood in one another's arms on the dance floor. "The trick is learning that that's a painful way to live and getting out of it. And then, hopefully, learning from the mistake. Try not to draw the same teacher, the same lesson again. Grow. Reach out. Start over, but take what you've learned and put it into play in the new relationship."

Cam didn't want to leave Gus's arms. But the music had ended and the other couples were heading back to their tables, so she reluctantly stepped out of his embrace. Inwardly, Cam wanted to move closer to Gus, to stay in the circle of his arms and be held by him. Seeing the smoldering look in his eyes as he watched her, Cam felt her mouth go dry. The expression on his face was clearly readable. He wanted her. In all ways.

Swallowing hard, Cam whispered unsteadily, "The music's stopped...."

"The music we make here—" Gus released her and pressed his hand to his heart "—with one another, Cam, makes me happy. It's ongoing...."

With a jerky nod, Cam gazed up at him. How courageous Gus was compared to her. She felt like an emotional coward of the worst sort. "I—I wish I had that kind of courage, Gus," she said, then turned and walked quickly back to the table. Suddenly she was more scared than she'd ever been. Even staring down a Black Shark combat helicopter paled in comparison. Cam wanted to run. Anywhere. Now.

Chapter 11

"Four weeks," Wild Woman said to Cam as they walked across the revetment area after landing the Apaches. They'd been on a grueling, five-hour final test with the student pilots.

"An unending nightmare," Cam agreed as she walked with Jessica. Taking off her helmet, she ran her fingers through her damp, flattened hair. She cut a smile toward her friend, who was taking her own helmet off. "But it looks like we've made the grade with all of them."

Chuckling, Wild Woman nodded. "Yeah, Luis and Antonio took the challenge. I didn't think they would, but those rich boys dug deep and bailed their collective butts out of the hole they'd dug for themselves."

"Yes," Cam said, relieved, "they have."

"Did Antonio pass?"

"Yeah, barely. I'm givin' him a seventy-five per-

cent, the lowest mark you can have and still pass,''
she told her wryly. ''He tried his best, though his
nerves got to him. He's flown better before, so I'm
giving him a passing grade.''

The sun was warm as they walked toward the barracks, across from the revetment area where the aircraft were parked. Cam sighed. The fresh, warm air
felt good on her face.

''How about Gus? I'm sure he passed?''

''Yeah. I'm giving him a ninety percent.''

''That dude is good. I'm glad we switched the students around every three days. I really looked forward
to flying with him. He's incredible. He's got great
flight hands.''

Cam's heart thumped in her chest. ''Yes...yes, he
does.'' Ever since that night on the dance floor, she'd
retreated from Gus—out of fear. And to his credit,
he'd backed off, too. They kept everything strictly
business between them now. Cam missed the warmth
that she'd always seen in his eyes when they were
alone together. Well, she had no one to blame but
herself. She'd been in a constant state of grief since
that night on the dance floor. Her fear overcame her
desire to open up and get to know him better.

Opening the door to the barracks, Wild Woman
gestured for Cam to enter. ''Well? What now? Are
you going to call Morgan and tell him these three are
ready for real-time drug interdiction?''

Nodding, Cam led the way up the stairs to the second floor. ''Yeah, I will.''

''Where does that leave us? Do we get to go back
to BJS?''

Sadness moved through Cam as she unlocked the

door to her office. "Yes. I'm gonna miss you and Snake. You're the reason these guys are ready to do their job." Pushing the door open, she walked in and hung her helmet on a peg. Divesting herself of her chicken plate—the mandatory bullet-proof protective jacket they always wore while flying—she hung it next to the helmet on a wall hook.

"This has been a great diversion," Jessica said, sitting down, her helmet in her lap. She smiled at Cam, who sat down behind her desk. "Snake and I sure are gonna miss those weekends over at Club Flamingo. We had fun dancing every night with those great Latino guys. You won't find those kind of men down in Agua Caliente," she said with a scowl.

Chuckling, Cam shook her head. Agua Caliente was the closest town to the BJS base in Peru. It sat at the foot of Machu Picchu, one of the largest and most sacred temple sites of the whole Inca empire. "No, not there. But hey, you girls always found guys to dance with in Cuzco." Of course, it was a forty-five minute helicopter ride from their base to the city, situated at eleven thousand feet in the heart of the Andes Mountains.

"Yeah," Jessica pouted, sliding down in the chair and spreading her booted feet out before her.

Snake entered the room, her helmet beneath her left arm, her clipboard in her hand. "Hi, girls. Mind if I join this party?"

Cam smiled. "Not at all," she said, gesturing for Vickey to come in. "We got business to attend to, anyway."

Shutting the door, Snake took the second chair in

front of Cam's desk and sat down. She grinned at Wild Woman. "Well, did Antonio ante up?"

Laughing, Wild Woman said, "Yeah, the dude passed. How about your boy?"

Snake grinned and handed Cam her final report. "I'm passing Luis with a seventy-five percent. He froze in the clutch, but he's flown better than that in earlier sessions. He's got the heart, just not the nerves yet."

They all smiled at one another.

Cam looked at the reports on the men's flights. "Well," she murmured, going through each page of the official flight forms, "looks like they've carried the load."

"Yeah," Snake chuckled, setting her helmet down beside the chair. "I'll give 'em that. They decided to stop sulking and pouting like a couple of schoolboys and took the bit in their teeth and ran with it."

"They didn't have a choice," Wild Woman snorted. "They feared being embarrassed and shamed before their fathers more than anything else. It was a good hammer to hold over their heads so they'd haul ass and produce like they were supposed to."

"They've come a long way in four weeks," Cam agreed, dropping the reports back on the desk. She folded her hands over them and gave her cohorts a sad smile. "And I have you two to thank for that."

"Hold on," Snake said, lifting her long, thin hand. "If it weren't for the planning you did, they wouldn't be anywhere. So give yourself credit in this dance, too, Cam."

"Oh, I do, but I'm the C.O., Snake. I'm expected

to come up with bubble gum and wire to fix a problem.'' She grinned, though her heart was heavy.

Wild Woman looked over at Snake. ''So, now that our boys have passed through the collective fires of female hell, you know where that leaves us, don't you?''

With a sigh, Snake sat back and ruffled her brown hair with her fingers. ''Yeah, home to BJS. Damn, I'm gonna miss all our dancing, Cam. This has been a lot of fun. A great break.''

''I know,'' Cam whispered, blinking back tears. Opening her hands, she said, ''I'm gonna miss you two.''

''Yeah, you're stuck here with the three of them,'' Wild Woman said. ''Gus is easy to be around, but I think you're going to have to keep riding roughshod over Luis and Antonio. I'll bet they try to slough off now, with us gone. They won't have one of us always watching them in the cockpit.''

''We'll be going down to two Apaches,'' Cam said. ''I'll be doing a lot of flying to make sure they stay in line.''

Rubbing her hands, Wild Woman said, ''Yeah, we get to fly this third bird all the way back to BJS. I'm lookin' forward to it!''

Snake gave her a dark look. ''You would, you crazy woman. Who wants to sit with their butt in that cockpit for twenty-some hours?''

Snickering, Jessica said, ''Well, hey, it gives us a chance to practice our in-air refueling. We need to have that on our record every year. I'm lookin' forward to seein' that C-130 herky jerky coming out of the blue and trailin' a fuel line from its wing. We'll each get a chance to do it. I'm kinda excited.''

"You get excited over the weirdest stuff," Snake growled, rolling her eyes.

Cam didn't relish the idea of a long flight for her friends, either. Still, it meant that Maya would have one more Apache to add to her squadron, and that was good. Cam was sure Maya was looking forward to having her pilots back, too.

"So, you gonna hand out the BJS2 squadron patches to them in a little while?" Wild Woman asked.

"Yeah, I will. They've earned them."

"They've got to *keep* earning them," Vickey said darkly. "I know Gus will. I'd love to have that guy with us down at BJS. He's hell on wheels up in the air. He's all combat mode. But Luis and Antonio? Nah."

"You're prejudiced," Cam teased her lightly. Her heart squeezed when Gus's name was mentioned. How much she missed their private, searching conversations. "Well," she sighed, opening a drawer and handing them two sets of orders, "here are your passports back to BJS. You'll take off at 0500 tomorrow morning."

Grinning wickedly, Vickey looked at Wild Woman. "Great! Wanna kick up your frisky heels tonight, girlfriend? Club Flamingo? One last hot rumba? A tangle of tangos? You up for it?"

Laughing, Wild Woman said, "In a heartbeat, Snake. Let's go get outta these army duds and into some hot mama movin' dresses with lotsa fringe on 'em!"

"Have fun," Cam told them as they stood.

"Why don't you come with us?" Snake invited as she opened the door.

Shaking her head, Cam said, "No...I'd cry all the time because I'm going to miss you so much. I would just rain on your party."

Nodding, Jessica smiled. "Well, we'll see you before we leave tomorrow morning?"

"That's a promise," Cam said. She had duties to perform now.

She saw Luis and Antonio standing tensely outside the door. Their faces belied their stress and worry as to whether or not they'd passed the final flight test. "Ask Mr. Dominguez to come in, will you, Snake?"

"Sure," she called, lifting her hand. "See you mañana...."

Gus was the last man to be called into Cam's office. Her heart picked up in beat as he quietly entered, still in his flight suit. How handsome he looked. Her gaze centered on his mouth. Gus had a beautifully formed mouth, and Cam had stopped counting the times she'd wondered what it would be like to kiss him and to feel those lips against her own. As he shut the door and turned around, Cam forced a smile she didn't feel.

"Congratulations, Gus, you've passed." She stood up and held the BJS2 patch across the desk.

Grinning, he took the patch, their fingertips briefly touching. In his heart, Gus felt an incredible sadness. Ever since the night he'd taken her out and spoken those words on the dance floor, Cam had retreated from him. He was so sorry those words had flown from his mouth.

"Thanks, Cam," he said.

"You're welcome. Sit down." Her heart beat even harder as he slowly sat down in front of the desk. Just the way he reverently touched the patch made her yearn for him to touch her in the same way.

Gus smiled gently. "Looks like I know what I'll be doing tonight—sewing this on my flight suit."

Chuckling, Cam nodded.

"Luis and Antonio looked relieved."

"Yeah, they passed. Barely. But they've got good training under them, so I feel confident in the next step—actual night interdiction."

Nodding, Gus looked down at the patch. Running his fingertips across it, he said, "So, where does this leave you? I know you were brought here to whip us into shape, to give us form and substance." Grief ate at him. Looking up, he held her dark green gaze. Was Cam leaving, too? Gus had never heard her say one way or another. After his faux pas at the restaurant, he wondered obliquely if she had put in for a transfer, to get away from him as soon as he graduated from training.

"Me?" Cam asked, surprised. She shut the desk drawer that held the flight tests. "I'm going to continue to command this little squadron of ours. Why?"

Glancing up, she saw his cinnamon-colored eyes lighten with obvious joy, and the look caught her completely off guard. It was then that she realized Gus still liked her.

The thought was euphoric. He was still going to be her X.O. She was still going to have to work with him, closely—on a daily basis now, but on an equal footing.

"Oh…" Gus shrugged and gave her a boyish grin, "I just thought that…well, it doesn't matter. That's great news."

"Is it?"

Feeling her gaze dig into him, Gus smiled boldly. "Yeah, I'm glad you're staying." Hooking his thumb across his shoulder toward the door, he said, "Now, I can't speak for Luis and Antonio, but I'm glad you're still running our ship, Captain."

Warmth sheeted through Cam and she felt suddenly vulnerable and nervous. "It's been hard," she muttered, avoiding his warm perusal by nervously moving a number of papers on her desk.

"But worth it," Gus insisted. Seeing her nervousness, he tightened his lips. "You're a great leader and teacher, Cam. I hope you know that. Look how far I've come. I learned more from you and the other women in the past six weeks than I did at flight school. Your experience, your generosity and the way you taught us was a gift."

Cam's fingers froze over the papers as Gus spoke in a low, emotional tone. Within her, she felt the armor plating around her heart give way beneath his fervent sincerity. How many men had the guts to come clean and be honest with her? Gus had shown, nonstop, that he was someone she could always rely on. He'd never lied to her, as men in her past had done. He'd always been straight with her, and he could admit he'd made a mistake.

Chewing on her lower lip, Cam looked across the desk at him. His face was open and readable, as it always was when they were alone. The care radiating from his eyes was undeniable. "Thanks for your words, Gus. They mean a lot to me. And I'll pass them on to Snake and Wild Woman, too.''

Opening his hands, he took a huge risk. "Listen, Cam..." His voice dropped to a whisper. "I know you've been dancing on the edge of a sword around here since you arrived—learning how to be a C.O. and balancing it against army regs. And dealing with me as your X.O., I know, hasn't been a lot of fun. It's been trying on you." Gus saw her eyes narrow as she sat there, weighing his words. "Well, what I mean is, maybe you want someone else as your executive officer now?"

"What?" Stunned, Cam sat up, blinking.

Gus shrugged. "I'm gonna come clean with you, Cam. That night at the restaurant, well, I crossed some lines with you that I shouldn't have, militarily. But it happened. In my heart, I'm not sorry I said what I did, but I know it adversely affected you—and our relationship. I just want to give you the out to get another X.O., is all. I don't like the tension that's always hovered between us since then. It's got to be a special hell on you because you see me so often, working together as we do."

Sitting back, Cam wiped her mouth with the back of her hand. He was giving her a sad look, one that nearly broke her heart. Gripping the arms of her chair, she closed her eyes for a moment, then stared at Gus, who sat forward in his chair, his hands—those wonderful hands that had held her so gently while they danced—resting on his long, hard thighs.

"Gus, you have a way of forcing me to come clean, too," Cam muttered with a frown. "The least I can do is be honest with you." Looking up at the ceiling, she continued, "I've had three relationships with men. I have a flaw somewhere in me, and damned if I know why, but I draw the same kind of guy every time. A guy who wants to manipulate me into bed, lie to me, and take what he wants and then just walk away as if he has no responsibility toward me."

Gus sat very still. His heart ached—for Cam. He saw the pain in her eyes as she admitted her past to him. "That must have been terrible for you, because you're not that kind of person." Right now, he wanted to beat the hell out of all of those men, for he could see the damage they'd done to Cam. And how it was keeping her from trusting him. Rage flickered in him. Life was so unfair.

Taking a deep, ragged breath, Cam got up. She crossed her arms and began to pace behind her desk. The venetian blinds were open, allowing horizontal bars of light into the room. They reminded her of prison bars. Looking out at the revetment area, where a crew worked on the Apaches, she hung her head.

"I've been running, Gus," she admitted quietly. Turning, she looked over at him, tension swirling around the room. "Running from you, even though you aren't like them. I'm scared."

Swallowing hard, Gus wanted to get up, walk over and take Cam into his arms. That's what she needed, judging from the stricken look on her face. His heart, however, cautioned him. She would rebuff him, he knew. "I understand now," he told her. "And, for what it's worth, Cam—" he opened his hands in supplication "—I'm sorry. As a man, I'll apologize for their selfish behavior toward you. You didn't deserve to have that happen to you. You're a good, kind person who's honest and likes to treat the world that way.'' He gave her a twisted smile. ''But not everyone in life is going to play by your rules, with your idealism.''

''Yeah,'' she whispered, ''I know that—now. One of life's little chucks under the chin—to tell you that not all people have your best interests at heart in a relationship.''

''People play games, Cam. You're not a game player—you play for keeps. You bring your honesty, your hard-work ethic, your high moral values and standards to the table with everyone you deal with.''

Amazed that Gus could see all that in her, Cam felt her heart lift a little. She felt some of the grief dissolve beneath his probing cinnamon gaze. When he stood up, her pulse bounded. He held her gaze as he slowly walked around the desk and stopped within a few feet of her.

''You don't have to apologize for those jerks,'' she muttered. Cam stood there, tense and tall, her arms wrapped around herself defensively. Gus wasn't stupid. He could read body language pretty well and he knew that she was feeling very prickly right now, even toward him—because he was a man. It had been men who had so deeply wounded Cam to the point where she no longer trusted any of them.

''Are you comfortable with me being your X.O. and knowing that I care for you on a personal level, too? That on some days, I might slip and be intimate with you? I'll try my darnedest to always be businesslike, Cam. You have my promise...but I'm human, too. I might slip. I won't do it on purpose. I won't manipulate you like those other men did, but

I'm an ordinary guy. Like on the dance floor that night—those words just came out of my mouth, straight from my heart, and I didn't even realize it until it was too late.''

Gus pursed his lips and held her dark, shadowed gaze. Seeing tears glimmer dangerously in her eyes tore at him. The desire to take two steps toward Cam, hold open his arms and ask her to come into them nearly undid him. It was so tough not to speak what was in his heart.

Choking back the tears that came out of nowhere, Cam slowly unlocked her arms and let them fall to her sides. How badly she wanted to move into Gus's arms. Cam knew from the searching look on his face that he'd hold her. And she'd be safe. And loved. Stunned by that realization, Cam stood there in shock, staring dumbly at him. Words jammed in her throat and she couldn't speak for a long moment.

"There isn't a day that goes by here, Gus, that I don't look forward to seeing you," she finally murmured brokenly. "And it scares the hell outta me admitting it to you."

"Because you think I'll use it against you? That I'll try and get you in bed and then walk away, like they did, right?"

"Stupid, isn't it? But yeah…"

"Listen to me, Cam." Gus took a huge risk and reached out, sliding his hand against her jaw and cupping her flushed cheek. He saw the tears trail silently down her face. Groaning softly, he rasped, "I won't *ever* do that to you. First, I need to earn your trust. Without trust, we have nothing. We can go no-where." Her flesh was warm and firm beneath the palm of his hand. When Cam closed her eyes and nuzzled her cheek into his hand, Gus held his breath. Elation soared through him. Cam's action shouted volumes. She could have slapped him. She could have jerked away. She could have gotten angry and told him to back off, but none of that had happened. Instead, she was trusting him enough to allow this intimate moment with her. The tears, however, were unstringing him.

"Just...let me hold you, Cam? I'll just hold you for a moment. I think you need to be held. I can do that for you. No manipulation. Just two humans being here for one another?"

A sob jammed in her throat. Gus's face blurred as she willed herself to look up at him. His hand was warm and stabilizing. Cam ached to ask so much more of Gus, but her fear overrode that. Two feet of space—that's all that was separating them. That's all she had to walk. Gus was offering her a safe haven against her pain. Her past. Getting up the courage, Cam tried to smile through her silent tears.

Without a word, she stepped forward.

Groaning softly, Gus placed his arms around her tense shoulders. "Come here, Cam...." he whispered harshly against her ear. Her chestnut hair tickled his nose and cheek. Wrapping his arms around her, he drew her gently against him. Closing his eyes, Gus realized a fragile truce was being built between them, and that Cam was giving him a gift. As she shyly, hesitantly slid her arms around his shoulders and laid her head against his chest, Gus sighed raggedly. Little by little, Cam relaxed against him. Feeling her torn emotions, Gus didn't try to force her to do anything but what was comfortable for her in that moment.

"You're a priceless gift to me, Cam," he said in a low tone. Smiling against her hair, his cheek against her head, Gus felt her sink more surely into his arms. He held her gently, lovingly. And as he felt Cam begin to relax and fit the contours of her body against his, he felt a sob wrack her. Automatically, his arms tightened for a moment around her shoulders. "That's it, let it out. Let it all out, Cam. You're safe with me. I promise…. Just get it all out and I'll hold you…."

Chapter 12

"Don't worry, they'll do fine," Gus reassured Cam as they stood just outside the barracks, the harsh floodlights breaking up the darkness around them.

Cam absorbed Gus's nearness like a sponge. It was dark, and in the distance, she watched Luis and Antonio climbing into the Apache helicopter, the ground crew ready nearby.

"I just worry," she said, frowning as she crossed her arms against her chest.

Chuckling, Gus stood inches behind her. "Hey, you've flown with these guys every day for the last month. If they don't have their night ops down pat by now, and interdiction rules memorized, they're never gonna have them." He glanced at her shadowed profile. Seeing the concern etched in her face, Gus fought the need to put his hands on her shoulders and tell her not to worry. But he couldn't. They were in full view of the crew and it wouldn't be proper military etiquette.

"This will be the first night they're going up alone."

"You'll be here. You've got the iridium phone. You'll be in contact with them," he coaxed. "Besides, aren't you tired of flying with each of these guys? Aren't you looking forward to a night off?" Gus was worried about Cam. Since her two friends had left, he'd seen Cam turn back into a twenty-four-seven workaholic. He'd done what he could to take work from her and give her a breather, but she still had to do the biggest share.

"I know…." Cam whispered. She twisted her head to look up at his dark, serious face. How handsome Gus was to her. And how lonely she'd been without their daily meetings out at the grove. Everything had changed since Wild Woman and Snake had left. She had to fly each night with either Luis, Antonio or Gus, five to seven hours, teaching them interdiction in real time. The entire duty rotation had changed. She was flying every night, without a break. They had only two Apaches available, and while one flew, the other was being serviced. Gus wasn't up to speed yet on the finer points of interdiction himself. Cam had spent most of her time getting the two Mexican pilots qualified so they could work with one another. Tonight was their first trial by fire, without her guiding them.

"Hey," Gus whispered, briefly touching her shoulder, "come on, Mama Hen in the Sky. Let's go to the grove—something we haven't been able to do for a long time." He looked forward to the rare personal time with Cam. Ever since she'd walked willingly into his arms, laid her head on his shoulder and cried her heart out, things had changed between them. Gus was earning Cam's trust one small step at a time. She was worth it to him. Even though he had his own devils to contend with—his fears that she was in a dangerous profession and could get killed just as the other woman he'd loved—Gus couldn't fight his powerful attraction for Cam.

Cam hungered for his touch. As Gus's hand grazed her shoulder, her flesh tingled with wanting of him, and she turned, searching his face. "You know what? That sounds wonderful. Since we only fly at night, our whole world has been turned upside down. We're awake all night and sleep all day."

"Not exactly great," Gus agreed as Cam fell into step with him. They walked along the concrete path around the barracks, then moved away from the lights on the building. In the distance, Gus could hear the Apache revving up for takeoff. Cam had the iridium phone in her left hand. He hoped the two pilots, who had made an amazing about-face, would do everything by the book tonight so Cam wouldn't have to worry about them so much. If they screwed up, it was on her record, her watch. He didn't want to see her career torpedoed like that. She didn't deserve it.

"Where's your guitar?" Cam asked. How she missed hearing Gus play it. This last month, their former routine had been shattered, and she had discovered just how much she needed this hour alone with Gus. The grove had become a place of healing for her on so many levels, a place where she could, for a little while, leave her responsibilities behind.

He gave her a slight smile as he walked at her side. "It's already on the picnic table, waiting for you."

Giving him a narrowed look, Cam murmured, "Why do I think you've had this all planned out, Mr. Morales?"

With a boyish grin, Gus said, "Oh, I dunno, Ms. Anderson. Do I look like the type who has a plan up his sleeve?"

Chuckling, Cam said, "That's one of the many good things about you, Gus—there're no games. No manipulation." He wasn't anything like the men in her past. The afternoon Gus had held her in his arms, so many of the old walls and fears had dissolved within Cam. The last month had been tentative, hopeful, scary, and yet happier than she could ever recall. Gus made her want to trust him. His honesty at every juncture was evident.

Swinging his arms as they stepped off the asphalt and onto the sandy earth leading to the grove, he said with humor, "I can't say this isn't something I didn't cook up. It is." He held her hopeful gaze. "It's something you need," he said enigmatically.

"Uh-oh, I'm in trouble now," Cam laughed. His returning laughter lifted her spirits and made her heart pound with joy.

"Nah," Gus teased. Once inside the grove, he slid his hand into hers. In quiet moments, especially in her office with the door closed, Cam allowed him the privilege of touching her hand, her shoulder. And as her trust in him grew during the last month, she'd come into his arms on her own, just to be held for a quiet moment. Gus knew the gift she was sharing with him and never made a move to go beyond what Cam silently asked for. Oh, how he wanted to kiss her! But he didn't. He waited. If he pushed his will on her, the fragile trust between them would shatter. And there was no way Gus was going to let that happen. His desire for Cam was held firmly in check. He was going to behave.

Cam squeezed his large, warm hand as he led her into the grove. "What have you done, Gus? I can see that wicked glint in your eyes." Breathless because she needed this playfulness, Cam grinned up at him. His hand tightened around hers as if to quietly reassure her that it was going to be a good surprise.

"Oh," he hedged, "just some small stuff." And he led her to the table. Cam stood at his side, lifting her arm and placing it around his waist. Shocked by her bold move, and yet glorying in it, Gus lost his smile. Gently, he wrapped his arm around her shoulders. Cam leaned against him, her head resting against his chest. Joy sang through him. Clearing his throat and trying to think coherently, because he hadn't expected Cam's response, he gestured to the long redwood bench.

"I got your favorite dessert," he told her in a conspiratorial tone. "A cream puff." He'd found out that Cam loved them. One night she'd enthused about her mother's ability to make the world's best cream puffs.

Touched, Cam moved out of his embrace to the small baker's box sitting on the bench. "Ohh, Gus, you shouldn't have!" she cried, quickly opening it.

Just watching the childlike expression on Cam's face as she leaned over and opened the box did Gus a lot of good. Picking up his guitar, which had been lying on the table, he straddled the bench behind Cam and settled the instrument against him.

"Sit down and enjoy your just dessert," he teased, as he began to strum the instrument.

Laughing, Cam turned around and straddled the same bench, facing Gus, the box between them. He'd thoughtfully included several large paper napkins, and she placed one on her left thigh and one on his right. The music he played was beautiful to her. Picking up the first huge cream puff, which was oozing with whipped cream, Cam placed it on the napkin on his knee.

"This is yours," she told him, grinning. Picking up the second one, she eyed it wolfishly. "And this is mine!"

Gus watched as Cam eagerly bit into the pastry. She knew how to attack it without squishing all the whipped cream from the center.

"You're pretty good at that," Gus said, impressed. "When I eat one, it squirts all over the place."

Chuckling and closing her eyes, Cam enjoyed the pastry. "Mmm, this is wonderful, Gus! Thank you so much. It's so thoughtful of you!" Opening her eyes again, she gave him a huge smile.

Gus grinned. Cam had whipped cream on both sides of her luscious-looking mouth. She quickly slurped it away with the tip of her tongue and attacked the pastry again with great relish.

"Good thing cream puffs don't fly. They wouldn't stand a chance with you," he stated humorously.

Laughing, Cam melted beneath his dark, smoldering gaze. Still in his flight uniform, with a few rebellious strands of hair dipping down across his brow, he looked dangerously handsome to her. "Why don't you eat yours?" she challenged.

Shrugging, Gus said, "I'll get it all over me."

"Chicken."

Rising to her bait, he placed the guitar on the table beside him and reached for his pastry. "Okay, here goes...."

Cam gave a cry as Gus bit into it, and whipped cream spurted everywhere, including a blotch on her cheek. When he pulled the pastry away from his mouth, he had cream on his face, hands and uniform.

"What a mess you are!" she said, easing to her feet and scooting closer till their knees met. She picked up her napkin and began wiping cream off his smiling mouth. Drowning in his darkened, narrowed gaze, Cam found her hand slowing as she dabbed at the remainder.

"I warned you," he growled huskily, setting down the cream puff and wiping his hands on his own napkin. "You've got a big splotch of whipping cream near the side of your mouth. Want me to kiss it away?"

Heat shot through Cam as he gently cupped her face and tilted her chin slightly upward. Gus wanted to kiss her. And she wanted to kiss him. Her hand came to rest on his chest and Cam gazed wonderingly up into those warm, cinnamon-colored eyes that held such love for her. It *was* love, Cam realized despite her stunned, spinning senses. She saw his strong mouth curve into a gentle smile as he cocked his head and studied her.

"Y-yes, kiss the whipped cream away," Cam whispered unsteadily, her voice hoarse.

"Sure?"

"Very sure, Gus."

"This has to be mutual, Cam...." And it had to be. He saw the desire in her huge and luminous eyes. Gus saw fear in them, too, but he hoped that the trust he'd earned would allow Cam to surrender to him. His fingers tightened briefly beneath her clean jawline. Her skin was warm and firm. How badly he wanted to touch it, touch her and kiss her.

Closing her eyes, Cam stretched upward. "Kiss me?"

Never had two words meant so much to Gus. Leaning down, he met her halfway, his mouth moving slowly, provocatively across her parting lips. She tasted of sweet cream. Grazing her lips, Gus smiled and licked off the spot of cream from Cam's cheek. Hearing her moan softly, feeling her fingers tighten reflexively on his flight uniform, Gus placed a soft kiss on each of her closed eyes.

"You are," he breathed, "the most beautiful flower in my garden of life, Camelia Anderson." He allowed his lips to trail down to the tip of her nose, and then lower, to her parted lips. "You are so beautiful to me. Like the delicate flower you are, everything has to be right for you to bloom, to flourish. I want to help you do that, *querida*. Darling...."

Lost in the heat of his strong mouth closing over hers, of his breath, warm and moist, flowing across her cheek, Cam surrendered to Gus. She felt his hands move in a caressing motion across her hair, cherishing her as if she were some fragile, breakable treasure. Never in her life had she felt so loved, so cared for. His mouth was strong and giving, searching and coaxing. She tasted the whipped cream, the sweetness of him, and felt the power of him as a man, held in check.

Moaning, Cam felt his arms move around her shoulders as he drew her more closely against him. Sitting on the bench with their knees pressed together didn't allow for complete contact, but she didn't care. Holding him close like this was enough. Her breathing became shallow. Hungry for his continued touch, Cam felt her lower body begin to throb with an ache that moved upward toward her heart.

"I need you...." Gus rasped against her wet, slick mouth. "In every way, *querida,* whenever you say the word..." And he crushed his mouth against hers as she met and returned the fire that had exploded between them. Pain knotted deep in his lower body. Oh, how he wanted to make slow, delicious, mind-blowing love to Cam! Gus knew in his heart that he could please her and show her that not all men were selfish takers, interested only in their own needs. Her mouth was strong, searching, eager, as he met and matched her sweet assault. Beneath that cool exterior lurked a woman of immense passion, he realized with happiness as he threaded his fingers through the strong, silken strands of her hair.

Moving her hands across his chest and up his thickly corded neck, Cam eagerly traced every inch of Gus. The male odor of him was like a perfume to her flaring nostrils. Heart thundering in her breast, she eagerly slid her lips against his. As his tongue moved in a slow, sensual dance against hers, she shuddered. She wanted to mate with him, to become one with him, and that desire shook her as she'd never been shaken before.

Tearing her mouth from his, Cam drowned in his smoldering, hooded eyes, which were focused on her like those of a predator. "I need you, Gus. I'm afraid, but I can't stop...." And Cam leaned upward and pressed her lips against his. Feeling a groan ripple through his chest against her flattened breasts, she shared that wonderful animal sound with him. As his fingers slid across her scalp caressingly, Cam lost herself in his arms. Somehow she knew she was safe with Gus, that he wouldn't take advantage of her. Everything was so right. So beautifully right...

Lost in the explosions arcing through him as her mouth caressed his over and over again, Gus felt his control disintegrating. Alarmed, because he didn't take Cam's words to mean that she wanted to go "all the way" physically, he prayed that he was reading her right. Otherwise, he could botch this and send her running.

Cradling her in his arms, Gus moved his mouth more slowly, sipping from her wet, warm lips. Laving her lower lip with his tongue, he covered her mouth with his, smiling against her. Cam was trembling. So was he. Savoring the weight of her arms around his neck, the pressure of her fingers opening and closing against his back, he absorbed her thirst for him. Feeling euphoric, he finally reached up and smoothed her hair away from her cheek.

"You are so beautiful," he whispered to Cam, their noses almost touching. Watching her eyes open, those long chestnut lashes flutter up to reveal her drowsy, desire-filled gaze, Gus gave a very male smile of appreciation.

"You make me feel that way," Cam whispered unsteadily. Just being in Gus's arms was wonderful. "I've never felt how I do now, Gus. You make everything seem so right. So good."

His mouth curved ruefully as he traced her arched brow with his index finger. "That's because we trust one another, *querida*. We've laid a good foundation, don't you think? We've had time to get to know one another. We've talked a lot out here." Gus lifted his head and glanced appreciatively around the quiet, darkened grove. Looking back down at Cam, he saw her mouth part and a soft smile touch the corners.

"Yes…we have."

"I'm going to turn you around so you're more comfortable," he told her.

Nodding, Cam eased away. Gus positioned her so that she was straddling the bench like him, her back against his chest, her head resting on his shoulder. When his arms went around her waist and captured her hands across her abdomen, Cam sighed.

"Better?"

"Much better."

"We're not pretzels anymore."

Laughing softly, Cam looked up and drowned in his dark, narrowed eyes. "No…"

"That's for teenagers," Gus chuckled. "At our age, comfort is better."

"Mmm, this is nice," Cam agreed, and she sighed, feeling languorous and sated on so many levels. Moving her fingers across his clasped hands, she added, "I don't know how you did it, Gus."

Holding her close, he pressed a kiss to her hair. "What, *querida?*"

"Got me to trust you." Cam frowned and traced his thick, hard knuckles with her finger. The back of his hand was darkly haired and silky.

"It was easy," Gus confided. "The first time I saw you, the doors of my heart just sprang open."

"Really?"

"Yeah. Kinda took me off guard."

"Because of the woman you loved and lost?"

Nodding, Gus rested his cheek against hers, content just to have Cam in his arms like this. It was an unbelievable gift. His heart was still pounding in his chest, and his lower body was in knots of need, but he refused to allow his raging desire to affect this moment. Everything was perfect. Perfect. Cam was in his arms, trusting him, and maybe…loving him? Gus wasn't sure about that. He did know that whatever they shared, it was mutual.

"Yes, losing her ripped my heart out of my chest," Gus said quietly. Feeling Cam's hands tighten comfortingly around his own, he closed his eyes. "I'm still not right with it all, Cam. I'm scared, too, in a different way than you. But scared just the same."

Cam nodded. "I'm always amazed at how our fears stop us." How wonderful it was just to be held by Gus, to be talking like this. She had been starved for such intimacy, she realized, for a long time. In part, Cam knew, the closeness of her women friends at BJS had filled that need in her. When she left for this assignment, however, she'd been cut off from that lifeline.

Gus compressed his lips and he tasted Cam on

them. Aching to love her, but knowing that wasn't possible now, he said, "You fear trusting another man. I fear having a relationship with a woman in a dangerous profession again."

"You're helping me get over my fear," Cam told him softly as she grazed his hand with her fingers. Gus tightened his arms briefly around her in response.

"And I'm getting to be friends with mine, too."

"Where does this leave us, Gus?"

"Afraid but moving forward, I think," he said, giving a short laugh.

Nodding, Cam closed her eyes. "Yes, I feel the same."

Sighing, Gus murmured, "We just need to keep pacing ourselves with one another. And we need to keep talking. I'm not a mind reader and neither are you. The last thing I want to do, Cam, is misread you or assume. That can get us into hot water real fast. The *last* thing I want to do is shatter your growing trust in me."

"Just keep doing what you do so well, Gus." She looked up and smiled at his very serious face. "You seem to have this sixth sense about me, what I need and when I need it. I'm in awe of it, to tell you the truth. I don't trust myself in thinking I know you, or where you're at, because I never could with the other men I was involved with, so I'm relying more on you than me. Does that make sense?"

He gave her a one-cornered smile. "Yeah, it does, *querida*. It just puts more pressure on me to read you right the first time, though. I'm afraid I'm going to screw up with you…and that if I do, it will wreck what we have."

Cam shook her head. "No, Gus, it won't. I've known you for a long time now, in a lot of very different and difficult situations, and you've been steady as a rock for me. Your morals and values, the way you treat me daily, have never changed, no matter what was happening around us." Searching his eyes earnestly, Cam reached up with her hand and slid it along the curve of his jaw. "I trust you—with my life. Just know that, okay? I trust you, Gus."

Those were words he'd prayed to hear. At the same time, as he caught her hand and pressed it against his cheek, they scared him even more. Unwilling to call what they shared love, because it was just too much for him to grasp at this time, Gus whispered, "I've always trusted you, Cam. You hold my life, my heart in your hands, whether you know it or not."

"I didn't know that, Gus." She sighed deeply. "I'm so inept at reading men."

"You're innocent," Gus said in a hushed tone, pulling her hand from his cheek and placing a slow, warm kiss on her palm. "Don't be hard on yourself. Innocence is forgivable in my book."

Her palm tingled deliciously as he rested his lips against it. Every fiber within her screamed to make love with Gus, but Cam knew it wasn't time. At least, not yet.

"I've never thought of myself as an innocent," she said, humor tingeing her tone.

"Well, you are in my eyes," Gus said, pressing a second kiss to her palm.

"You're wonderful, Gus," and Cam smiled up at him, into his deeply shadowed face, carved with the harsh lines of life. "Thank you for everything to-night...."

"Even the cream puffs?" He chuckled. Gus knew their time was drawing to a close. He knew Cam had to get back to her office and stay alert in case the Apache crew needed her help.

"Especially the cream puffs," she said, laughing softly. As Gus lifted her hand and kissed the back of it, she felt giddy. Effervescent and free.

"Hmm, I wonder if they're really aphrodisiacs in disguise. I should bring them to our next secret meeting in the grove."

Cam sat up and turned toward him, laughing fully. "Gus Morales, you are an incredible man." She placed her hand against his heart. Growing serious, she met his hooded gaze. "I don't know what life will throw at us, but I want you to know this—I'm in it for the long haul with you. I don't want a one-night stand. I'm not built that way and I think you know it. I want the time to get to know you. I want to laugh with you. Cry with you. I want to talk, and share life with you."

Pressing his hand to hers, Gus said in a rasping, emotional voice, "Cam, we want the same thing. Only our lives aren't our own here. Not really. We're going to have to make precious hours like this one happen when we can."

Nodding, Cam whispered, "Let's make them happen, Gus. For both of us."

Chapter 13

"Nasty night out," Gus grumbled as he leaned down, frowning at the green HUD screens in front of him. Cam was flying the Apache over the harsh, high desert in northern Mexico, roughly a hundred miles south of the Texas border.

Cam gripped the controls, trying to keep the Apache on course despite the rain and wind whipping them around. "Yeah, our first time together on a night flight in over a month and we get this."

The darkness was complete except for lightning bolts that sizzled cloud-to-cloud around them, or danced toward the earth. A U.S. Army radar balloon tethered at the border and floating three hundred feet off the earth, had detected two aircraft, one fixed wing and the other a helicopter, coming in over a well-known drug route. BJS2 had been called to intercept them.

At five thousand feet, the Apache strained and bobbled as Cam hit one jolting air pocket after another. Sweat stood out on her brow. She had her nightscope, which was hinged on the right side of her helmet, positioned beneath her right eye, allowing her to see objects out there in the darkness. It was a necessary piece of high-tech equipment. With her other eye she continued to monitor the instrument panel in front of her. The soothing green color served to calm her heightened sense of anxiety somewhat. Cam didn't have a good feeling about this mission, but she said nothing to Gus. After all, it was only an intuition she had, and so far, nothing had confirmed it.

"I hate thunderstorms. They destroy our night vision capability," she groused. Sitting in the upper cockpit, with Gus below her, separated from her by an armor-plated wall, Cam pushed the nightscope away with her gloved hand. It was useless with lightning dancing around them. They had to fly through the edge of the huge storm in order to reach the validation point where they'd intersect their targets.

"I can see why," Gus agreed. Peering at the HUDs, he saw the two aircraft approaching from the right. "I've got 'em painted on the screen." He placed his gloved index finger on the television-screen image in front of him. "One's a Cessna 150 and the other is a Bell helicopter, according to the identification."

"Helluva night for either of those Tinkertoys to be out here," Cam said. "They must have a lot of coke on board to risk flying in a storm like this."

"Yeah," Gus said grimly, "a 150 is too light to withstand violent up-and-down drafts. If that pilot is in the wrong place at the wrong time, he'll get smashed into the desert below, like a fly hit by a flyswatter.''

Chuckling, Cam said, "The flyswatter being a nasty downdraft that pushes him to the ground before he knows what hit him.''

"Well, as we know, druggies will do anything, fly in any kind of weather or circumstances, to get drugs across the border.''

Grimly, Cam turned the Apache to the south on an intercept course as Gus called out the coordinates. "It's bad out here tonight. Those pilots have got to be sweating it out, too,'' she muttered.

"They're at fifteen hundred feet and going lower. They sure don't want to remain on radar very long.''

Cam knew that drug-running pilots were well aware of the radar balloons placed at certain points along the U.S.-Mexico border. The balloons were a first-warning line of defense to pick up their approach. Drug pilots tried to fly beneath the reach of radar, sometimes as low as fifty feet above the ground, or what was referred to as "nap of the earth flying.'' It was dangerous at any time. Especially dangerous tonight, given the turbulence caused by the storm.

"Uh-oh, they're turning west. I think they're trying to avoid this storm altogether.''

"Right,'' Cam agreed grimly, easing the Apache downward to intercept them. "They'd have to. This storm would kill 'em and they know it.''

"Okay, they're both hugging the earth. One thousand feet. Twenty miles ahead. We're going out of our box.''

"That's okay.'' The "box'' was an area they normally flew in on a known drug route. They would often fly Bravo or Alpha box, specific latitude and longitudes, in a rectangular flight pattern at five thousand feet, hoping to intercept a drug flight coming north. Gus would have to notify the base back at Tijuana that they were moving out of the box now. That way, military personnel would know where they were located in case they had engine trouble and had to go down. Rescue teams would know what their last location coordinates had been.

Looking around, Cam saw the roiling, cauliflower-shaped clouds light up for a second above them. Right now, even with the jostling they were experiencing in the storm's turbulence, they were still safer in the Apache than those two pilots were in their lightweight aircraft. Her heart was pounding a little, and anxiety enveloped her. Cam didn't like storms, didn't like flying anywhere near them. Akiva and Joe's Apache had been struck by lightning and suffered severe software damage on their last mission, and she had no wish to be placed in the same position.

"They're outta the storm's reach," Gus said, following the radar images on the HUD, "and going down to five hundred feet."

"What's the terrain under us like?" Cam asked. This was territory they'd never flown over before. But fortunately, the Apache's state-of-the-art equipment gave them a good look at the terrain.

Gus chuckled darkly. "Brutal. My people's land. My mother was born about fifty miles east of here. It's high desert, very dry with lots of canyons and caves. It's not hospitable. No water."

"Nice place to visit but not live in," Cam said,

smiling tightly. Her eyes narrowed as she continued to sweep her gaze over the instrument panel. In the dark, a pilot could get vertigo. Especially with lightning causing havoc with her eyes and brain. It was more important than ever for her to watch her instruments and trust them. Guiding the Apache swiftly downward, she saw that they would intercept the other aircraft in a matter of minutes.

"Right on," Gus said. Reaching for his night-vision binoculars, he waited as Cam placed the Apache in position to get a positive identification of the two aircraft. The first thing they had to do was get close enough, without giving away their position, to retrieve the numbers on each aircraft's fuselage. Then Gus would type them into his computer and send a request to the Federal Aviation Agency's computers in Washington, D.C., to find out if either of the other pilots had filed a flight plan. Every plane was required to have one, especially if crossing from one country's airspace to another's. Aircraft without flight plans were very likely drug runs.

The registry of the plane, and the owner's name, would pop up on Gus's HUD as well. Those names would be cross-referenced with the FBI database in D.C., which held a list of pilots known to fly drugs. A match there—a frequent occurrence—confirmed it was a drug run. If there was no match, but the plane had been involved in other suspected drug flights— even searched and found clean—that info, too, would pop up on his screen.

All they needed, however, was a thumbs up from D.C. to confirm there was no flight plan. That meant they could go to work and force the pilot to land at the nearest airport, where Mexican soldiers could apprehend and search the plane.

"This is strange," Cam muttered. "Two aircraft flying together? You'd think they'd realize that two make a bigger dot to be picked up on the radar screen."

"Yeah," Gus said. With the turbulence so bad, he held the binoculars in his lap, gripped in both hands to prevent them from flying around the cockpit and injuring him. "Makes me wonder if they're really drug flights...."

Shrugging, Cam said, "I don't know. If they are, this is a new tactic, and we need to be super alert."

"It's odd that one's fixed wing and the other's a helo. Usually it's one or the other."

"A lot of things aren't adding up on this miserable night," Cam muttered. They were less than a mile from the fleeing plane and helicopter now. She would bring the Apache closer, without lights on so that they wouldn't be detected, and Gus would get the numbers on the fuselage by looking through the night-vision binoculars. At least that was the plan.

"Druggies are always tryin' new things," Gus stated. They were within a half mile of the fixed-wing craft. Turning in his seat, the harness biting into his shoulders, he lifted the binoculars to his eyes. Even in the rain, he'd be able to read the numbers. "Stay the course, I've got 'em sighted, Cam...."

Using all her flight skills, she held the Apache as steady as possible. For the most part, they were out from under the storm cloud, and the wind was lessening. That made it easier to fly the gunship and she was grateful. Rain was still falling, but conditions weren't as bad as before.

"Steady..." Gus murmured. "Steady...I got 'em!"

Cam grinned, hearing the crow of triumph in his voice. Within seconds, Gus had typed in the numbers and sent them on for verification.

"Bingo!" he said shortly. "It's a Javier Rios flight, a drug lord from southern Mexico."

"Excellent," Cam said with a short, tense laugh. "Akiva and Joe must be doing a good job down there. He's been sending more and more flights north to avoid interdiction by them over the Gulf of Mexico, where Akiva and Joe's black ops base is located."

Before Gus could answer, he saw something on his HUD that made his eyes go wide.

"Rocket! Rocket being fired at us!" he yelled. Disbelievingly, he saw the helicopter, which was half a mile behind them now, firing—at them!

Cursing softly, Cam saw the warning on her HUD screen as a shrill warning went through her headset, indicating that they were being painted by an enemy's firing array. Where the hell had that rocket come from? Mind whirling, she instantly took evasive maneuvers.

"Get online. We're returning fire!" Cam barked at Gus.

Too late!

She had wrenched the Apache out of the path of the rocket. The only problem was that the rocket was a heat seeker, and it followed the heat of the Apache's engine.

"Look out!" Gus screamed, and he threw his hands outward to brace himself.

Spinning the helicopter around, Cam tried to avoid the hit. Out of the corner of her eye, she saw a yellow flame. It was the rocket—coming directly at their tail rotor assembly. Fear filled her. She groaned as she worked the controls, trying to avoid being hit.

Seconds flew by, though to Cam they seemed to drag. Tensely, she gripped the controls. Her breath jammed in her chest. *No! Oh, no!*

The rocket exploded upon impact as it grazed the tail rotor assembly. Fire arced all around them. Cam felt the Apache shudder. The blades whapped loudly as the helicopter began to slowly turn in a circle, out of control.

"Hang on!" she yelled at Gus, her nostrils flaring. Cam knew what would happen. The tail rotor was gone. Without it, the Apache would turn in endless circles until it smashed into the ground.

Darkness cloaked them suddenly as their instrument panels went offline. Panic surged into her throat and sweat popped out on her brow. They were going down! In a hurry!

Mind whirling, Cam calculated their chances. They had been five hundred feet above the ground when they were hit. She had no idea what kind of terrain lay below them. Feverishly, she worked the pedals with her booted feet and twisted the cyclic and collective to try and stop the Apache from spinning. Vertigo chased her. She shook her head savagely, trying to clear it.

In the distance, a bolt of lightning flashed. It gave just enough light for Cam to see the vague outline of a canyon coming up. They were falling into it! The walls were steep and narrow. Breathing hard, she gasped. The blades would strike the rock! Hands gripping the controls, she wrestled with the sinking helicopter. She heard Gus gasp as well.

In the middle of their uncontrolled free fall, Cam dimly registered the fact that the helicopter shadowing the plane had been the craft that had fired at them. It had been a setup! They'd fallen for it. She hadn't taken adequate precautions. Her mouth flexed grimly. The earth was coming up fast!

"Prepare for crash!" she cried out.

Seconds later, the blades of the Apache struck the wall of the canyon, sending a sickening shudder through the bird. Jerked savagely one way and then another, Cam felt their slowing descent. Chunks of rock struck the canopy. The Plexiglas groaned but didn't shatter.

The helicopter suddenly groaned and turned on its side, causing Cam's harness to bite painfully into her shoulders. She let go of the controls and, trying to brace, threw her arms up to protect her face. Simultaneously, she lifted her feet away from the pedals. If she didn't, the impact would break her legs and possibly crush her feet.

The Apache's descent was slowed even more as the flailing rotor blades hit the wall of the canyon again. The blades snapped and sliced like scimitars hurling through the blackness, shrieking as they spun. The bird tipped backward, the tail hitting the ground first.

The impact was horrific. Cam cried out as she was flung toward the front of her cockpit. Her harness held, but the jolt was savage, straining every muscle in her body. Pain shot through her neck and shoulders. Slammed to one side and then the other, she heard the scream of metal being ripped apart. Helplessly she flung out her arms as the bird keeled over, nose first now, tossing Cam in her harness like a rag doll.

Every second felt like a separate nightmare. The Apache slammed down on its port side. Cam's helmet struck the cockpit Plexiglas, shattering it all around her. She felt the final death throes of her bird before it finally lay without moving.

"Gus! Gus! Can you hear me?" Cam cried, fumbling for her harness release.

"I hear you!" he gasped. "Get outta here! That helo could have followed us in. They could finish us off! Get out! Hurry!"

Cam knew the score. Whipping her gaze across the cockpit controls, she saw they had no electricity. No way to call for help. But the bird had a transponder. It would start emitting a signal immediately.

"Get out!" Gus shouted.

Another bolt of lightning illuminated the canyon briefly. Cam managed to unharness herself. She reached to the right and twisted the release mechanism on the canopy, which popped open. Relief swam through her. She wasn't seriously hurt, just bruised. Wind rushed into the cockpit, and so did the rain. Grunting and groaning, Cam threw herself out of the cockpit headfirst. She struck the fuselage and then bounced off, hitting the ground hard.

Above, she heard a helicopter approaching. On

hands and knees, spitting sand out of her mouth, she yelled, "Gus! Where are you?"

The night was so black she couldn't see anything.

"Here!" he groaned.

Scrambling to her feet, Cam took off her helmet and dropped it as she headed drunkenly along the bird's fuselage, leaning against it to steady herself. Rain whipped into her face and she raised her gloved hand to protect her eyes.

"Where?" she cried. "Where are you?"

The helicopter that had shot them down was fast approaching. Breathing hard, Cam held out her right hand as she stumbled over rocks.

"I'm here!" Gus yelled.

Cam nearly tripped over him. Quickly, she fell to her knees, her hands reaching, searching. "Gus?" Her voice was strident, off-key. "You hurt?"

"Yeah...dammit. That chopper's coming, Cam. Help me up! We gotta get away from this bird. They're gonna take it out!" And he reached out and connected solidly with her hand. Cam was strong, he discovered. Holding his broken left arm close to his body, he gritted his teeth and stood.

"This way!" Cam yelled. The whapping of the chopper's blades was puncturing her eardrums. Any second now, Cam knew the helicopter would fire another rocket at them. Gripping Gus and wrapping her arm around his waist, she gasped, "Come on!" as he leaned heavily on her. Slipping on unseen rocks and gravel, she lunged away from the Apache and headed down the canyon.

Another bolt of lightning flashed. Panting and dizzy, Cam staggered unevenly beneath Gus's weight.

He was groaning, obviously trying not to cry out. In the second's light, she saw a bend in the canyon. Only fifty feet away! If she could get them around that corner of rock wall, they might be safe from a rocket fired at the Apache.

"Run!" she begged breathlessly. Gripping Gus hard against her, Cam surged ahead, digging the toes of her boots into the hard, sandy soil.

Gus gasped. Pain made him dizzy. He tried to run and felt Cam steady him as she aimed for the bend in the canyon. It was their only chance! Breath tearing out of his contorted mouth, he tried to concentrate. *Run!* He had to force his wobbly, weakened legs to run! Somehow, he had to force his attention to the present.

Faintness rimmed his vision, and Gus felt himself physically failing. Felt himself leaning more heavily on Cam, until she groaned. *No! No!* He loved her! This couldn't be happening! They couldn't die now!

Those thoughts cleared his pain-filled senses briefly. Gathering his strength, Gus swung his feet forward, one in front of the other. The rocks and gravel made the surface slippery and dangerous. They ran brokenly, stumbling, almost falling. They had to make it to that bend or they were dead!

Breath ripping from her burning lungs, Cam swung Gus ahead of her with one, last superhuman effort. She heard the rocket being fired. They had only seconds. As Gus flew off his feet ahead of her, Cam dived headfirst after him.

Slamming into the earth, the breath knocked out of her, Cam heard a tremendous explosion behind them. The entire canyon lit up like Fourth of July fireworks.

With a cry, she rolled to the right. Safe! She was safe! Fire vomited past them with a roar. The wall protected them! As Cam scrambled to her knees, covered with sand and grit, her eyes widened enormously. The fuel from the leaking tanks on the Apache had exploded. The fireball raced past them and shot high into the night sky. The odor of burning aviation gas permeated her senses. Nostrils flaring, Cam threw herself farther behind the wall and landed squarely on top of Gus.

He cried out.

Cam rolled off him, gasping for breath.

As the fireball began to dissipate, the drug helicopter flew past them and on up the canyon.

"Gus!" Cam staggered to her knees and twisted toward him. In the light of the fire still crackling and popping from the destroyed Apache, Cam saw his shadowy figure lying on the ground. His teeth were gritted and he was holding his left arm. His face was stretched with pain. Looking down, Cam saw that her hands shook as she reached out to touch his left shoulder. The dark color of blood stained the entire upper arm of his uniform.

"No!" Cam cried softly. She gently held Gus down when he started to get up. "Don't move, Gus, don't move!" she chanted as she reached into her flight suit. She always kept a Swiss Army knife with her; now she needed it. Pulling it out and opening the blade with shaking fingers, she quickly cut away the fabric. It gave with a sickening, ripping sound.

Cam winced. "Oh, God..."

Gus lay there gasping for air. Sweat rolled into his tightly shut eyes and he clenched his teeth. Hearing

Cam's soft cry sent fear through him. He felt her hands on his arm as she carefully pulled the sleeve away. "I—broke it on impact," he rasped.

Swallowing hard, Cam could see blood spurting from beneath his arm. Worse, she could see the whiteness of bone sticking out of his torn flesh. It was a compound fracture, the worst kind.

"Just hold still," Cam said in a shaky voice. Digging into the left pocket on her thigh, where she kept all her emergency medical items, she found several dressings. Tearing them open, the paper fluttering away, Cam placed them where she saw blood spurting out. Gus was losing a lot of blood. Fast.

"This is going to hurt," she sobbed near his ear, "but I gotta do it. You're bleeding, Gus.... Just hold still...." And Cam pressed the dressing up beneath his arm and then applied downward pressure on top of his biceps, hoping to stop the bleeding. If she couldn't, Cam knew, he'd lie here dying before her eyes. Swallowing hard, she shut her eyes and concentrated. Gus couldn't die! She loved him. It had taken this crash for her to admit that to herself. What a fool she'd been to dodge the truth of how she felt toward him.

Gus groaned, his body arching upward. Closing his right fist, his hissed out a string of oaths in Spanish.

"I'm sorry...I'm sorry..." Cam sobbed. "I've got to stop the bleeding. This is the only way...." And she bent protectively over him, tears stinging her eyes.

Heart pounding with dread, Cam tried to get ahold

of her emotions. The crash had ripped away any pretenses. As she knelt over Gus, in an unknown canyon, without any prayer of rescue, Cam knew she loved this man, heart and soul. But was it too late?

Chapter 14

Cam shuddered inwardly as the dawn appeared, turning the sky over the canyon a dirty red color. She sat huddled against Gus, who was sleeping intermittantly, his head resting against her shoulder, his left arm in a makeshift sling. The coolness in the canyon depths made her shiver.

It had rained off and on for the rest of the night. Soaked, they had clung to one another, striving for warmth. Shaken and bruised, Cam studied the yellow and ochre walls of the canyon, sandstone cliffs that rose nearly a thousand feet straight up. They were lucky to have survived at all.

Gus stirred. Cam gently eased him into a sitting position. She saw him grimace, his right hand moving immediately to his left one in its sling.

Anxiety threaded through Cam. She saw how leached out he appeared, and she didn't miss the pain in his expression as he slowly opened his eyes. He studied her in silence.

"Are you okay?" he asked finally, his voice thick and rough.

Nodding, Cam whispered, "Yeah. Cold. Bruised. But okay. How's the arm?" She gestured toward it.

The bleeding had finally stopped with direct pressure, and Cam had never been so grateful. Looking at Gus in the grayish morning light, she could see the dark stain of blood all the way down his flight uniform to his waist. It was a grim reminder that he could have died last night.

"It hurts like hell," he muttered.

"What I'd give for some pain meds for you," Cam exclaimed, sympathy in her voice.

"I'd settle for a glass of water." He rubbed his face, trying to get alert.

"Oh, yeah," Cam said, as she slowly got to her knees. Her entire body ached. She felt as if she'd been in a multicar crash at high speed. There was a tightness along her shoulders and into her neck. *Whiplash.*

"Stay here," she said as she got to her feet. Dusting off her uniform, she ran her fingers distractedly through her hair. When she flew, she kept her hair tied up in a rubber band at the base of her neck. During the crash, the band had broken. Now her loose hair was littered with ash and sand.

"I'm going to check out what's left of the Apache," she told Gus, and rounded the corner of rock wall that had protected them from the explosion. The gravel crunched beneath her booted feet. Down in the narrow canyon lay the blackened, charred remains of the once proud Apache. Wisps of grayish smoke still rose from it as Cam approached it. The air reeked of spilled fuel and melted metal.

They had carried ammunition, but no missiles, and Cam was glad. The missiles could have detonated upon impact and she and Gus would have died in the cockpits. Running her hand through her hair again, Cam stood looking at the wreckage. There was nothing left to retrieve, she realized, now that the rain had doused the fire. No iridium phone call for help. No state-of-the-art computer equipment linking them with the outside world. Nothing.

Turning on her heel, she looked at the wall behind her. It was scorched and blackened from the original blast. Compressing her lips, she realized once more how narrowly they had escaped from death. By getting around that wall they had saved their lives.

Sighing, Cam frowned and walked around the crash site, looking for anything they could use. Right now, they were in high desert—outside the box where the search planes would start looking for them—and without water. The prospects were daunting. She knew that Gus hadn't had time to radio back their position; everything had happened too quickly.

Still, they were alive, and as Cam retraced her steps to see how Gus was doing, hope clung stubbornly within her heart. Unshaven, his hair tousled, he was sitting there, back against the wall, cradling his broken arm, his right hand resting beneath his left elbow. Pain was etched in his face, darkening his eyes. Cam's heart lurched as she knelt down on one knee near his left side. Reaching out, she gently grazed his bearded cheek. "At least," she said, "we're alive."

"That's a big one," Gus agreed, lifting his head

and holding her narrowed gaze. "Anything left of our bird?"

Shaking her head, Cam said, "No…nothing."

"I didn't get a radio message off to base."

"It's okay. We didn't have time."

Gus hung his head and scowled. "I should have seen that coming. I should have been monitoring that damned helo. I'm sorry I let you down."

"No," Cam sighed, "that was my call. I *knew* better, Gus. This is an old trick that the drug dealers used to play on us down in Peru. They would have two helos about two miles apart trying to sucker us in and shoot us down. We almost lost a couple of our Apaches to them before we caught on to their change of game tactics." Grimacing, she looked up. "I did lose one. I was commander on this flight. It's my fault. I knew better. I had that feeling, and I was ignoring it. Dammit…" She rubbed her dirty face with her hands.

"Hey," Gus rasped, reaching out with his right hand to touch her leg as she stood near him, "don't do the blame game. Neither of us knew that helo was armed with rockets."

"I'd just gotten a report yesterday," Cam said, regret in her voice as she held Gus's gaze, "from BJS. It came from Akiva and Joe. They said that Luis Rios, Javier's son, who runs four or five helicopters to shadow their coke shipments in fixed-wing aircraft, had been using that tactic with them as of late, and to be on top of it."

"That was a day ago," Gus said.

"Doesn't matter, Gus. As commander, it's my job to take these reports seriously and to change our in-

terdiction approach as a result. I didn't.'' Her mouth
flattened. Cam knew it would be a horrible black
mark in her personnel jacket. More than likely she'd
get yanked from her position as C.O., and someone a
lot wiser and sharper would replace her. Cam shut her
mind to that possibility. Right now, they had to survive this ordeal and get Gus medical help.

"They'll understand, *querida*."

The endearment brought tears to Cam's eyes.
Kneeling down, she touched his thigh, then reached
out and slid her fingers across his hair before she allowed them to come to rest on his cheeks again.
"You know what? When all this was happening, the
only thing I was praying for was for us to survive."
She felt the warmth of tears running down her cheeks.

Gus lifted his uninjured hand to take hers and kiss
it gently. "We're going to be okay, *querida*. And
we're going to make it out of here." Her hand was
dirty, smudged from greasy black smoke. Her face
was streaked with a fine layer of gray dust that her
tears had made tracks through. Whispering her name,
Gus cupped Cam's cheek, wiping away the tears with
his thumb.

"We're going to get out of this."

Sniffing, Cam sat back on her heels and self-
consciously wiped her face with trembling fingers.
"D-do you remember anything about the map of this
area, Gus?"

He nodded. "Yeah, I do. That's what I was searching for in my brain while you were gone." He pointed
down the canyon toward the opening, which wasn't
far away. "I remember last night seeing a Yaqui village about twenty miles to the south of us, from our

last location before the rocket was fired. Now—'' he gave her a lopsided smile filled with pain ''—it might be closer or farther away, because we were dancing around in the sky so much, trying to shake that rocket. But I know it's south of this canyon. I saw the canyon marked on my HUDs, and for whatever reason, I remember thinking that it was a Yaqui village probably a lot like the one my mom was born in. So I *know* it's there and I know the approximate location.''

Getting hold of her escaping emotions, Cam whispered, ''good,'' and ran her tear-damp fingers along the dusty fabric of her flight suit. ''I'm so glad you remember that. I didn't.''

Giving her a grin that felt more of a grimace because of the way his arms was throbbing like fire itself, Gus said, ''Funny how we all remember certain things at certain times. You know, I had the weirdest thing happen to me in the middle of that firefight.''

''What?'' Cam saw his dark brows draw down, a quizzical look on his face.

''I would swear that seconds before we got hit, I saw this jaguar covering our Apache. I know it sounds stupid, but I saw this apparition...or ghost, or whatever you want to call it. I saw the cat leap at us and the helicopter became a part of the cat.''

''Didn't your mother say she had jaguar medicine?'' Cam asked, fascinated by what Gus had seen.

''Yeah...that's right.'' Gus gave a short laugh. Grimacing because even laughter caused him pain, he looked up at her. ''Yeah, jaguar medicine. She said it protects her.''

''Well,'' Cam said wryly, ''I'm not Indian, but it

sure sounds like you either have a jaguar guardian angel or your mother's spirit is helping us survive.''

Shaking his head, Gus said, ''You know, looking back on the whole thing, I remember how after that cat surrounded us, the rocket hit us. I remember thinking we were dead. I heard this growling sound in my helmet and felt a weird vibration going through me, and it wasn't the Apache coming apart around us. I heard you curse and I knew you were doing everything in your power to get us down and out of there alive. And it was weird, Cam. I felt like I was above the Apache, like a detached observer, just looking on. I saw you. I saw myself sitting there. And I saw the bird on fire.''

Cam smiled slightly. ''This isn't as weird as you think. Maya, our C.O., is from the Jaguar Clan. We don't know a lot about it, or her, but talk goes around BJS about it. She has special powers because she's a member of that clan. Maya has this extraordinary sense about things. More than intuition. Snake, Wild Woman and I have all flown with her, and we've seen the power of the Jaguar Clan in action through Maya.''

''Maybe we were saved by my mother's Jaguar blood?'' Gus wondered aloud. ''This is the first time it's ever happened.''

''When we get back home,'' Cam said, ''I'll be sure to share this with Maya. I'll bet she'll know what happened to you. She can clear the mystery of what happened, and maybe help you understand it better.''

''Yeah, because I never felt my arm break. I never felt the pain, Cam, until you helped drag me away from that bird.'' Gus shook his head, wonder in his voice. ''I never felt the crash.''

Rubbing her aching shoulder, Cam muttered, ''I sure as hell did. I feel like I've got whiplash.''

Gazing at her, Gus felt his heart open. ''You had to be in your body to get us down safely,'' he said. ''You'd have felt everything. For whatever reason, and I don't know how it happened, I wasn't in my body during the crash.''

''Be nice if your were that way now. I can see the pain in your face.''

Nodding, Gus said, ''No kidding.''

Looking around, Cam took a deep breath. ''Well, come on. We've got a long walk ahead of us. I want to take advantage of the cloud cover and time of day. We'll lose less water this way.''

Frowning, Gus said, ''Go alone, Cam. I'd just slow you down.''

Her heart pounded once, strongly. She stared at Gus, her lips parting. ''No way!'' Her voice echoed down the canyon. ''I'm not leaving you here!''

''Hey, calm down,'' Gus said gently. He raised his hand toward her. Cam's face was a mass of raw feelings, and he saw the anger and anguish in her eyes. ''I'm really weak, Cam. I lost a lot of blood. I don't even know if I *can* walk. You can't carry me, not with this arm the way it is. I weigh more than you do.'' Gus forced a smile he didn't feel.

Cam's face grew dark and her mouth twisted. ''Gus, I'm *not* leaving you!'' She heard the desperation in her voice. Inwardly, she was shaking like a leaf caught in a massive storm. Her stomach knotted. ''How do I know if I leave you that the druggies won't come back here looking for us? Hunting us down?''

Gus touched the holster positioned against his right thigh. "I'd hold them off."

Snorting, Cam rasped, "Not for long! We each have one clip in our pistol and another on reserve and that's it! There's no way I'm leaving you here, Gus. I just won't!"

The anguish in her voice tore at him. Tears were splattering down Cam's cheeks. He saw the turmoil in her eyes, the way her mouth contorted and her lower lip trembled. Feeling bad, he said, "Listen to me, will you? I'm in no shape to go anywhere. You can walk a lot faster without me. Twenty-minute miles, Cam. You can make it there in ten hours."

"Tough. You're coming with me, Gus. I don't care if it takes twice that long, I'm not leaving you behind." Her voice had risen to an almost hysterical level. Shaking, Cam scrambled to her feet. "I left Maya. I swore after that that I'd *never* leave another person in the field. I just won't do it!"

Closing his eyes, Gus remembered how Cam had told him of the awful decision she had had to make on a previous mission. She had to leave Maya, who was unconscious, behind to be captured by the druggies, or stay with her and be captured along with her. Opening his eyes, Gus held Cam's teary gaze.

"This isn't the same, *querida*," he said in a quiet tone meant to soothe her. "I'm not Maya. There are no druggies. This is different."

"It's no different to me!" Cam cried. She leaned down and slid her arm beneath his right armpit and around his back. "Now get up, Gus! We're doin' this together or not at all!'' And she reared upward, taking his full weight with her.

Weakness seeped through Gus. Cam's quick, strong movement caused him to grow temporarily light-headed. Wrapping his good arm around her shoulders, he steadied himself against her as his feet found purchase beneath him. Knees feeling mushy, he gasped as the effort created waves of unrelenting pain up his left arm.

''Hold still....'' he rasped.

Cam was breathing hard, but holding Gus firmly. Unmoving, she saw his face blanche almost white. Her heart sank. Maybe he was right. Maybe he couldn't be moved. Cam felt him struggling to get his feet beneath him and become stable. A gasp tore from his taut lips as he managed to stand on his own. She loosened her hold slightly, but not much, unsure if Gus really could balance himself.

Though he understood why Cam wouldn't leave him, Gus knew they'd be in trouble if they tried to make the trek together. But he also knew that because of her past, Cam would rather sit here in this canyon waiting for search parties to find them, than leave him alone. Oh, he knew that Luis and Antonio had probably put in a call for help when they saw he and Cam hadn't returned to base on time. That was a given. But the search would be concentrated within the box designated by their FAA flight plan. Rescue aircraft wouldn't be searching outside of it for days, not until they'd combed that area first. Without water, Gus knew, they could die before they were found. The rain that had fallen wasn't enough to create puddles. The desert had been dry and instantly sucked all the moisture up.

Grimly, he forced himself to stand on his feet, planting them apart. Feeling Cam's strength, her steadying arm about his waist, he kept his right arm around her shoulders just in case. Biting down hard on his lower lip, he allowed the waves of heat and throbbing pain to pass through him. Slowly, the pain began to ease as he remained still and standing.

"You know what?" he said, his voice scratchy and low.

"What?" Cam breathed, watching him closely.

"I think we can do this...."

Her heart soared with gratefulness. "Okay," Cam muttered, "then let's try, Gus. One small step at a time. I know every time you put your foot down, it's going to jolt that broken arm of yours...."

"Yeah, and I don't want to rip open that artery that's just clotted shut, either," he reminded her dryly. "I don't want to bleed to death."

"No," Cam whispered, her voice off-key, "I don't want you to, either."

Raising one eyebrow, Gus asked, "You ready, partner?"

Cam fought back the tears. She was highly emotional at the moment. Part of it was the letdown after surviving a fiery crash, the aftermath of the huge surge of adrenaline. The other was fear of abandoning Gus. He didn't fight her on that, and she was relieved. "I'm ready, partner. Let's go. One small step at a time."

Girding himself, Gus nodded. "Yeah, very careful, mincing steps."

"I'll hold on to you," Cam swore. "I won't let you go. I promise."

Those words packed a lot of power and emotion behind them, Gus realized, as he began to take tentative, careful steps forward. Cam matched her stride to his. Every step jolted his arm. It was agony. But it kept his head clear. The sand beneath them was littered with gravel and small rocks. Gus concentrated on not slipping.

"At this pace," he groaned as they moved slowly down the canyon toward the exit point, "it will take us two days to reach the village."

"That's okay," Cam said. As they left the canyon behind and climbed slowly upward, the desert around them gradually revealed itself. Above, the low-hanging clouds, like strips of bumpy cotton kept the rising sun at bay. There was cactus here and there on the flat yellow reaches. In the distance, very far off— maybe fifty miles, in Cam's estimation—rose dark blue mountains, their peaks sharply pointed. Gus headed in that direction.

The desert floor was a dark yellow color due to the recent rains. The only vegetation was cactus.

"We're in luck," Gus told her. "See that cactus just ahead?"

"Yeah."

"It's a prickly pear. You got your Swiss Army knife on you?"

Cam nodded. "Yeah. What do you want me to do?"

"Let's stop here, let me rest for a few minutes." His knees were feeling like jelly. "First knock off some of those oval, flat pieces. With your knife, cut out the thorns. And then we can skin them. The pulp inside will give us the water we need.''

Heartened, Cam gently helped Gus into a sitting position, his legs crossed. ''Sounds good. My mouth feels like dried plaster.'' It was tough to form words properly, and she had been slurring them as a result of her mouth being so dry. The idea of a water source bucked up Cam's spirits.

Gus watched as Cam did exactly as he instructed. The prickly pear was a series of leathery, leaflike appendages, oval shaped, growing out of one another. They didn't have a lot of thorns, and contained enough water to survive on.

As Cam nudged the thorny pieces toward him with her boot, he drew his knife out of the lower pocket of his flight suit. Unable to open it, he handed it to Cam, who straightened the blade and gave it back to him.

''Thanks,'' he said. ''Now watch me. As a kid, my mom taught me how to skin a cactus without ending up like a pincushion in the process.'' And he flashed Cam a grin.

Kneeling in front of Gus, she watched him expertly dethorn the prickly pear. Placing the tip of his boot on one end of it, he made several criss-crossing cuts through the tough, leathery surface. Once the skin had been scored, he used the tip of his knife to pull it off, leaving only the pulp. He was good at dethorning the fruit and she marveled at his skill and speed, even using only one hand. ''Who would ever think that something like that, taught to you as a kid, would come in handy now?'' she laughed. Hope pounded through Cam. Gus looked a tiny bit better. He was still wan, but there was some pink to his cheeks beneath his dark growth of beard.

"Yeah, you never know," Gus said, returning her smile. With her help, he skinned the cactus. "Now, cut up the pieces into bite-size chunks."

Cam followed his instructions, then held up the first morsel. "Here…"

Taking it, Gus popped it into his mouth. The water in the cactus tasted delicious.

"Try it," he urged.

Cam took a piece herself. The cactus was firm and fibrous, and she tasted a slight astringent bitterness, but water was released as she chewed.

"You can chew on it, get the water out and either swallow it as a food source or spit it out." Gus grinned and took another piece she handed him. "The only bad news about this is your stomach might feel a bit nauseous because you aren't used to the taste or texture. But you should be able to keep it down."

Nodding, Cam knelt there sharing the cactus with him. Her stomach did roll, but she wanted to absorb the life-giving water too much to allow the sensation to stop her from eating.

Within twenty minutes, they'd sated their thirst. Gus looked better, and Cam felt stronger. Without water, it would have been a terrible journey, she knew.

"I'm glad," she told him, wiping her fingers on the thighs of her flight suit, "that you have desert survival training."

Grinning, Gus said, "You'd better hope we find that village sooner rather than later."

"Why?" Cam ask, melting beneath his warm

smile. She saw life coming back to his eyes, and her heart soared. As she stood, Cam stopped fooling herself. She loved Gus. Unequivocally. Without reservation. The crash had brought it all home to her. As she put their knives away, she wondered if he loved her.

"Because we need protein," Gus said as she helped him stand. The pain was intense as he leaned against her for support. Her arm, wrapped firmly around his waist, steadied him. "Protein in a desert comes in the form of critters. Insects." He saw her wrinkle her dirty nose.

"Ugh, I remember the survival training the army gave us back in school." Shivering, Cam muttered, "I sure hope we find that village soon. I *hate* eating bugs!"

Chuckling, Gus looked around the flat, quiet desert. He heard the lone cry of a coyote somewhere off in the distance. The day was getting brighter, and he saw rifts and openings in the clouds above, where slashes of blue sky appeared.

"I dunno," he said congenially, teasing her, "I've eaten my share of them. My mother's people know which ones are tasty and fortifying if they can't find a rabbit or peccary to eat instead."

Snorting, Cam felt his teasing banter bolster her hopes. The love she felt for Gus ballooned. Having him beside her—his strength, his warmth and closeness—was really all she ever needed.

"We've got pistols. I'm all for finding some poor rabbit to be our meal tonight," she muttered. "Let the bugs live."

Chuckling even though it hurt, Gus gave her a warm look. "You know what, *querida?*"

At the endearment, Cam felt heat spread from her neck to her cheeks as he held her gaze. They walked slowly, but together. "What?"

"I'm glad you're here. And I'm glad you decided to haul my sorry ass along for this walk."

Grinning, she said, "Thanks, Gus. That means a lot to me." And it did.

Sighing, he looked across the desert. "This is a beautiful place. Full of life. Most people don't ever think of the desert as being alive, but it is." He tightened his arm briefly around her shoulders. "And I'm glad I'm sharing it with you...."

Chapter 15

"I'm inspired," Gus told Cam as they camped within a small cave they'd found near sunset. She hunkered over a small fire just outside the cave, turning a freshly killed rabbit, which she'd skinned, over the fire. The meat was browning and sizzling.

Cam gave him a dirty look as she held the rabbit over the flames. "Yeah, so was I. There's no way I was gonna eat bugs tonight, Morales."

Grinning tiredly, he sat on the yellow sand and leaned against the wall. "See? I'm good for you in exciting and unexpected ways," he teased. Seeing Cam return his smile lifted his tiredness momentarily. Supporting his aching, swollen left arm with his right hand, he absorbed Cam's features as the shadows of the night stalked them.

Giving Gus a warm look, Cam tried to keep her worry to herself. Twice today, as they'd rested, she'd pulled off the bandage to check his arm. There was little bleeding, thank God. Still, his entire upper arm was swelling up like a balloon because the bone needed to be reset. Anxiety ate at her. She saw how wan Gus looked. Throughout the day, he'd been courageous in not complaining of the pain she knew came with every step.

The rabbit was a fat one. Cam had been looking for any kind of animal on their walk toward the village. Luckily, a male jackrabbit with long, black-tipped ears had bounded out in front of them. She'd used her pistol and shot the animal. Though she'd felt badly about it because she didn't like killing anything, she knew that in order for them to keep going and hopefully reach help by tomorrow, they needed food as fuel. Slowly turning the rabbit over the flames, she shifted the stick it was skewered on between her hands.

"That sure smells good," Gus murmured. The desert was quiet tonight after the storm the night before. The thirsty earth had soaked up all the rain that had fallen and was now a pale ochre color once more. He watched Cam from beneath half-closed eyes. They'd found a small pool of water in a rock crevice which had sated their thirst earlier.

"I'm starving, too," Cam said.

"You should be. You practically carried me all day long." Gus was surprised at her strength, both physical and internal. He knew Cam wasn't going to leave him behind. The stubborn set of her mouth and the burning look in her eyes told him that.

"How many miles do you think we made today?"

she asked, pushing her hair off her forehead. How she wished for a brush and comb.

Mouth quirking, Gus said, "Maybe ten… It's hard to judge out here."

Nodding, Cam said, "Yeah. That's what I thought. Around ten."

"If all things are equal," he said, "and we didn't fly too far from the last position on my HUD, that village should show up sometime tomorrow evening if we can keep the same pace as today."

Cam shoved the end of the long, sturdy stick into the ground and surrounded it with large rocks, leaving the rabbit at just the right height to sizzle over the flames. Getting up, she scoured the area illuminated by firelight to find more pieces of dry wood for their campfire. With mesquite shrubs growing nearby, sticks were easy to locate. Gathering them in her arms as she walked, her boots crunching on the yellow sand, Cam looked up.

The sky was darkening swiftly now; only a hint of the peach-colored sunset remained, a thin rim on the western horizon. Just above the eastern horizon was a glowing white star. Turning back toward Gus, Cam said, "That's got to be Venus in the east. Isn't she beautiful?"

The cave opening faced east, so it was easy for Gus to see where she was pointing. His gaze moved back to Cam as she placed the fuel near the fire. "What I'm looking at is beautiful. In fact, she makes the planet Venus pale in comparison." All day Gus had wanted to establish intimacy with Cam. But their dangerous situation hadn't warranted it. Now, he hoped, it would. When Cam lifted her face, shadowed by the flickering light, he saw the surprise in her features.

"You're prettier than any star or planet," he said, giving her a slight, one-cornered smile. No matter how he sat or what position he tried, Gus couldn't relieve the pain in his arm. It was growing worse, but he wasn't going to tell Cam that. She was worried enough, and knowing her, was probably feeling as if the responsibility for the loss of their Apache rested solely on her shoulders. All day he'd seen her waging an internal war between sadness and guilt over the incident.

"Thanks…" Cam said, giving him a shy look. "I've never had a guy see me like that before." And she hadn't. Gus had a very poetic and romantic side to him, a side she loved….

There was that word again. Frowning, Cam picked up the stick with the meat on it and began to rotate it slowly over the flames once more. The crash had shaken loose all her suppressed feelings toward Gus. Did he love her? Could he love another woman who took risks? She had no answers. And she didn't have strength to devote to anything but their survival right now.

Somehow, Gus wanted to take Cam's guilt and worries away. He understood where she was coming from, and he knew there would be a military inquiry into the Apache being shot down. But that didn't mean Cam would lose her C.O. position and be drummed out of the army, as she feared.

"Tell me something," he said. "What would you do in your life that you haven't done already if you could?"

"Uh-oh," Cam said with a quiet laugh, "the philosopher is coming out. Are you bored, Gus? Sitting over there, helpless? Feeling like you should be helping me or doing this?" Cam pointed at the rabbit on the skewer.

Forcing a smile, Gus felt buoyed by Cam's laughter in spite of the relentless pain that moved like grinding waves up and down his arm and shoulder. "Yeah, you're right on all counts. Are you a mind reader, *querida?*" He purposely used that endearment. Instantly, he saw Cam's narrowed eyes soften. Her mouth relaxed, too. How he wanted to take her into his arms and hold her, and whisper to her that all would be well. But he couldn't....

Shaking her head, Cam tested the meat. "If I was a mind reader, I'd have known that that helo was armed with rockets." The meat was dark brown and oozing with juices now. Cam peeled back a piece to see if it was done inside. It was. *Good.* Getting to her feet, she took the rabbit over to Gus. Sitting down on his right side, facing him, she held the rabbit between them.

As she pushed the end of the stick into the ground so that the meat hung between them and they could peel off chunks to eat, he gave her a thoughtful look.

"Thanks. You're saving my neck, yet again."

"You owe me, Morales. Big time."

Enjoying her teasing, he popped the first bit of meat into his mouth. It was hot and delicious, just what he needed. "I like owing you," he teased back. He saw her grin. "This is good. You're a great chef, Ms. Anderson. Five star, if I don't miss my guess."

"Let's stick to the owing one another, shall we?"

Cam forced herself to eat slowly and savor every bite of meat. Her stomach had been in knots all day with worry and anxiety. She hadn't realized how hungry she was until just now. But maybe it was the company she was keeping, too. Eyeing him tenderly, Cam saw that several strands of his hair dipped onto his brow. With her left hand, she pushed them back into place. She liked touching him.

"I'll write you an IOU," Gus said with a grin. "And you can collect it from me once we get back to base."

"You're on," Cam chortled. And then she became serious. "You know, the only good thing about this," she confided, "is that I can touch you whenever I want. I don't have to worry about prying eyes or military regs getting in the way."

His flesh tingled briefly where Cam had slid her fingertips against his brow. "I agree. We should use this time productively." Catching her hand as she lifted it away, Gus pressed a long, slow kiss to the back of it and then released it. The surprise in her eyes made him feel good. Without a doubt, Gus knew he loved her. Fiercely. Without compromise. Wanting to broach the topic with her, but not knowing when would be best, he watched a look of languor come to her eyes for a moment after he'd kissed her hand.

"You are so gallant," Cam whispered. Her skin tingled where his strong mouth had caressed her flesh. No other man had kissed her hand with such a flourish. No other man had kissed her hand at all. Gus was a throwback to an age where gentlemen were truly that, and treated women with remarkable respect.

"Me? What about you, *querida?* I don't think *gal-*

lant is a word reserved exclusively for men, do you?''
He ate another chunk of the meat and held her gaze.
''Gallantry is like chivalry.''

''Is that how you see me?'' Cam wondered out
loud.

''As a heroine? Yes. Courageous. Fearless.''

''Forget the fearlessness,'' Cam growled. ''I was
scared as hell up there last night. When that rocket
was fired, I about died. I just wasn't expecting it. I
should have foreseen the possibility, but I didn't. I
was too focused on getting the numbers off that first
plane.''

Shaking his head, Gus wiped his greasy fingers on
the thigh of his uniform and then reached out. ''Stop
it, will you? I've never seen anyone savage themselves like you do, *querida.*'' He stroked her cheek
in a loving gesture. Maybe he couldn't come clean
with his feelings toward Cam yet, but Gus wanted her
to know that he cared deeply for her, anyway. Judging
from the softness in her eyes after he caressed her
cheek, he knew he could lift her spirits and stop her
from worrying so much. It was a wonderful discov-
ery. A powerful one. Maybe he couldn't help her
gather firewood, make a fire or find meat, but he could
tend the garden of her heart and emotions. In that
way, he could help her.

''I just can't shake it, Gus. I screwed up with Maya.
I've screwed up here. All I do is screw up.''

''No, you don't,'' Gus growled. ''I don't think any
board of inquiry is going to hold you accountable for
what happened last night. We lost a rotorcraft, but we
survived. They can replace the Apache. We're a lot
harder to replace.''

Pursing her lips, she saw that the rabbit was pretty much eaten. Taking the carcass off the skewer, she picked delicately at it and found a few more morsels, handing them to Gus. He needed it most because pain was stealing his energy, sapping his strength.

"Maybe you're right," she muttered.

"I know I am." Thanking her for the last bits of meat, he made sure she got half of them, anyway. Cam had already dethorned more cactus, skinned it and cut it into bite-size chunks. He handed her some. It served as a vegetable with their meal.

"I can't say I'm thrilled with prickly pear," she told him, chewing on a small piece to get the fluid out of it. The water from the small pool they'd found earlier was gone and Cam knew they had to get as much fluid in them as possible.

"No, it's not exactly a Starbucks mocha latte, is it?" He smiled.

"What a die-hard sense of humor you have." Cam looked out of the cave mouth. The darkness was complete. Above them, a canopy of stars twinkled overhead. From somewhere out on the desert came the lonely, serrating cry of a coyote.

"I don't like the other choice," Gus told her.

Cam turned around, her back to the wall, only inches away from him. She needed his closeness. His optimism. Tipping her head back against the rock, she sighed and closed her eyes.

"You're my counterpart," she told him in a low tone. After wiping her fingers on her flight suit, she opened her eyes and found his hand. Slipping her fingers into his, she closed her eyes again and sighed.

"You make me happy, Gus. You have a way of pulling me out of a tailspin of darkness."

"Isn't that what people who care for each other do?" he asked, squeezing her hand.

Right now, in that instant, Cam wanted to turn to Gus, seek refuge in his arms. It was impossible under the circumstances, so she focused on feeling the warm strength of his hand around hers. "Yes...it is...."

Frowning, Gus took a deep breath. Just getting to talk to Cam helped ease some of the pain he was in. "Listen, I need to talk with you, *querida*. I don't know if this is the right time or not, but here goes...."

Cam opened her eyes slightly and slanted him a look. The firelight outside the cave highlighted Gus's sharp, strong profile. She saw that his brows were knitted. "Okay..."

"The crash," Gus began in a low tone, "changed a lot of things for me, Cam. Before it...well, I thought I had my life pretty well figured out. But now I find I don't. Maybe I never did, and I was just fooling myself."

Her heart beat a little harder. Feeling his hand tighten around hers a little more firmly, she whispered, "Go on...."

"When we were falling out of the sky," Gus said, "I thought we were going to die. And I had only one regret."

Heart hammering as she felt his tension, she asked, "What was that?"

Lifting her hand, he kissed the back of it tenderly and held her probing gaze. "That I hadn't told you I love you, Camelia Anderson. That I was too scared because of my past to say anything. I didn't think I could ever put my heart on the line again with a woman who had a dangerous profession. I found out that wasn't true, *querida*. As we fell out of the sky, I was crying inside because I'd never said those words to you. I didn't want to die, or have you die without knowing that I love you...."

Gulping, Cam sat up and turned toward him. Gripping his hand, she stared into his smoldering cinnamon gaze. "You love me?"

"Yeah. Why are you asking it that way?" His mouth hitched up slightly. "You're looking at me like I'm an alien from outer space who just landed in front of you."

"Well..." Cam hesitated, looking to the right, then the left, and finally back at Gus. He had such a tender and patient expression on his face, filled with love for her. That was how he felt. An incredible warmth spread through Cam's chest and moved downward.

"I never thought," she began lamely, "that you could...well, like me, much less love me. I just never expected that, Gus. I knew your past. I tried to tell myself that because of it, there was no place for me in your life."

"And where did you want to be in my life?" he whispered, holding her sparkling green gaze, which glimmered with tears.

It was put up or shut up time, Cam realized. Gus was being brutally honest with her. He deserved no less for his bravery. She held his hand between her own and stared down at it.

"I didn't dare dream that you could love me, Gus, the way I was falling in love with you." Her voice broke. "From the moment I saw you, my heart was doin' crazy things. You seemed unreal to me."

"Why unreal?"

"Because—" Cam cleared her throat nervously "—you seemed too perfect, like the guy I always dreamed about meeting and falling in love with. But I always thought that guy was a dream. That a man like you could not exist in reality." Cam managed a self-deprecating smile as she looked up and connected with his heated eyes. Her body responded hotly to that look.

"Dreams can come true," Gus told her. "I ought to know. The woman I never thought would exist is here right now with me, and holding my hand."

"Oh, Gus…"

"We're both knee-jerking from our past," he said. "We're both fearful, for different reasons."

"Yeah…" Cam muttered. "There's that word again—*fear*."

"Amazing how much fear runs our life, eh?" Gus grinned a little through the haze of pain. Despite that, he felt his heart opening and the resulting warmth turn down the pain a few notches. It was a miraculous thing. Moving his fingers along her slender wrist and long fingers, he whispered, "I think we've faced the worst fear of all—death. And we've survived, Cam. Maybe we oughta reorder our attitudes and tell fear to get the hell out of our lives so it doesn't muck up anything else for us."

"How long have you felt like this toward me?" she wondered, her flesh tingling wildly as he traced each of her fingers and then the palm of her hand.

"Since the minute I saw you."

"Then…we both—"

"Yeah, got knocked over the head and heart by one another."

"Only," Cam said wonderingly, "neither of us had the guts to admit it to ourself, much less to one another."

"Yep," Gus said. "But air crashes have a way of leveling the playing field, you know?"

Nodding, words choking in her throat, Cam slowly got to her knees. She faced Gus, her thigh against his as she gently placed her arms around his neck. Taking care not to put any weight on his left shoulder, she smiled at him. Their noses were inches apart. She could feel the warmth and moisture of his breath against her skin.

"Your courage deserves to be rewarded, darling…." And she leaned down and found his mouth with her own.

Gus raised his right hand and slid it across her strong back as he cherished the feel of her tentative, searching lips against his. Groaning softly, he whispered, "I wish I could love you right now, *querida.* We'd lie down here, together, in one another's arms. We'd make this night sing with our happiness…."

Moaning his name, Cam drowned beneath his poetic words. Truly, Gus was a romantic of the most wonderful kind. She felt his hand graze her shoulder and then move in a slow, exploring caress down her spine. Oh, to be loved by him! Her body ached to be touched, tamed and molded by his hands. That was impossible, so Cam simply absorbed the feel of his mouth claiming hers strongly and hotly. As she ran her fingers through his hair, massaging his scalp and memorizing everything about him, Cam's joy soared. Gus loved her. She found that amazing. Wonderful. Humbling.

Gus didn't want their kiss to end. Cam was being so careful not to bump him or touch his left shoulder as she kissed and caressed him. When she eased away, he saw the rose color in her cheeks, the brightness in her eyes and the love that shone in them—for him.

"What we have," he told her huskily, "is so rare...." Taking her hand, he kissed it tenderly. "Life is so tenuous, *querida*. I want to take every minute I have and live it with you."

"I feel the same, Gus," she whispered, her voice off-key. Cam's mind went to all the sordid possibilities that could destroy what they'd just admitted to one another. Gus was right: life was so tenuous. Last night they'd nearly died. Today they had professed their love to one another. Feeling beat up inwardly, yet glowingly alive, Cam knelt at his side, unable to speak.

"Come on," Gus urged her gently, "let's get ready to go to bed. We've got a long day ahead of us tomorrow, and a good night's sleep will help a lot."

Biting back her worry, Cam nodded. "I wish I could sleep in your arms."

"So do I, *querida*. Someday. Soon," he promised.

Worry edged out her joy as she released his hand and slowly got to her feet. Things had to be taken care of around their camp before she could join him. He slowly moved from his sitting position and laid down on his right side, placing his right arm beneath his head as a pillow.

Cam smiled down at him. "I'll be there in a little bit. I want to get rid of this rabbit carcass first. We don't need a pack of coyotes coming to visit us tonight."

Gus nodded and smiled. "You're a great outdoorswoman, *querida*."

Cam had other worries other than coyotes, but she didn't mention them to Gus as she moved out of the cave. How did she know for sure that the druggies who'd shot them down wouldn't try to find them? She'd underestimated them once. She wasn't about to do it again. By tamping out the fire and sleeping in a cave, they were less likely to be found.

No, life was tenuous, as Gus had said. And they weren't out of danger yet—not by a long shot.

Chapter 16

Gus staggered drunkenly against Cam as she supported his full weight. Her cry of relief at the sight of the Yaqui village, not two miles in the distance, made him continue putting one foot in front of the other. The sun was low on the western horizon, sending long shadows through the brush and cactus that littered the hard sand surface around them.

Cam could barely contain her joy, though she forced herself to continue the same, slow pace. Gus was sagging more and more against her as the day wore on. He had a fever and that worried her greatly. That meant infection from the compound fracture. Now, more than ever, the urgency to get him to a hospital for treatment and surgery thrummed through her.

"We're going to make it!" Cam said, her voice breaking with joy. The Yaqui village was small and laid out in a circle around a main flat, dusty plaza. Squinting, she saw a number of women in long, colorful cotton skirts moving about the adobe buildings.

Grimacing, Gus whispered, "Yes...." His head swam with fever. He wasn't always sure where his feet were going to land. Yet Cam was so strong and steady for him. A fierce love of her swept through him. Today had been a special hell on him. When he'd awakened early in the grayness of the dawn, he had broken out in a heavy sweat with a raging fever. All day he'd fought the vertigo, the throbbing, pounding pain in his left arm, and kept trying to think clearly. Without Cam, her soft coaxing voice, her strong arm around him, Gus knew he'd never have made it this far. It seemed with every step her determination to get them to help grew. Amazed by the strength he felt radiating from her, Gus truly began to appreciate her inner toughness and resiliency in an emergency.

"Listen," he gasped, carefully stepping forward, "the Yaqui..." He grimaced, tightening his lips and closing his eyes as Cam steadied him.

Breathing savagely against the pain, Gus opened his eyes. Cam kept up their slow, mincing pace. "The Yaqui," he rasped. "They have a woman leader and a man leader, though they're matriarchal. They'll speak some Spanish intermixed with their own language. In case I go unconscious, tell them that I'm the son of a Yaqui woman. They'll give you extra special care. They take care of their own, Cam. Okay?"

"Yeah," she said, "I hear you." She saw several people walking toward them now that they had been spotted. "I just pray they have a phone—anything—so we can get you help pronto."

"Don't be disappointed if they don't," Gus warned her. Sweat dribbled into his eyes and he blinked it away. The fever was making him feel light-headed. He knew his temperature was high, maybe 103 degrees. If it went any higher, Gus would become delirious. Already he was seeing things that weren't really there. Every once in a while, he'd see a gold-coated jaguar with black crescent-moon spots walking near him. He'd blink and the apparition would disappear. And then, as he gave in to the fever again, the jaguar would reappear. Not wanting to mention it to Cam for fear of scaring her even more than she already was about his deteriorating condition, Gus forced himself to concentrate on one thing only: putting one foot ahead of the other.

Heart speeding up, Cam raised her hand as three people, all middle-aged, began to trot toward them. Hope flared in her. "They see us, Gus. They see us!"

Hearing the joy in her voice, he groaned. The ground was flat, but small pebbles made the sole of his boot roll, causing him to momentarily lose his balance. Cam's arm would automatically tighten around him to keep him upright. Hanging his head, he clenched his teeth. His left arm felt like a huge, swollen sausage. And it looked like it, too. Gus worried about losing his arm. If they couldn't get him medical help soon, he worried that partial loss of his arm's function would be the very least he would suffer. If that happened, he could no longer fly. Traumatized by the possibility, he pushed that aggravating fear away.

Within twenty minutes, Cam met with the village elders. Two were women in their fifties, with steel-gray hair and black, flashing eyes. The man—she assumed he was the other leader—was also gray-haired, with dark brown, weathered skin. As they drew to a halt, Cam saw their eyes widening. First she saw fear there as they stared at them. And then, when Gus raised his head and began to speak in Yaqui, Cam saw the fear go away and relief replace their original looks.

She knew only Spanish, and not the mother tongue of these short, thin people. They were dressed in colorful cotton garments, with leather sandals on their feet. The man carried a rake over his shoulder, as if just coming from a garden somewhere near the village.

Gus smiled tightly. "Okay, Cam, here's the deal. They have no phones. Senora Marquez, the woman to your left, who's wearing the red skirt, is the leader of this village. Her husband, Juan Marquez, is also a leader. He's the guy with the rake." Gus halted, pain ripping through him. Biting back a groan, he said, "I told them who I was. They want us to come back to the village with them."

"Good," she said, smiling and nodding to them in thanks. They smiled and nodded back.

"There's more," Gus groaned. "There's a drug dealer that comes once a week to their village. If these people don't find peyote buttons on the cactus, and give them to him to sell, he pistol whips someone in the village. They're basically unprotected out here. They have no way to defend themselves against this guy."

Frowning, Cam looked around at the flat stretches of the desert, at the mountains, jagged and black, rising loftily behind the small town. "Well...does this guy come by car?"

"That's the bad part," Gus whispered. Sweat ran into his eyes. He could feel himself beginning to weaken. His knees felt like jelly. "He flies in by helo once a week. And he's armed. His name is Robert Clark. He's a *norteamericano* drug dealer. Apparently, he works for a local drug lord out of Tijuana. That's all they know."

"I see," she said grimly, looking around. "Okay, let's get you to the village, Gus. We'll worry about these other things later. Right now, all I want to do is contact someone for help."

With all the water she wanted to drink and hot food to eat, Cam felt like her old self within the next two hours. The Yaqui village was small; perhaps thirty people lived here, all related to one another. Gus lay in the headwoman's adobe home on a pallet of soft grass with a blanket thrown across it. The medicine woman, Senora Ramos, had cleaned Gus's wound, placed damp, warm herbs around the ugly red, swollen flesh and rewrapped it with a clean bandage. He was sleeping, the fever having taken a terrible toll on his strength.

Worried, Cam walked around the village. Night was coming, the eastern sky darkening while the red-and-peach-colored sunset spread in a breathtaking wash on the western horizon. She was followed everywhere by curious children of all ages. Their Spanish was broken, but she managed to converse with them. Earlier, Senor Marquez had taken her outside the village that wrapped around the plaza, to where the helicopter would land.

Cam had seen how the dust had been disturbed by a powerful blast of rotors. When she tried to find out what kind of helicopter the drug runner flew, the kindly gentleman had shrugged and opened his hands. He'd smiled, revealing a gap where his two front teeth were missing. More than anything, Cam wanted to know if the chopper was armed.

Her thoughts swung back to Gus as she reconnoitered the area around the village. It was flat desert with a lot of brush, and a few stubborn trees that defied the heat and still survived through the summer. The Yaqui had a well, a shallow one, but it supplied water to their massive gardens, which were sprinkled about the area.

"Señor?" Cam asked as they walked back toward the center of the village. "When does this helicopter come to your town?"

Shrugging, Juan said, "No one knows when he will fly in on his devil bird, Senorita Camelia." He waved his hands in a frustrated gesture. "You will hear him coming. The devil bird is loud. Everyone—" he waved his hands, sadness in his tone "—runs and hides in their adobe homes. They fear him. He lands over there and comes with his gun drawn. If I do not bring him a bag of peyote buttons right away, he will go through each home, tearing it up, breaking our pottery, ripping things apart, to find them."

"The bastard," Cam whispered tautly. She flexed her fists in rage. "How long has he been doing this?" She looked down at the lean farmer, who wore a long-sleeved, white peasant shirt and a pair of faded jeans that were frayed on the bottom.

"Just the last year, *señorita*. He came out of nowhere—" Juan pointed to the west "—out of the place of death."

Cam nodded. That was where Tijuana lay, to the west of them. "How far from this city are we, *señor?*"

Laughing, Juan shrugged. "Oh, many, many hours, *señorita*. The nearest phone that you speak of is fifty miles farther to the south. There is a Catholic mission, a small one—there at San Anselmo." He pointed in that direction.

Grimly, Cam's mind spun. Fifty more miles. "And you have no way to get there? No car? A truck?" She'd not seen a single vehicle.

"No, *señorita*. *Nada*. None. You must walk. Oh, you could take one of the donkeys that we use to plow with, to plant our corn every year, but you are much larger than the poor beast. You would do best to walk there."

"I see...." Cam said. They entered the village, where long shadows were falling across the main plaza. A number of black pots hung from tripods there, the small fires beneath them tended by women. The odor of rice and beans wafted temptingly through the dusk. Dogs and children were standing around each cooking pot, which was being stirred by a woman.

"Tomorrow," Juan said, patting her arm, "I will have Jose, my son, who is our strongest young man, take you to San Anselmo. Your man, Senor Morales, is very sick. He needs help we cannot give him."

Nodding, Cam halted at the door of the man's dark brown adobe home. There was a bright red wool blanket in place of a door. The house had three rooms. Thanks to their generosity, Juan and his wife had given up their bedroom to her and Gus. "Thanks, Juan. And yes, if Jose could be ready to leave early tomorrow? Say at dawn? We might be able to make San Anselmo in a day's time."

"*Sí, sí,*" Juan agreed eagerly, gesturing for her to enter. "Come, come, my wife makes tortillas for dinner. Please, come in…."

Gus groaned as he felt a damp, cool cloth being pressed against his hot forehead. Lying on his right side, a lumpy pillow beneath his head, he barely opened his eyes. Because his fever was high, everything was blurred in the semidarkness. Seeing Cam leaning over him, cloth in hand, her eyes filled with worry, he managed a twisted smile.

"You're the most beautiful apparition I've seen so far," he muttered. Feeling thirsty, his mouth gummy, he tried to sit up.

"Take it easy," Cam whispered, and supported him as he eased into sitting position so that his back was against the earthen wall. Searching his washed-out face, and seeing the fever in his darkened eyes, Cam reached out and wiped his sweaty face with the cool compress. "Are you thirsty? Hungry? It's nearly 2100."

The flickering of an old oil lamp in the corner of the room made shadows dance before Gus's eyes. Blinking, he saw a jaguar, he'd seen the same one earlier, sitting in the doorway where a dark blue cotton blanket separated this room from the next one. He was having another feverish hallucination.

Lifting his chin, he looked up at Cam. "Yeah...I'm thirsty...."

Nodding, Cam reached for a bottle of water. "Let me help," she murmured, crouching at his right side. Gus looked terrible. When he tried to lift his hand to help guide the bottle to his lips, his fingers shook badly.

"Easy," Cam crooned softly as she placed her arm around his shoulders. Gus was weak—alarmingly so. His hand fell limply at his side. He couldn't hold it up at all. When she held the lip of the flask to his mouth, he drank deeply.

Dribbles of water trickled from the corners of his mouth when Cam took away the bottle. Sated, he tried to lift his right hand again. He couldn't. "I feel like a baby," he confided, his voice husky. "Useless..."

"You've got a high fever," Cam whispered as she sat back on her heels next to him. "Are you hungry, Gus? You need to eat. You have to keep your strength up. Senora Marquez slaughtered a chicken. She made you some delicious chicken soup. Want some?" Cam hoped he did.

"These people shouldn't be cooking their precious chickens for me," Gus said, frowning. He saw a pottery bowl filled with hot, steaming soup nearby. But he wasn't hungry. The fever had him in its clutches.

"Hey, you're like a son to them," Cam chided with a smile. "They wanted to do something to help you, Gus. You're one of their own. Everyone is worried for you."

"I'm worried for myself," he joked weakly. He

watched as Cam reached for the bowl and brought it over to him. She sat down facing him, the wooden spoon in hand.

"Tomorrow morning, early," Cam told him, as she placed a spoonful of clear broth into his mouth, "I'm leaving for a Catholic mission, San Anselmo. It's a day's walk from here. They've got a phone, Gus. Once I can get to a phone, we're home free. I can call in the help we need." She gave him a tender look as he patiently slurped the soup she fed him.

"You're going with a guide, aren't you?"

"Yes. Juan's son, Jose."

"Good," Gus muttered. He forced himself to eat half the contents of the soup bowl, a mixture of shredded chicken, potatoes and onions. The soup was salty and tasted good, but his stomach was roiling threateningly because of the constant pain he was in.

"You did good," Cam said, giving him a soft smile as she wiped his mouth afterward. "Keeping water and food in you right now is the best thing possible. It will keep you going."

Snorting softly, Gus looked around the shadowed room. It was small and warm. There was a square window, but no glass in it, only a blanket pinned into place. "I feel like a weak baby—completely helpless, *querida.*"

Arching at the endearment, Cam put the bowl aside, along with the damp cloth. Gus's uniform was dirty and damp with sweat. She wanted to get him out of it, but feared that moving his left arm might start the bleeding again. No, he might be in dirty clothes, but he was stable, so she let that idea pass.

"I had a dream about us," Gus told her in a quiet

tone as she came and sat cross-legged facing him. "A little while ago…"

"Yeah?" Cam smiled, reaching out and grazing his darkly bearded jaw. The stubble only accentuated Gus's high cheekbones, showed how sunken his cheeks had become in the last two days. Trying to put her worry aside, Cam allowed herself the privilege of wrapping her fingers around his good hand, which lay at his side. His fingers were hot and damp. She could see the wildness, the fever, gripping him.

"Nice dream…" Gus tipped his head back and closed his eyes. "We were at this incredibly beautiful place, like a Garden of Eden. There was jungle around, and in the distance, big, beautiful mountains with snow on the peaks."

"Sounds nice," Cam murmured, "but it sure isn't around here."

His mouth twitched in a slight smile. Squeezing her hand, he said, "No…I don't know where it was. You were with me. We were sitting on this sloping, grassy hill that had an oval pond at the bottom of it. The water…" Gus forced his eyes open and drowned in Cam's tender look "…was incredible, Cam. It was like living, vibrating turquoise. It was clear, and as I sat there with you, the desire to walk down there and step into it was almost overwhelming." He closed his eyes and quirked his mouth. "I knew if I walked into that water, if I submerged myself in it, I'd be healed."

"Wow," Cam murmured, "that's pretty far out. Wish I knew where this place was. You need it."

Hearing the humor in her voice, he nodded slowly. "Yeah, this place…I'm telling you, I felt like I was there. It was so *real*, Cam. So real…"

"Well," she whispered gently, "maybe when you go to sleep in a few minutes, you'll go back there. Next time, get in the water, okay? We need all the miracles we can lay our hands on now."

The humor revived him slightly. Gus opened his eyes. "Help me lie down? I'm so dizzy I feel like I'm going to pitch over...."

Getting to her feet, Cam eased Gus onto his right side. Once he was as comfortable as he could be, she tucked several blankets around his shoulders to keep him warm.

"Thanks..." he whispered wearily. "I love you, Camelia Anderson. All the way. With all my heart."

His gritty words flowed through the quiet room and touched her heart. As sick as Gus was, and in such unrelenting pain, he could still share that with her. Getting down on her knees, Cam leaned over him. Gus had already shut his eyes. His brow was beading with sweat again. She could see the pain and how it pulled his face into lines of unrelenting tension.

"And I love you, Gus Morales. Sleep, just sleep..." She stroked his damp hair with her hand. "Go back to that beautiful garden with the pond."

Her words lulled him into a deep, spiraling sleep. The fever had him once again. Even with his eyes shut, Gus could see the female jaguar sitting near the curtained doorway. She was looking at him with sparkling sun-gold eyes. A sense of care and protection emanated from her. As he felt Cam's hand stroking his head, Gus sensed, for the first time, that things were going to work out. Cam's words—that she loved him—embraced him and flowed through him. How nurturing she was. Like a sponge, he absorbed each of her tender touches. Tomorrow was a new day, he told himself. Tomorrow, Cam would go for help. Maybe by tomorrow night he'd be in a hospital getting the medical attention he needed.

As Gus drifted off, he heard the low, rumbling growl of the jaguar, who seemed to be very close to him now. He couldn't see her, could only feel her strength and presence. In his fevered brain as he spiraled into sleep, Gus thought it must be his mother's guardian, or perhaps his own, come to protect him. He had grown up listening to stories of the mountain and desert jaguars that had once roamed this part of Mexico. Oddly, Gus felt comforted by the apparition. That, and Cam's closeness. Hope flowed through him as he drifted off into the dark, feverish realm of sleep.

Chapter 17

Cam didn't want to leave Gus, but she knew she had to. He lay huddled beneath the warm blankets they'd shared last night. She'd lain against his back, her body curved against his. Half the night he'd been delirious with fever. Only when she slid her arm around the dampened waist of his flight suit, pressing her palm against his chest, did Gus cease his restless thrashing. He stopped muttering in Yaqui and Spanish, two of the three languages he'd grown up with.

Picking up the holster now, Cam strapped it around her waist and buckled it. Dawn was just touching the horizon, so the room was shadowed. Though she was barely able to see him, Cam made sure that a bottle of water was within Gus's reach for when he woke up. And she picked up his pistol, which had eight bullets left in it, and put it near the water. Her mouth tingled in memory of the kiss she'd pressed to his

damp brow. Worried, Cam knew she had to meet
Jose, who waited in the next room, and make that
long, fifty-mile trek to San Anselmo. Giving Gus one
last look as he lay sleeping deeply, she whispered, "I
love you, Gus Morales. I'll be back, I promise...."
And she quietly exited the room.

Jose, tall, lean and in his mid-twenties, nodded def-
erentially to her as she slipped into the main room.
He wore a backpack on top of the lightweight dark
green jacket over his upper body. Handing Cam a
threadbare blue knapsack that sat on the wooden table, he said, "There is food and water in there for
you, *señorita.* Are you ready?" And he smiled.

Liking the young man's quiet manner, Cam nodded. She quickly slid her arms into the knapsack
straps and adjusted it against her back.

"I'm ready, Jose. Let's roll. I want to get to San
Anselmo before dark." She saw his dark eyes sparkle
as he opened the curtain at the front for her.

"I hope you are in good shape for a lot of trotting
and little walking then," he teased in a low tone.

Outdoors, the morning was crisp, clean and cold.
Cam could still see the stars above them. Everything
was quiet. It was a peaceful quiet that fed one's spirit.
Turning to Jose, who stepped out from the blanketed
doorway behind her, she grinned at him.

"Let's start our trotting then, shall we?" Cam
wanted to get to San Anselmo as fast as they could,
even if it meant pushing herself to her maximum. She
hoped that her daily three-mile runs and regular work-
outs at the gym at the base would hold her in good
stead.

"*Sí, señorita,*" Jose said. He put an old, floppy

cotton hat with a wide brim on his head. Handing her another one, he said, ''The sun is going to be merciless today. Wear this to protect your head and eyes.''

Cam nodded and put the cap on. ''Thanks, Jose. Now I look like one of your people.''

Laughing softly, Jose said, ''*Sí*, you do. Shall we?'' And he took off at a trot across the hard-packed earth of the plaza, heading due south.

A growl of warning vibrated the air around Gus. He jerked physically, sending pain radiating from his left arm into his shoulder and neck. The sensation pulled him out of a deep, deep sleep. Where the hell was a *growl* coming from? His eyelids felt like weights, Gus discovered. He felt so weak he couldn't seem to force them open. He was warm and it felt good to just lie still.

Another growl. This time it felt like the animal, a big cat of some kind, was sitting right next to him and making the sound, which vibrated through his entire body. That forced Gus to drag open his eyes. Feeling fear, he slowly rolled onto his back, his right hand stabilizing his left elbow to minimize the pain. The room was a murky gray. Was he dreaming again? When the fever went high, he'd have hallucinatory dreams—nice ones, the only good thing about it. His fever was down now, he realized. It always seemed to be lower in the morning, and then, toward noon, would start to climb and he'd become delusional for the rest of the day and late into the night.

Right now, as he lay there, the blankets twisted about him, Gus tried to shove the sleep from his barely functioning mind. The first thing he realized was there was no big cat next to him. The room was empty. Cam was gone, too. Vaguely, he recalled that she was going to get up at dawn, meet Jose and hike to San Anselmo today.

A wave of relief moved through him. She was going to get them help. That was good. Gus was quite worried about his broken arm, and the fact that he couldn't feel any sensations in his left hand at all now. Was there nerve damage? If so, that meant he might never be able to fly again, and that scared him.

Cam... He lay there, eyes closed, feeling such a fierce love for her. She had kissed him so tenderly last night that it had brought tears to his eyes. With the unrelenting fever, Gus found himself highly vulnerable to the emotions he normally kept closeted within. Not now. Cam's gentleness with him brought out every emotion he'd ever known. And when she'd come to lie at his back, curving her long, firm body against his, he remembered feeling loved and protected by her. It was then that he'd drifted into a healing sleep, with her palm pressed against his chest, over his beating heart. Yes, Cam owned his heart. And his spirit. She was such an incredible woman.

Another sound, far off, caught his scattered attention—helicopter blades turning. Frowning, Gus felt sweat beading his forehead once more. Blades. Helo blades. What time was it? Lifting his right wrist, he held his watch close to his face so he could read the glowing dials. The fever made his vision blurred and slightly out of focus.

It was 0800. Gus dropped his arm across his belly and lay still. Was he hearing a helicopter because he was hallucinating once again? Did he want to be rescued so badly that his fevered mind was making up the sound, as it did that big cat's growl? Or that female jaguar he'd seen off and on at the entrance to the room? Blowing a frustrated sigh from between his lips, Gus decided it was probably that. But his fever was lower, and although his mind was sluggish, he didn't seem to be hallucinating. Maybe the cat's growl in his ear had just been a bad dream.

Hearing excited Yaqui voices outside in the plaza, Gus frowned. The helicopter sounds were growing stronger. It was flying closer and closer to the village. *Was* he hallucinating? Gus opened his eyes. With a huge effort, he slowly and carefully moved to a sitting position, his right hand cupping his left elbow. Giving his head a slight shake, he keyed his hearing.

No, those were helicopter blades! Suddenly, Gus gasped. Could it be a rescue helo? One from Tijuana? Maybe Luis or Antonio had found them? His heart beat hard in anticipation. Lifting his chin, Gus looked toward the blanketed entrance. Outside, he heard more and more excited voices. Yes! That had to be a rescue team!

Hoping that Senora Marquez was in the house, Gus called for her, though his voice was rough and weak. Again, he called for her in Yaqui.

No one came.

The helicopter was almost upon them. Gus could hear the strong whapping of the blades, and it made his heart quicken with joy. The aircraft was landing just outside the village, so close that the vibration was palpable. They were going to be rescued!

As he heard the helicopter power down, the shriek-

ing of the engine die away, Gus took a deep breath.
How badly he wanted to get up, but he was still so
weak. Cam had set a bottle of water and his pistol
nearby, he noted. Anxious to meet whoever had come
for them, Gus focused on trying to get up.

It was then he heard a scream—the scream of a
little girl. And then he heard the shouts of panicked
adults. Frowning, Gus tried to hear what they were
saying. It was impossible.

He heard a warning growl—again. This time it
seemed to be over his head and shoulders, the sound
vibrating down through him.

What the hell was going on? His mind churned,
confused, as he sat there.

More shouts. Screams. Someone was begging for
something.

Something was wrong. Desperately wrong. Gus
cursed.

It couldn't be a rescue team, then. So what was
going down? Feeling shaky and unsteady Gus forced
himself to his knees. Throwing out his right hand,
knees spread, he assumed a tripod position to halt the
dizziness that threatened to pitch him headfirst onto
the earthen floor.

Another scream. Very close this time.

Suddenly, the curtain was ripped aside.

Gus jerked his head up.

"*Señor!* The *bandito* is here! Quickly! You must
hide!" Senora Marquez whispered.

Gus saw the fear in the older woman's eyes. He
saw blood dribbling from the corner of her mouth.
Someone had struck her.

"What the hell is happening?" he demanded in Yaqui.

Senora Marquez quickly stepped into the room, wringing her hands. "*Señor,* the drug man is here—Robert Clark! He holds little Maria hostage, a gun at her head. He demands peyote buttons, but we have none! It is the wrong time of year. They do not grow now. But he wants some!" She gave a sob. "He is threatening to kill Maria if we don't bring him any."

Gus grabbed the pistol, which was inches from his hand. He forced himself to his feet. Staggering badly, he leaned against the earthen wall. Breathing hard, the pain clearing his mind, he looked at Senora Marquez.

"Where is he?"

Pointing, Senora Marquez said, "Near his bird. He is holding Maria there and demanding we bring the sack of peyote buttons to him."

Rubbing his sweaty face with his right arm, Gus rasped, "Tell him to come in here, *señora.* Lie to him and tell him the sack is in here. Tell him he has to come and get it."

Her eyes grew huge. Eyeing the pistol in his hand, and then his face, she whispered, "You mean...?"

Grimly, Gus rested his back against the wall. He could barely stand. His knees felt shaky and unsure. "Get him in here," he told her harshly. "I'll do the rest. Just make sure the little girl isn't with him, all right?"

Eyes widening, Senora Marquez made a fervent sign of the cross. "Aiiee, yes, yes, I hear you, Senor Morales."

"Just get the girl out of the way. And keep everyone else away from here. I don't want one of our bullets to hit anyone. Understand?'' His heart was beating hard. Gus knew this plan could backfire. He could die.

"Yes, yes, I understand.''

"Vamoose!'' he ordered her.

Turning, Senora Marquez turned and fled from the room. He heard her crying for Senor Clark, her voice strident and high.

Cursing softly, Gus saw his Kevlar vest lying in the corner of the room. Well, the bulletproof garment wouldn't do him any good now. He didn't have time to try and don it, and couldn't do so with his broken arm, anyway. Cam had removed it so she could tend to his broken arm.

Situating himself in the corner opposite the blanketed door, Gus waited. He felt incredibly weak, and fought to save his waning strength so he could lift the pistol at the right time and drill Clark before he shot him first.

Would the plan work? Gus's mind spun with questions. There were few options. He didn't have the strength to walk out of the room and confront Clark. Besides, if Clark was holding the girl hostage, Gus didn't have the accuracy to hit him and not the child. No, this was his only choice.

Dammit. Nervously, Gus wiped his beaded brow once more with the back of his good arm. Pain was stalking him in earnest now, throbbing unrelentingly through his arm, shoulder and neck. It shredded his concentration.

He heard voices—raised, angry voices. A child was crying pitifully. More screams. More begging.

Breathing hard, Gus wondered if his plan would backfire. Maybe Clark would shoot Maria anyway. Maybe he would refuse to come into the room. Chest rising and falling with each breath, Gus waited, half standing, half leaning against the wall. His legs were trembling badly and his knees felt like jelly. Closing his eyes, he sent a prayer to his mother and asked for help. He recalled her telling him a long time ago, as a child on her knee, that his jaguar spirit guide was there to give him help. All he had to do was ask for it.

Well, he was asking now, because if he didn't get physical strength from somewhere, he was about to slide down the wall into a heap. Breathing chaotically, Gus struggled to stay standing. Opening his eyes, he felt an incredible surge of heat spiraling up from his feet, running up both his legs toward his head. A moment later he felt an incredible surge of strength. What the hell was going on?

Gus wasn't sure. What he did know was that he felt incredibly stable and suddenly very strong—much stronger than he thought possible, given his broken arm and feverish state. Unable to sort it all out, Gus heard the raised, angry voice of Clark outside the adobe structure.

"You'd better not be lying to me, Marquez. If you are, I'm shootin' your husband in the head. You hear me, bitch?"

Holding his breath, Gus waited.

He heard Clark come through the first blanketed door, cursing darkly as he did so.

"Which room?" he snarled.

"Th-there...in there, Senor Clark..."

Gus heard Senora Marquez's trembling voice. Lifting the pistol, he prayed he could hold it in position. Any second, Clark would come through that blanketed entrance.

As Gus stood there, back to the wall, time seemed to stretch out endlessly so that every second passed in slow motion. His heart was beating hard in his chest. Perspiration was streaking down the sides of his face. And then Cam's face appeared before him.

How much he loved her! Wanted to spend his life with her! But he could die, right now.... *No! No, I want to live. Let me survive this. Please...I want to love her...to share my life with....*

Nostrils flaring, the point of his pistol wavering slightly as he aimed it at the blanket, he waited. There was no sound. Everything quieted. Gus suddenly felt as if he were out of time and space. It was such a surreal feeling, that he wondered for a moment if all of this was simply a nightmare he was experiencing during his delusional fevered state.

The blanket was ripped aside.

Robert Clark was a tall, lean man with frosty blue eyes, black hair and a black mustache. He was wearing civilian clothes, a suede tan jacket over a white shirt and black chinos. The gun he held was raised in caution.

When he saw Gus, he halted for a second. His eyes widened tremendously as he stared at the U.S. Army pilot in the shadowed corner. Was he seeing things?

"Drop the gun, Clark," Morales ordered, his voice deep and threatening. When the drug runner ignored the order and raised his weapon, Gus fired. The crack of the gunshot caromed around him, hurting his ears.

The pistol bucked in his hand. Gus saw Clark knocked off his feet, landing hard on his back in the room beyond. The pistol flew from his nerveless fingers.

There were shrieks and screams, panicked sounds surrounding Gus as he forced himself out of the corner. Drunkenly, his legs rubbery once more, he moved as fast as he could toward Clark, who lay unmoving on the floor of the next room. Breathing hard, Gus kept the pistol aimed at the druggie. Seeing a red stain in the center of the man's chest, rapidly eating into the white of his shirt, he staggered to a stop. Breath tearing in gasps from his mouth, he saw Senora Marquez at the door, her hands pressed to her mouth, her gaze on Clark.

"Get someone to check his pulse," Gus rasped. Leaning against the doorjamb, he felt the strength begin to drain out of him, like an ocean tide leaving the beach and retreating back out to sea. Sweat stung his eyes. He blinked several times.

The whole village seemed to be crowding around the doorway. Senor Marquez came forward, moving cautiously around Clark.

"Get the gun," Gus ordered weakly. "Get it away from him."

Leaning down, Senor Marquez picked it up as if it were a snake that might bite him. He started to hand it to Gus.

"Lay it at my feet," he said. "Then check his pulse. On the side of his neck. See if you feel anything?" Gus thought the man was dead. He hoped so. Every second, he felt weakness stalking him once more.

Gus saw the eyes of the villagers crowded in the doorway, looking at him and then at Clark. There was such terror on their faces. A sense of satisfaction moved through Gus. He didn't like killing anyone, but he had no problem doing so to defend these people.

"There is nothing!" Senor Marquez said, holding his brown, work-worn fingers against the man's throat.

"Good," Gus rasped. He closed his eyes. "Get him out of here. Go bury him…" And that was the last thing he remembered.

"Gus? Darling? Wake up. It's Cam. Gus?"

Cam's low, urgent tone filled his darkness. Gus felt heavy. He also felt the constant, gnawing pain in his arm and shoulder. But something else—a warm hand caressing his bearded cheek—caught and held his attention. Then he felt her lips upon his mouth. Soft. Tender. The kiss drew him out of his sleeping state.

Forcing his eyes open, Gus felt Cam's lips ease from his. Focusing on her face, he saw that her green eyes were glittering with tears. But she was smiling.

"Uhh…what happened? Are you okay?" The gunfight started resurrecting from his clouded memory.

Laughing softly, Cam whispered, "Yes, darling. I'm fine. Everyone is okay."

Forcing himself awake, Gus saw that the room was filled with daylight. Cam was kneeling over him, smiling. Her hair was tousled and in need of combing, but even in its wild state it was like a chestnut halo around her head.

"W-what time…?" he asked, his voice thick and rasping.

"Eight hundred hours."

"You're back?"

Cam sat down next to him, her hand on his right shoulder. Gus was feverish. She understood his mind was shorting out. "Yes. We saw the helicopter coming in. Jose recognized it as the drug dealer, Clark. We were roughly six miles away when we saw it heading for the village." Cam quirked her mouth. "When Jose told me that, we headed back here at a dead run. Of course, six miles is a long way, Gus. I couldn't run that far. By the time we got here, you'd taken Clark out." Her voice quavered and her smile disappeared. "You could have been killed, darling."

Giving her a ragged smile through his pain, he rasped, "I didn't have many options left open to me. The bastard had a little girl hostage…."

"I know," Cam murmured soothingly, running her hand across his damp hair. "You were wonderful. It was a smart call, Gus. The Marquezes told us everything."

He saw her eyes lighten and become mischievous. Joy radiated around her and her cheeks flushed a rosy hue. Just feeling the caress of her hand on his head made him feel peaceful. Hopeful.

"What's up?"

"A lot. Clark's helicopter is available to us to use. Do you realize that?"

Blinking, Gus muttered, "No…I didn't think…"

"You're injured and feverish, that's why," Cam soothed. "I just put in a call to our base in TJ. I got ahold of Luis. I told him everything. Then—" Cam smiled broadly "—I contacted the Naval Medical Center in San Diego. I told them we were coming in shortly, and that you were wounded. I gave them all the information on your broken arm, Gus. They're waiting for us, darling. Are you ready to leave here and head out?"

Tears jammed into Gus's eyes as he stared up at her. He saw tears rolling down her face, too. He heard the quaver, the relief and joy, in her hushed tone.

Gripping her hand in his, he whispered brokenly, "Yeah...I'm ready to go home, *querida.*"

Chapter 18

"Hard to believe we were out in the desert wondering if we were going survive only seventy hours ago," Gus said dryly. He lay in a private room of the Naval Medical Center in San Diego. Cam sat on the edge of his bed with her hip against his blanketed thigh, facing him.

Cam slid her fingers into his. "It was like a bad dream," she agreed quietly. Morning sunlight was streaming through the eastern window. Outside, Cam could see the sprawling city, the streets filled with rush hour traffic. Since she had nothing to wear except her dirty green flight suit, she'd gone out and bought some civilian clothes.

Gus gave his left arm a worried glance. It was encased in a movable cast and suspended at an angle that promoted the best healing. At least he'd be out of the contraption by tomorrow morning and into a regular sling. That was progress. Looking up at Cam, he saw that she'd recently washed her chestnut hair, which curled around her shoulders. Dressed in a long-sleeved pink blouse and dark blue slacks, she looked like a young college woman and not the combat pilot she was.

"You're worried about Maya's reaction to the loss of the Apache, aren't you?" He squeezed her hand gently as he saw her green eyes become shadowed.

"Yeah, I am…and what's worse, Gus, I haven't heard a *thing* from her. Normally if you call Maya, you get a fast response." Biting down on her lower lip, she gazed at him, absorbing his caring concern.

How much better Gus looked now. He was clean and freshly shaved, his dark hair combed and tidy. Cam knew he had his own worries, but he wasn't going there. The break in his arm had been severe. Because he hadn't gotten prompt medical attention, there had been some nerve damage that affected his left hand and fingers. The doctors weren't sure at this point whether he would ever regain full use of his hand or not. Gus faced being drummed out of the army as a helo pilot if that happened.

Cam didn't know how she'd handle it if it were her, but Gus seemed easygoing about it. When he'd awakened shortly after the operation and the navy surgeon, Dr. Hannah Orbson, had told him of the possibility, Gus had given her a lopsided grin. He'd lain there and announced that no one was going to take him out of the seat of the Apache for any reason. He'd do the physical therapy it took to get full use of his hand back—or else. Cam loved him fiercely for that kind of spirit. She wasn't sure she'd have taken the news as well.

"I missed you last night," Gus told her now in a low tone, holding her worried gaze. Cam had been given a voucher for a room at a nearby hotel. The navy was taking care of her basic needs because Morgan Trayhern had made a call to the right people to see that she was not only okay, but given full and complete access to Gus.

"I didn't sleep well, either," Cam confessed, giving him a gentle smile. Lifting his hand, she brushed a kiss on the back of it. "I like sleeping with you."

"A bad habit," he teased.

Cam laughed shortly. Tension thrummed through her. Why hadn't she heard from Maya? She was afraid her C.O. would pull her from the BJS2 team and relegate her back to pilot status in Peru because of the screwups. It was only a matter of time, Cam was sure, before she'd hear her sentence from her larger-than-life leader. The iridium phone had been burned in the crash, so the only way Cam could reach Maya was through the Perseus office. Morgan had made sure the information was passed on to Maya, though Cam hadn't been able to talk to her directly. And she wanted to. She wanted to apologize for the loss of the twenty-million-dollar Apache.

Just then the door opened. Cam thought it was Gus's breakfast being wheeled in, since it was 0800. Her eyes widened. Major Maya Stevenson, in full U.S. Army uniform, stood there. Her black hair was knotted at the nape of her neck, just above the collar of her jacket. Cam's lips parted. It was the first time she'd seen Maya in her Class A olive green uniform, with the many ribbons above her left breast pocket, and the gold wings above them. Generally, she saw Maya in her plain black flight uniform, which had no markings whatsoever because they were a black ops, except for the squadron patch.

"Maya!" Cam gasped. She released Gus's hand and stepped forward quickly as her C.O. closed the door quietly behind her.

"You two are a sight for sore eyes," Maya said, grinning. She took off the hat she wore and hung it on a peg near the door. As Cam came to attention, she muttered, "Relax, will you?" Then she opened her arms. "Come here!"

With a sob, Cam relaxed. When Maya smiled and opened her arms, Cam felt such relief. This was her C.O.; to hell with army regulations when prying eyes weren't around. The fierce hug she gave her told Cam better than anything could that Maya wasn't angry with her.

"It's so good to see you, Maya," she whispered, quickly wiping away her tears.

Maya grinned and patted her shoulder. "Makes two of us. Gus? How are you?" She moved to his bedside and looked down at him. Extending her hand, she gripped his right one, squeezing it gently.

"I'm fine, ma'am." It was the first time he'd seen the legendary leader of the Black Jaguar Squadron. Gus stared up at her. She was powerful, warm and charismatic. Bowled over by the energy swirling around her, Gus absorbed her smiling features and her large, emerald green eyes, which danced with life. When her hand met his, he felt a distinct electrical spark, and even now, as she stood holding his hand, he felt those tingles moving up his right arm and into his left one. There was immediate warmth, almost an unpleasant burning sensation at the break site. Blinking, Gus knew something was happening, but he didn't understand it.

"Just receive the healing," Maya murmured. She looked over as Cam came to stand on the other side of the bed.

Gus nodded. Who could tell this woman no? Beginning to understand why Cam idolized her C.O., Gus found himself drawn to Maya himself. She was such a strong, nurturing woman—bold, yet with a fierce tenderness. She had the look of a warrior, but she wasn't aggressive. No, more like a powerful cat who knew her abilities and didn't need to show them off to anyone.

"Well," Maya said, humor in her tone, "I hear we lost an Apache. The good news is that you two survived. I'd rather lose a bird than two of my best pilots." She gave them each a measured look of pride. "I'm proud of what you did to survive."

Relief started to trickle through Cam. She stared at Maya. "Then...you aren't angry? It was my fault, Maya."

Shrugging eloquently, Maya said, "I read your report, which Morgan passed on to me. How could you or Gus even begin to think, in the middle of a thunderstorm, at night without a visual, that a lousy little civilian helicopter would be armed with rockets? It's one of those things, Cam. Accidents do happen. All you can do is learn from them and not make the same mistake twice."

Gus began to feel the heat flowing into his left arm

become more intense, almost painful. Remembering that Cam had said Maya came from the mystical Jaguar Clan, he realized she must be a medicine woman, like his mother. His mom used to lay her hand on his forehead when he had a fever or flu, and make the illness go away. Only now, whatever energy Maya was pumping into him was powerful. When she moved her intelligent green gaze to him, Gus had the distinct feeling she was reading his mind.

"Just a little longer, Chief Morales. I want you back flying a lot sooner than that year the docs are giving you." Her lips twisted enigmatically.

"A year?" Gus muttered. "No way." He focused on the energy she was giving him.

Cam sighed. "Thanks for your help, Maya. I never expected it."

"Why wouldn't I be here?" She grinned dryly. "Of course, having to fly commercial and in this get-up—" she gestured to the army uniform "—isn't something I looked forward to, but regs are regs. I miss my black flight suit. Infinitely a lot more comfortable," she chuckled.

Cam brought a chair to Gus's bedside and sat down. She saw the look of awe on his face as he kept his gaze riveted upon her C.O. "Are you healing him?" Cam asked.

"Well," Maya murmured, "let's put it this way. My jaguar spirit guide is sending Gus energy to help heal up that nerve and bone damage. You feelin' pretty uncomfortable about now, Gus?"

Giving her a twisted grin, he said, "Ma'am, my mother, who is Yaqui Indian, is a medicine woman for her people. When you sent that heat through me,

I knew what you were doing. It's okay, and I know it will help. I'm grateful. I want to fly again, more than anything.''

Maya's black brows rose. ''Really? You'll do *any-thing* to get back into the seat of an Apache, Chief?''

''Yes, ma'am, I will. If I have to move heaven and earth to do it, that's what I'll do.'' Gus looked over at Cam. ''I want to fly with her again. We're good together. Even though we got shot down, I blame myself for what happened. It was a bad night, ma'am. The winds were throwing us around. We had lightning dancing all around us, destroying our night vision. There was no way we could get a visual on that helo that shot us down.''

''At ease, Chief. You don't need to convince me of what happened. Akiva and Joe down on the Gulf, at their black ops base, face the same weather conditions almost nightly when they interdict drug flights there. I'm aware of the circumstances. No one is finding either of you culpable. Nothing is going into your fitness reports that will indicate any unprofessional conduct. So take a deep breath and let's get past this, shall we? I have other fish to fry with you two.''

Gus gave Cam a warm look. He was so relieved that she wasn't going to be singled out as at fault for the incident. ''That's good to hear, Major. Thank you...from both of us.''

Releasing his hand, Maya patted him in a motherly fashion and then smiled slightly. ''You're welcome. Well, Gus, you said you'd do anything to get healed up so you could fly again?''

He felt the heat begin to saturate his broken arm.

The discomfort was slowly leaving after Maya had released his hand. "Yes, ma'am, I did."

"You meant it?" Maya shifted her gaze to Cam, who was frowning, obvious questions in her eyes.

"Yes, I did. Why?" Gus saw a feral smile cross the major's mouth, as if she were a cat and he, an unfortunate mouse that had just been trapped. Gus could feel so much around the woman, and yet he wasn't able to translate all of it to understand it—or her. Cam had said she was powerful, and now he clearly knew it was true.

"Okay, you two," Maya murmured as she took out some folded papers from inside her blouse and handed a set to each of them, "here are your TDY orders for the next two weeks." She opened Gus's and gave it to him to read. Cam took hers and carefully unfolded the typewritten orders. "TDY" meant temporary duty, so the two pilots knew they were being sent someplace, but not where. Maya waited in silence as they read the new orders.

Cam frowned. "Village of the Clouds? I've heard of that place. From…Inca, your twin sister."

Gus frowned, too. "Is this a military base? A hospital?"

Grinning, Maya said, "Yes to all the above. Gus, when you were delirious, you remember seeing a female jaguar? A big one with black half-moon spots over her golden coat?"

Jarred, Gus blinked. Maya stood before him, serious now, her hands folded in front of her body. Stunned, he took several seconds to respond. His mind whirled with questions. How could she know that? The mystery surrounding this woman shocked him. "Er...well, yes... But it was a hallucination brought on by my high fever," he managed to reply. Shooting a glance at Cam, who was smiling at him, he wondered where this conversation was leading. Seeing merriment dancing in Maya's eyes and a smile on her lips, he wondered what the hell was up.

"Yes, well, you see, Gus, you weren't actually imagining that jaguar. She's real. As real as you or I, right now. She's your spirit guardian.... Your mother is a member of the Jaguar Clan. Did she ever tell you that?"

"Er...yes..." Gus's head was spinning with a hundred questions. The jaguar was *real?* How?

Maya's smile widened. "Yes, she is. That means you, as her direct descendant can go to the Village of the Clouds for training, if you want it. It's also a place where people go to heal. There's a small pond known as the Pool of Life. If you go sit in that healing water, it will heal any disease or wound." She pointed toward his left arm. "If you want full use of that arm again, you have to go there and bathe in the waters every day for two weeks. It's not going to be dog duty, Gus. The place is like a Garden of Eden. You saw it already. You visited it in your dreams. Do you remember? The green slope leading down to that beautiful water?"

Dumbfounded, Gus nodded. "Yes, ma'am, I do recall that now...but I thought it was all—"

"I know, hallucinations brought on by high fever." Maya chuckled darkly. "Sometimes, when we're sick, we go to another place to heal, to help ourselves, Gus, and that's what you did. Would you like to know more about this place and what it offers you, since by heritage you can become a member of the Jaguar Clan if you want?''

Gus looked up at Cam. "Has she got the same set of TDY orders?"

Maya laughed softly. "Yes, she does. I think Cam deserves a little R and R with you, Gus. She's been busting her hump for months squaring this little TJ operation and getting it in order."

"But," Cam said worriedly, "what about the BJS2 mission? If I'm not there to run it?"

"Snake and Wild Woman are coming up to stand in for you two for the length of the TDY," Maya told them. "And my X.O., Dallas Klein, will run the place for you. When you return from the Village of the Clouds, they'll come back to BJS and me." Maya held Cam's worried gaze. "And upon your return, Cam, you're still the C.O. Gus is still your X.O. Things will move on just like they did before this happened."

Frowning, Gus muttered, "But…I won't be able to fly at that time. I'll just be a deskbound X.O., and Cam's going to need another pilot."

Maya's grin turned sardonic. "Really, Chief? Well, I guess you're gonna have to trust me on this one, aren't you? By the time you return to TJ, you'll be ready to fly."

Cam laid her hand gently on Gus's left arm. "Darling…believe her. I know it sounds impossible, but when Maya was wounded in action when Dane was flying with her down in Peru, and they mixed it up with a Black Shark, Inca flew in from Brazil. She laid her hand on Maya's wound and healed it instantly. We all got to see it.

"A number of us dragged Maya down from that Apache cockpit, and she was hemorrhaging. Our doctor got the bleeding stopped, but Maya was dying because she needed a blood transfusion. Luckily, Dane had the same blood type. A day later, Inca flew in—she's a well-known healer from the Jaguar Clan. All she did was lay her hand on Maya's arm where it got sliced open, and in ten minutes the wound was *gone.*"

Hearing the hope in Cam's voice, Gus gave Maya a strange, assessing look. The major stared back at him, her gaze bold and confident. "Two weeks?" he challenged huskily.

"Two weeks, Chief. I know you don't believe me, and that's fine. But you'll see." Maya moved to the door, picked up her cap and settled it on her head. She gave them a broad smile. "Morgan is sending you an overnight, top-secret packet. In it are your commercial airline tickets to Tarapoto, Peru. And Mike Houston, his right-hand man, who is also a member of the clan, has put in written directions on how you are to get to the village from there. Have a good trip...." She lifted her hand and waved to them.

"I don't believe this," Gus whispered. The place in his dream *was* real. He sat on the same grassy knoll that led down to the oval-shaped Pool of Life and it looked just as he had imagined. Except in reality Cam was at his side, dressed in a loose-fitting white cotton top and slacks. Her feet were bare, snuggled in the green grass. The sun was warm, but not hot, the sky a light blue, with rolling clouds. In the distance the peaks of the Andes, clothed with snow, were barely visible.

Cam sighed and put her hand on his right shoulder. Gus wore a pale blue, short-sleeved top and loose, cotton pants. He, too, was barefoot. Around them, the jungle closed in, embracing the beautiful spot as a lover would. The profusion of orchids in the trees overhanging the aquamarine pool below did indeed make this look like Eden in Cam's mind.

"This place is mystical," she said. "And so wonderful. Walking over that bridge earlier today and meeting Alaria and Adaire, the keepers of the village, was like meeting old friends. I swear, they're like grandparents to us."

Nodding, Gus stared at the vibrant water of the pool. The color was unearthly. It reminded him of that translucent hue he'd seen on icebergs in the Atlantic as they drifted southward. "I felt such love for them instantly."

"Me, too..." Cam sighed. "Why don't you go into the water, Gus? Alaria said you need to do it once a day for about ten minutes."

Nodding, he slowly stood up and walked down to the edge of the pool. Cam went with him. She helped him out of his shirt by unbuttoning it and gently removing it from around his arm, which was in a removable plastic cast. Kneeling down, she tugged off his pants, leaving him in a pair of boxer shorts. She then divested him of the sling and eased open the cast and removed it. The ugly red scar where the doctors had operated to put his bones back in alignment was a glaring reminder of their traumatic crash. It hurt Cam just to look at it.

Getting down on her knees, she dipped her fingers into the placid water. "Ohh, it's so warm! Like a hot tub." She twisted her head to look up at him, smiling. Cam knew that Gus really wanted to believe Maya—that by doing this, he could be healed. His two left fingers, the last two on his hand, didn't work at all. He couldn't move them.

Understanding his anxiety, Cam said, "Come on, I'll help you in, Gus. Nothing ventured, nothing gained."

Taking a deep breath, Gus set aside his questions and stepped into the pool. The gently sloping bottom was sandy and the water was deliciously warm and soothing. Instantly, he felt a delightful bubbling sensation against his flesh wherever the water embraced him. Moving out to the center, which was neck deep, Gus turned and looked up at Cam, who stood on the bank. He loved her fiercely. He wished he could make love to her, but it was impossible right now with his arm the way it was. Seeing the hope burning in her eyes, he said, "It tickles."

"What does?" she asked, laughing and sitting down at the edge, placing her feet in the water.

"That's the feeling," he told her, looking around the glade. "The water is like champagne bubbles all around me. I can feel their warmth and it's like...well, going *into* me. It's a strange sensation, but it feels good."

"Yes," Cam said, startled, "I feel it, too!" She pointed to her feet and ankles, which were immersed in the pool. "Wow, this is something else, Gus! Oh, won't it be wonderful if it helps your arm and hand?"

Hearing the hope in her voice, Gus nodded. Indeed,

he felt the water working energetically around his wounded arm, felt heat penetrating the wound and moving down his limb to his hand. To his surprise, he tried to flex his fingers. They all moved. Gulping in surprise, he tried it again. Before, his last two fingers would not flex because of the nerve damage. Now they did.

"I moved them," he exclaimed in a strangled whisper, giving Cam a wide-eyed look of surprise.

She grinned. "Yeah? Your fingers? They moved? Really?"

"Yeah…they did!" Gus flexed them again as if to persuade himself it had really happened.

Tears flooded Cam's eyes as she sat there, watching Gus in the center of the pool. His face looked at peace for the first time. The strain of the accident was gone, all the tension washed away from his strong male mouth. A soft breeze riffled his hair, lifting a few short strands and settling them against the smooth line of his brow. There was such hope burning in his cinnamon-colored eyes as he looked down at his left arm through the jewel-toned water.

Her heart pounded with hope. Hope for him. And hope that he'd fly at her side once again. Never had Cam wanted anything more. She trusted Maya. And she believed her statement that Gus could be whole once more, even if he himself was uncertain. He hadn't spent three years with this mysterious and powerful woman as Cam had.

"Just stand there and let yourself heal," she called to him softly, tears trailing down her cheeks. "I love you, Gus Morales, and I *know* you're going to be a hundred percent in two weeks."

Chapter 19

Gus ambled into their thatched hut, which sat beside a creek of cool, burbling water. It was dark. The weather was warm, in the mid-seventies. The village was quieting down for the night, for there was no electricity here. He'd grown used to the low light, the candles set in glass globes in every hut. To the left was their sleeping room. Seeing Cam sitting on their large pallet, with a globe flickering in the corner, giving her just enough light to write in her diary, he halted in the doorway and smiled softly.

She didn't hear him come in. He'd been quiet on purpose. Tonight was the last night they'd be here at this incredibly wonderful, healing village. He'd already said his farewell to the grandparents, Alaria and Adaire, who together ran this mystical community. Tomorrow morning, Gus and Cam would cross that wooden bridge over the stream and move out into another world, another life.

His heart expanded with joy. Cam would be at his side. He couldn't get any luckier than that. His lips curved in a wider smile as he observed her writing, her chestnut hair alive with red-gold highlights, her brow scrunched in concentration.

Gus hadn't understood the importance of being given a journal upon their arrival here, but now he did. Every day one of the teachers at the village would lead a number of them in some kind of visualization. They would then write down their experience afterward, their emotional response to it. The next day, the same group would gather with that teacher and share the experiences they'd had. The amazing thing to Gus was that all of them had the same experience. That told him that whatever was going on was real, and not a figment of his imagination. No, the last two weeks had been empowering to him and had given him a clearer understanding of his own Yaqui grandmother, and the valuable heritage she'd passed on to him.

"I want to take a photograph of you through my heart's eyes in this moment," he whispered to Cam.

Instantly, she lifted her head as she heard Gus's low, deep voice. His words cascaded over her like a warm blanket. In the thirteen days they'd been in the village, they hadn't made love because of his broken arm. But how she looked forward to sleeping near him, even if she couldn't snuggle in his arms.

"That's a beautiful thing to say," she murmured.

"I'm looking at a beautiful woman. Why wouldn't I say that?" His mouth drew into an enigmatic smile. Eyes widening, Cam realized he was leaning casually on the doorjamb—against his left shoulder. The one that had been so badly injured.

"Gus, aren't you in pain?" she asked, pointing to his arm. This was the first time she'd seen him do that. He had already regained the full use of his fingers and hand, just as Maya had promised. It was a miracle, but then, Cam had realized very quickly, miracles were an ordinary part of life here at the village.

"Hmm?" He glanced down at his left side. "No, I'm fine. There's no pain. Nothing."

Relieved, Cam rested her hands on the diary and smiled up at him. "That's so wonderful, darling. I can't believe it, but it's real. You'll be able to fly again when we get back to TJ." She saw his hooded eyes narrow on her. Heart pounding in anticipation, Cam wondered what that look meant. Gus held something in his hands, but she couldn't see what it was.

"In a way, I'm glad to be going back," Gus told her, glancing down at what he was holding. It was a small ring he'd fashioned for Cam in the last several days. He'd asked Adaire if he had any silver wire around, and the old man had beamed. Taking Gus to their craft shop, a large thatched hut at the outer perimeter of the village, he'd shown him much more. And for days, after lessons, Gus would go there and work. He'd made the ring for Cam—to symbolize a hope in the future for both of them.

Cam looked around and sighed. She gently closed her book and set it near the wall. "I know how you feel. But there's a part of me that doesn't want to leave this peace and quiet."

"But the other part, the warrior, wants to get back into action, right?" he chuckled. Pushing away from the door frame, Gus quietly shut the woven-palm door so that no one would accidentally enter the room. Then he turned back to Cam, who sat cross-legged on the soft, springy pallet stuffed with freshly dried grass. She was wearing a simple white cotton nightgown.

"You're right. I'm itching to get back to flying. I miss that most." She watched Gus walk across the room and close the purple curtains at the two windows, left by day to allow fresh air to flow in. Cam had grown used to his nightly routine. It was time for bed. He had just come from bathing, because he was wearing only his dark blue cotton pants, and the black hair spread across his broad bare chest still looked damp.

Coming to the pallet, Gus knelt down in front of her, less than a foot away. Cam's face was free of tension. He'd never truly realized the pressure on her until he saw how peaceful she seemed during these two stress-free weeks. As she lifted her chin and smiled up at him, her lips parting, he groaned inwardly.

"I made you something," he said in a low tone. "Hold out your hand. I want to give it to you."

Thrilled and surprised, Cam did as he asked. When he placed the piece of jewelry in her palm, the slight touch of his fingers on her skin sent wild tingles of longing up her arm, to her heart.

"Oh, Gus. It's a ring!" Cam picked up the delicately made piece and looked at it closely.

Nervously, Gus said, "I want this ring to symbolize us, *querida*. Our future...our possibilities with one another." He waved his hand. "I used gold and silver wire, weaving them together to make a stronger band.''

Amazed by his painstaking work, Cam noted that seven tiny polished stones were woven into the ring, each a different color. ''It's like a rainbow ring,'' she whispered in awe. In the candlelight, the precious stones glinted and gleamed. It's beautiful, Gus...so beautiful!'' Cam choked up with emotion as she held his hooded gaze.

''It's for a beautiful woman who stole my heart the first day she walked into my life. I loved you then, Camelia Anderson, but I was a scared guy. There you were—a confident woman warrior, smart and foxy, who had three years of combat under her belt—my teacher and commander.'' He managed a sour smile. ''I didn't know I'd become your executive officer. That blew me away, but in a good way, because I wanted to spend as much time with you as I could. Through it all, I hungered for you, *querida,* even though I never let on to it.''

Smiling softly, Cam said, ''No...you never did. You're very good at hiding your motives, Gus Morales.'' She smiled into his eyes.

''And I had my own monsters to wrestle with,'' he told her huskily. ''I had my past to settle—the loss of another warrior woman I'd loved.''

''I understand,'' Cam said. ''I was afraid to love you, too, Gus, for different reasons.'' She gazed back at the ring, still in awe. The fire within each colored stone was breathtaking. Her fingers tingled as she touched the object. This was no ordinary ring, she realized.

Gus took it from her and held her left hand, her

long, graceful fingers extended toward him. "We've both faced our fears and worked through them," he said in an emotional whisper. Seeing her eyes tear up and fill with love for him gave Gus the courage to go on. He slid the ring onto her finger. It fit perfectly. "This ring symbolizes our love for one another, *querida*. What I hope for us in the future. I know we're in a dangerous business. I also know, now, that I'm going to savor every second I spend with you from here on out, because we may die suddenly."

Gulping, Cam drowned in his eyes, which burned with desire. "Oh, Gus…this is so beautiful! Your words, the ring…"

"Do you want to wear this ring for those reasons, *querida?*" He prayed she did, but he had to ask. He couldn't assume.

Tears drifted down her cheeks. "Oh, yes, Gus. Yes! I feel the same about you…about us. That crash where we almost died ripped away any misgivings or worries I had about us. Seeing you hurt like that, and knowing that you could die if we didn't get rescued, helped me get real clear real fast about my true feelings for you." Sniffing, she whispered, "I love you. I think I loved you from the moment I set eyes on you. I just didn't want to admit it. I was too scared."

Caressing her hand and gazing down at the delicately wrought ring, he murmured, "Two emotional cowards who finally got courageous enough to fight our own dragons to win the prize—one another?"

With a laugh, Cam nodded. She wiped her tears away with her other hand. "Yes…yes, exactly."

"That's what I wanted to hear," he murmured. Getting up, he went over to the corner and blew out the candle. The shadows in the room deepened, but bright moonlight pierced the semi-opaque curtains, filling the hut with a muted radiance.

Cam moved the blankets aside as Gus slid into bed beside her. This time, he maneuvered her onto her back and lay on his right side. With his left hand, he caressed her warm cheek.

"I want to love you tonight, *querida*."

His low, vibrating tone feathered through her. Cam sighed and smiled softly as his fingers grazed her temple, cheek and chin. "I've wanted to do this for so long, but your arm…"

"My arm is fine now," he assured her. Drowning in her dark green eyes, which were filled with yearning, he ran his fingers down her shoulder to caress her breast beneath the fabric. Her eyes fluttered closed. A soft moan of need rose in her throat as she pressed against his exploring hand. How guileless and trusting Cam was! That humbled Gus as nothing else could. Despite her troubled past with men, she was trusting him so sweetly. That was the power of love, he realized, as he leaned down to seek her lips.

Kissing Cam was like kissing a flower opening to the sun for the first time. Her lips were like soft, warm petals yielding to him adoringly. Gus realized that Cam was innocent and not very experienced in love-making. That cautioned him to go slow, to remember that she was new to real intimacy between two people.

"I want this night to be one you'll always remember, *querida*," he rasped against her wet lips. "Fly with me? Let me give you wings, Camelia. Come fly with me…."

His urgent words aroused her, and Cam moaned, "Yes... Gus, I love you...." And she arched against him, her own urgency real, her hunger making her body glow as if lava pooled in its core, ready to explode.

Lost in the haze and heat of his lips crushing hers, she scarcely registered the fact that he was tugging at her nightgown, slipping it up her body and running his warm hand over her bare skin. Cam reluctantly broke away from his searching mouth. Sitting up, she divested herself of the shift and set it aside.

Gus's eyes gleamed as he looked at her. "You're so beautiful." He reached out and caressed her small, firm breasts with his hand. Seeing the languorous look in her eyes, he smiled boldly and urged her to lie at his side once more. "I want to explore you," he whispered, kissing her nose, her chin, the length of her slender neck. "I want to learn every contour with my lips, my hands, and put it into my heart," he added, placing one wet, provocative kiss at the top of her breast, the side of it, and finally, closing his lips over the tight nipple.

Hands clenching, Cam closed her eyes as he suckled her and brought her fully into his arms. Swept up in a heated tide, she felt his strength as a man and reveled in it. Urgency filled her as his mouth left her nipple and found her mouth once more. Hungrily, Cam returned his passionate kisses. His breath was warm and rasping against her nose and cheek; his hand ranged artfully downward, exploring her rib cage, her waist and the curve of her hip. Even his wiry chest hair pressing against her sensitized breasts was a wonderful sensation.

When his fingers moved gently across her scalp, making it tingle, Cam rested her head on his right arm and looked drowsily up into his dark, burning gaze. "I ache, Gus…I ache for you…." she told him in a husky tone.

Cam saw the pleased smile come to his strong male mouth. Just having him trail his fingers through her hair was a wonderful and unexpected sensation to Cam. She felt like the most cherished woman in the world as he caressed her lovingly.

"That's good, *querida*. I ache, too. It's the ache of love…." Easing her upward, he lay on his back, grasped her wide hips and drew her above him. There was a look of surprise in her face as he did so, but under the circumstances, he had no wish to stress his newly healed left arm. Besides, his instincts told him that although Cam was not a virgin, it had probably been a long time since she'd made love, and this way he wouldn't accidentally hurt her.

He understood on some instinctual level that Cam needed to be given the freedom to flow with the needs of her body without him orchestrating their lovemaking. Gus knew that others had used her, forced her on her back and then, after their own gratification, got up and left her, not caring about her fulfillment. He was damned if that was going to happen tonight. Or any night they spent together. In the silent language of love, he was going to teach her about her womanly body, her own power and sexuality, and how she could reach the ultimate gift of it—with him.

As her legs straddled his narrow hips, she felt his erection graze her wet, throbbing core. A sigh tore from her moist, parted lips. When she rested her hands on his well-sprung chest, Gus moved teasingly against her, and when he settled her fully against him, the pooled wetness of her body met the hardened power of his. Fingers digging into the tight flesh of his chest, she moved downward of her own accord. A sense of newfound power, of being a woman, ripped through her like a bolt of lightning as Cam opened her body to him.

"Easy..." Gus whispered, gripping her hips to guide her. "Take your time, *querida*. This should feel good, not painful...."

His words drummed through her wildly pounding heart. Oh, how good Gus felt to her! Her body sang, the blood throbbing through her as she felt his masculine power at the doorway to her feminine darkness. Gulping, Cam could only feel right now. As he slowly eased his hips upward, and she felt him sheath a little more into her tight confines, the fiery sensations tripled. Breathing raggedly, Cam closed her eyes, lost in the hazy, exploding sensations. Never had she felt such joy, such honesty and beauty with a man as Gus was sharing with her right now. Oh, this was what love, real love, was about! In the spinning golden halls of her mind that were shorting out with the pleasure of their mutual coupling, Cam realized that Gus was controlling himself for her sake, to introduce her to a realm she'd never, ever explored before. Her breath was growing ragged. She wanted more.

"Take me," Gus rasped darkly. "Take me when you want, *querida*. I'm yours...all yours...."

With one powerful movement she did so, and the resulting pleasure moved through her like a tidal wave. Surrendering to her body's hunger, to her heart's desire to love Gus in every way possible, Cam sank downward. And then his hands were on her hips, moving her, grinding her body against his as he arched upward to create even greater pleasure for her.

Feeling as if she were in a storm, tossed by violent updrafts and air currents, Cam let the animal nature of herself take over. With each wet, gliding movement, the hunger grew, until finally an explosion unlike anything she'd ever experienced before took place within her. As Gus's large hands closed around her lower back, pulling her closer still, the violence of her climax took her by utter surprise.

Gus felt Cam stiffen. He understood what was happening. With a grimace of arousal, he finally released his tight control. As she arched her back with a sharp cry of pleasure, he quickened the rhythm between them, deepening his penetration and prolonging the pleasure for her. And just as her climax reached its peak, he allowed himself his final release into the hot, fluid depths of her loving body.

Cam groaned and slumped forward. Lost in a glowing haze, breathing hard, she lay across Gus, her head buried beneath his jaw. Weakly stroking his hair with her fingers, she felt their hearts beating in unison together like drums. Her mind was mush. She couldn't think, and speech was impossible. Wonderful radiating waves of warmth and light pulsing through her body held her total attention. Now she understood how sex, good sex, could be incredible, and she smiled against the curve of his sweaty neck. All the while, Gus was stroking her spent body, his strong hands moving gently down her spine and across her hips.

"You are my heart," he whispered into her ear, her silken hair tickling his face. "And this is what love...real love...is all about, *querida*. I wanted to show you that a man can love his woman as an equal partner. We don't always take and run, like you've experienced in the past." He smiled when she lifted her head to look into his eyes. "Loving is giving and taking. It's about sharing. It's about wanting to make the person you love happy." Reaching up, he grazed her flushed, damp cheek.

Drowning in his glittering gaze, which was filled with tenderness, Cam whispered brokenly, "I never knew, Gus...not until now...."

Satisfaction made him growl. "Well, now you know the difference, *querida*. This—" he stroked her shoulder and back caressingly "—is what we have to look forward to from now on. Pretty great, isn't it?"

Cam purred beneath his ministrations. "Yes...oh, yes!"

Sliding his hand to her cheek, he guided her mouth to his, cherishing her soft lips for a long, long time. When they finally eased apart, Gus whispered, "I'm going to love you forever, Camelia Anderson. Forever..."

Chapter 20

"Hey, welcome home!" Sergeant Angel Paredes called when Cam stepped into the barracks of the Mexican Air Force base in Tijuana.

Cam grinned and threw her arms around the Peruvian paramedic, who had worked at BJS since its beginning. They called her the Angel of Death because countless times Angel had managed to save the life of someone in the worst of circumstances—patients not expected to make it. She'd cheated death of many good people.

"Hey, great to see you here!" Cam replied. Glancing over her shoulder at Gus, she quickly introduced him to the Quero Indian. Angel was small and stocky, having descended directly from the Incas, proud rulers of an empire that had covered much of South America at one time.

Cam saw Angel's large brown eyes light up with

pleasure as she pumped Gus's hand. Then Lieutenant
Dallas Klein, Maya's X.O. back at the base in Peru,
appeared at the door. Giving the tall, slim, Israeli-born
pilot a huge grin, she called, "Hey, I'm relieving you
now. You can go home!"

Dallas laughed and rushed to embrace Cam. "Good
to see you! You look great, Cam. That two week R
and R did you a lot of good."

"Yeah, life is kinda wonderful now." Cam looked
around. "Where's the rest of my tiny squadron? Luis
and Antonio?"

"Oh," Dallas said with a mischievous grin, "I've
got them doing some serious work over the mountains. They're learning some finer details of nap-of-
the-earth flying, with Wild Woman and Snake in the
other Apache."

Chuckling, Cam moved into her office. It felt good
to be home. Her heart was light, her feeling about the
future of this mission positive.

"Take your chair," Dallas said, walking in behind
her. "Maya sent Paredes up here to give you your
official FAA medical exam. It's protocol, but it's
gotta be done before you and your X.O. can strap an
Apache on your butt again."

"Fine," Cam murmured. "Not a problem." She
ran her fingers over her battered old green metal desk.
Dallas was a neatnik compared to herself. Everything
was in little organized piles, unlike Cam's style,
which was messy at best.

As she sat down in her squeaky chair, Gus and
Angel entered the room, and Dallas went to the coffee
dispenser and started pouring cups of the freshly
made brew.

Gus closed the door and leaned against it, his gaze on Cam. She looked so happy, with her cheeks flushed, her eyes radiant. He knew why; their love was having the same effect on him.

Sergeant Paredes fetched her emergency medical pack and set it up on Cam's desk. "Let me check you two out, and then Dallas and I can take off, okay?" She gave them a swift smile as she pulled out a stethoscope and blood pressure cuff from her red canvas bag, which said Medic in Spanish and English.

"You first, Gus?" Cam asked as Dallas handed her a cup of steaming coffee. "Thanks, Dallas."

Gus nodded and eased away from the door. He knew the drill. Rolling up his right sleeve to above his elbow, he came over to where Angel had pulled out a chair for him.

"Right here, Chief Morales," Angel said, pointing to it.

Gus liked the energetic Quero woman. Her skin was a coppery color, and her black eyes reminded him of a night sky with stars dancing in its depths. "Gotcha," he murmured, and sat down. Angel was quick and professional, fitting the blood pressure cuff around his right arm.

After passing out the coffee, Dallas sauntered over to Cam's desk and rested her hip on one corner, her own mug in hand. "Maya said she sent you two to that village. I'm jealous. Angel has gotten to go, too."

"Well," Cam said, sipping her coffee, "I wondered why Angel looked so happy when she came back. Now I know why."

"Yes," Dallas chuckled, "I keep hoping my turn will come."

Cam gave her friend a narrowed look. "You've been with Maya since the beginning. You work with her day in and day out."

"Yes," Dallas murmured.

"And I think you know a lot about her...well, her other powers?" Cam wasn't sure how to approach Dallas on this topic. She didn't know how much Dallas knew about the mystery of Maya's past or how it figured into her present. Cam searched the woman's oval face, her shining sable hair and olive skin as the X.O.'s eyes grew thoughtful. Cam wondered if she'd made a mistake by asking at all. Still, she burned with questions.

Dallas took her time and sipped her coffee for more than a minute before answering her. "Maya has other powers. But from what she's shared with me, I wouldn't say they are superhuman ones. I've heard her say many times that anything she, or her twin sister, Inca, can do, anyone can, with proper training." Dallas looked over at Gus as Angel flashed a penlight into his eyes to make sure his pupils dilated properly. "Like Gus's broken arm..."

"Yes, that," Cam said. "We all know it's impossible for bones to knit and heal in less than six weeks, and yet in two weeks his serious break is *gone*. It's as if it never happened." She waved toward his arm. "Even the scar from the surgery is gone. I can barely see where it was."

Shrugging, Dallas murmured, "Maya has often said that truth is stranger than fiction, and that the world we live in is but a reflection of how we *want* to see it, not how it really is."

"I had a long talk with Grandmother Alaria. She's

the elder who runs the village along with her husband, Adair. I asked her about it, and she just laughed. She wasn't laughing at me, but rather, with me. Patting my hand, she told me that miracles are possible every breathing moment of everyone's life." Giving Dallas a questioning look, Cam muttered, "I felt like such an ignoramus there."

Nodding, Dallas said, "Maya refers to it as the study of metaphysics, or the unseen realms that surround us. She says they're there all the time, even if we're not aware of it. When we meditate, we become more in touch with the other dimensions and energies surrounding us."

"You seem to have a handle on this," Cam declared good-naturedly, "and you've never been to the village."

"I'm Jewish. We have the cabala. It's an ancient metaphysical and spiritual tradition that I think, at least from what Maya has shared with me over the years, parallels her beliefs very closely."

"Oh…" Cam said, frowning.

"Did you get asked to come back?" Dallas inquired.

Nodding, she said, "Yeah, they extended an invitation to Gus and me both to come back for training."

"That's a compliment to you, then," Dallas said, smiling slightly. She watched as Angel finished her examination of Gus.

"That arm looks incredible," Angel murmured, shaking her head. "Someday I'd like to go back to that place. Awesome!" She grinned up at her fiends. "Okay, next poor slob?"

Loving her upbeat spirit and teasing nature, Cam raised her hand. "I'm the next victim."

Laughter filled the room. Gus vacated the chair and rolled down his sleeve. With a flourish of his hand, he invited Cam to sit down in his place.

"Thank you, kind sir," she murmured, giving him a warm look filled with love.

"A pleasure, *señorita*," he answered. His heart blossomed with so fierce a love that he knew he wasn't able to hide it from either of Cam's colleagues. Somehow he knew they approved, and it made him feel good.

Dallas slipped off the corner of the desk and ambled over. She picked up Cam's left hand. "My...what's this? Isn't it gorgeous. New, hmm?"

Cam responded to her playful inquiry. "Gus gave it to me. He made it. Isn't it beautiful?"

"I was eyeballin' that thing, too," Angel said in a conspiratorial tone as she pumped up the blood pressure cuff around Cam's right arm.

Feeling heat come to her neck and cheeks, Cam looked up into Dallas's smiling eyes. She knew. And Cam wouldn't hide it from her best friends.

Gus came over, crossing his arms against his chest. "I made it for Cam while we were at the Village of the Clouds."

"You were inspired," Dallas said, holding Cam's hand so that the fluorescent light showed off the highly detailed, intricate work.

"Very," Gus answered, giving Cam a wink. He saw her lips pull into a grin.

"*He's* inspiring," Cam announced.

"I feel love in the air," Angel sang in a high

falsetto tone. She threw her hands up in a dramatic flourish.

"Calm down, Angel," Dallas laughed. "Angels of Death are supposed to be serious, you know?"

Giggling, Angel shook her head. "Angels of Death have gotta have the blackest humor in the world to work with the likes of all of you. Hanging ten over the surfboard of life out there every day. Just darin' those druggies to come try to shoot you down. Hell," she muttered, her mouth twisting in a mirthful grin, "if it wasn't for my humor, some of you would already have died and gone to Inca heaven."

Chuckling, Cam sat still as Angel placed the stethoscope against her chest to listen to her heartbeat.

"Don't laugh now," Angel said, wriggling her black, arched brows, "or you'll blast my eardrums."

"I know...."

"Just don't talk for a moment, okay? It's tough enough trying to hear your red-blooded American heart pounding because the guy you love is nearby. You laughing and making croaking sounds with that voice of yours only makes it worse."

Gus couldn't help but laugh deeply. Angel was leaning near Cam, stethoscope in place, her face intent. "Is she always like this?" he asked with a grin.

"Oh," Dallas said, "count on it. If you work at BJS, you have to have a die-hard sense of humor to carry you and your buddies over the hurdle when all hell breaks loose."

"Which," Angel said proudly as she straightened and took the stethoscope away from Cam's heart, "is daily. We boogie down there, Chief Morales. I come from Inca heritage, and we call this thing we do the dance of death. Every day one of our women flies to intercept a druggie in the air, she's layin' her life on the line—for all of us.'' Patting Cam's shoulder, she said drolly, ''You'll live.''

''Whew. I was worried.'' Cam pretended to wipe sweat from her brow.

''Yeah, sure you were.'' Angel gave Gus a sly look as she tucked her medical tools back into her red canvas bag. ''I prescribe doing more of whatever it was you were doing back at the village. Normally, you have low blood pressure, Cam, but now it's normal.'' She flashed Cam an evil, knowing grin. ''So do it daily.''

Gus couldn't curb his grin when Cam's face turned a bright red. He heard Dallas choke, trying not to laugh, her hand against her throat. Unexpectedly, Angel turned to him after she'd zipped up the bag and put the strap across her sturdy shoulder.

''I assume you're the prescription she needs, Chief Morales?''

Now he was the target. ''Er…''

''Yes, well, I can see you are,'' Angel said primly, giving Cam an even broader smile. ''This is the best medical condition I've seen Cam in. So I'm gonna sign the FAA medical certificate allowing her back to flight status.''

''What about me?'' he asked, suddenly alarmed. He watched as Angel walked toward the door, the huge red bag against her left hip.

Turning, she gazed at him seriously. ''You've passed, sir. Just keep doin' what you're doin'.'' She motioned to his left arm. ''Obviously, you got well in a helluva hurry.''

Relief flowed through Gus. He wasn't used to the raucous, intimate teasing between enlisted people and officers he was experiencing right now. Cam had warned him that the lines between them were greatly blurred and usually nonexistent down at BJS. Seeing the deviltry dancing in the Quero's eyes again, he gave a sour grin. "Oh, I think I can manage to do that, Angel."

"Good." Angel gave them all a fond look. "I gotta hoof it to the commercial airport in San Diego. The major wants me back pronto. And I want to see my guy, Burke, again." She waved her left hand, the ring flashing on it.

"You're always missed," Cam told her, meaning it. They had one doctor and two paramedics to take care of the huge squadron of women and a few men under Maya's command. It was a daunting task on good days. Elizabeth, a U.S. Army doctor, considered Angel her right hand. Without her around, she was usually overwhelmed by the many small medical problems that routinely happened in the squadron. But now that Burke, a special forces paramedic, had signed on to be with Angel, the load had been considerably eased.

"I know I am. I'm absolutely indispensable." She giggled as she opened the door.

"Better get on over to San Diego," Dallas said. "I've got a car and driver waiting downstairs to take you to Lindbergh Airport. And," she warned, arching one dark brow, "don't forget to let Burke know how much you missed him."

Angel grinned. "Roger that. Loud and clear."

"No one accused you of being slow on the uptake,

Sergeant Paredes. Adios, amiga. Have a safe trip back to Peru.'' Dallas lifted her hand to the woman.

"Adios," Angel call softly. She became suddenly serious. "Cam, Chief Morales? You stay *safe,* you hear? I don't wanna have to come back up here to requalify you for flight duty again...."

The room grew quiet when the Angel of Death had departed. Cam turned to Gus, who stood a few feet away from her, while Dallas finished her cup of coffee.

"I really miss the women of BJS," Cam said.

"Yeah, we're like a bunch of wildcats in the same bag, yowling, screaming and howling," Dallas chuckled. She put the cup near the coffee urn and looked over at Gus. "You took us in stride, Chief."

"Black humor is my specialty."

"It is," Cam told her. "You should hear him quipping in the cockpit when we fly."

"Good," Dallas said. She went over and picked up her helmet and gloves. "Well, we've officially changed commands, Cam. You're back in the hot seat again, and the chief is your X.O., again. I'm going to take some time to talk with the Air Force generals and give them a report on our actions here. I'll be leaving for Mexico City in an hour."

"I'll miss you," Cam said, going over to hug Dallas goodbye. As she released the Israeli from her embrace, she saw Dallas smile and nod.

"We miss you, but we know you're doing good work up here. Like Maya said, we've spent three years honing our combat skills, and now the rest of the world has decided we got what it takes, and wants us to teach them what we know."

"So the BJS pilots are like seeds in the wind, being blown here and there," Gus said.

"Bingo," Dallas murmured. She halted at the door, helmet dangling in her left hand, her green flight gloves jammed into it. "Morgan Trayhern and Mike Houston. Those two can't stop bragging about us, I guess, and the word is getting out at the top levels."

"Maybe BJS women are going to be sent around the world because we're the only ones who have the combat training needed to teach others," Cam said.

"Maybe," Dallas said, lifting her hand in farewell, "maybe our luck is changing. *Hasta la vista, amigos....*"

"Take care," Cam called after Dallas softly. The door stood partly open and Cam smiled, knowing Dallas had left it that way out of habit. Down at BJS, Maya always instructed her officers to keep their doors open, so they could be available to their people. Cam would try the same thing here, once they were assigned a permanent H.Q., which would probably happen after Dallas talked to the head honchos down in Mexico City.

"Welcome home," Gus murmured. He leaned over and pressed a kiss to Cam's smooth, unlined brow. How beautiful she looked, even in her genderless green flight suit. He knew what lay beneath that fabric—the heart of the woman he'd love until he died.

Sighing, Cam stretched up and kissed his mouth quickly. Hotly. But now was not the time for loving. "Sure is different from the Village of the Clouds, isn't it?" she murmured, releasing him and moving back to her desk.

"Yeah," Gus said as he ambled over and stood

near the desk as she looked at the flight schedule Dallas had drawn up for them. "But I have you. So I don't care where I am as long as you're at my side."

Touched, Cam turned the clipboard around for him to see. "Well, darling, it looks like we have the duty tonight. Together."

He took the clipboard and looked at it. "Yeah, Luis and Antonio are due back here in about an hour. They'll be exhausted."

"Dallas worked their butts off."

"That will make them appreciate your gentle but firm hand," Gus declared with a grin. Cam was a softy. Gus knew that as time went on, she'd grow into her role as C.O. of this mission. Much of her wavering was gone, replaced with a confident look— that of a leader who knew what she was doing and what she wanted to accomplish. As he set the board on her desk, Gus knew that his love for her gave her confidence, too. It was wonderful to see Cam growing daily before his eyes.

"Maybe it will," she said with a wicked smile. She saw the smoldering look in Gus's cinnamon-colored eyes and her body hotly responded. "Hey, you know this weekend?"

"Yeah?"

"Let's snoop around south TJ and see if we can find an apartment to live in. I don't want to keep living here, do you?"

Shaking his head, Gus said, "No. One apartment or two?"

"One."

"One bedroom?"

"One bed. The two of us in it."

"Roger. I hear you loud and clear."

Laughing, Cam sat down at her desk. There were a bunch of manuals to look through, read and then create written orders from. "Good."

Gus watched as she pulled the manuals in front of her. "Do you think Maya is going to mind about us?"

"It will be all right, Gus. She won't send you packing to another base, if that's what you're worried about. A number of her pilots have met guys—fallen in love and married them. They all work at BJS in one form or another." Cam knew he was worried about their intimacy. Normally, office romance was discouraged by the military. If they became engaged, as he and Cam had, then it was a dicey situation. Gus knew in a regular army mission he'd probably be sent away—permanently.

"Dallas liked the ring," he said, pride in his tone.

Lifting her hand, Cam looked at it, then sent a warm look in his direction. "Yes, she'll tell Maya. I'm sure that Sergeant Joanne Prater, Maya's desk clerk, will wag that tale all over BJS in short order— another woman pilot has crashed and burned and found a guy." She laughed and shook her head. "Prater knows what's gossip and what's top secret. When she hears Dallas describing your beautiful ring to Maya, she'll go racing out the door to tell everyone."

Gus smiled with her. "I hope someday to go down there, to BJS."

"I'm sure you will—with me."

He tapped the desk with his fingertips. "And we've been asked to go back to the village. Grandfather

Adaire said because of my Indian blood, and my mother's gifts, they want me to do more training.''

"I know," Cam said, leaning back in the chair. "Is that high on your list of things to do?"

"No...not yet," Gus murmured, holding her luminous green gaze. A fierce love swept through him. "My heart, my soul, are centered on you, *querida*. On our life here." He looked around, his brows dipping. "We're in combat mode every time we fly. Our lives are on the line. I just found you and I don't want to let you or what we have go." And then his mouth crooked. "Maybe in a couple of years I'll think about it. But not now..."

Cam slid her hand into the one he held toward her. "I like the old-fashioned approach we're taking, Gus."

"What? A year-long engagement? That's what my father did with my mother—courted her nonstop. And that's what I'm going to do with you. I'm going to show you how many ways you make me happy, how you make my life feel like it's filled with sunlight every morning when I wake up. Then..." he lifted her hand, leaned down and placed a moist kiss on the back of it "...if all goes well, I'm going to be asking you, next year at this time, to marry me."

"I like your plan, Chief Morales."

He reluctantly released her hand. They were on active military duty now, and personal wants and desires had to be laid aside. Still, it was tough for Gus to do. He'd made love with Cam last night, and early this morning once again, just before they'd left the village. His body tingled hotly in memory of her warmth, her fierce response.

"What do you say we go down and check out our steed then?" he suggested. Gesturing to the manuals, he coaxed, "Leave them for later. Let's get into some sunshine, blue sky and fresh air. Together..."

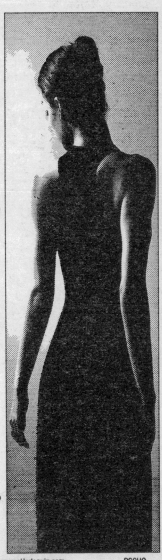

If you enjoyed what you just read,
then we've got an offer you can't resist!

Take 2
bestselling novels FREE!
Plus get a FREE surprise gift!

Clip this page and mail it to The Best of the Best™

IN U.S.A.
3010 Walden Ave.
P.O. Box 1867
Buffalo, N.Y. 14240-1867

IN CANADA
P.O. Box 609
Fort Erie, Ontario
L2A 5X3

YES! Please send me 2 free Best of the Best™ novels and my free surprise gift. After receiving them, if I don't wish to receive anymore, I can return the shipping statement marked cancel. If I don't cancel, I will receive 4 brand-new novels every month, before they're available in stores! In the U.S.A., bill me at the bargain price of $4.74 plus 25¢ shipping and handling per book and applicable sales tax, if any*. In Canada, bill me at the bargain price of $5.24 plus 25¢ shipping and handling per book and applicable taxes**. That's the complete price and a savings of over 20% off the cover prices—what a great deal! I understand that accepting the 2 free books and gift places me under no obligation ever to buy any books. I can always return a shipment and cancel at any time. Even if I never buy another The Best of the Best™ book, the 2 free books and gift are mine to keep forever.

185 MDN DNWF
385 MDN DNWG

Name	(PLEASE PRINT)	
Address	Apt.#	
City	State/Prov.	Zip/Postal Code

* Terms and prices subject to change without notice. Sales tax applicable in N.Y.
** Canadian residents will be charged applicable provincial taxes and GST.
   All orders subject to approval. Offer limited to one per household and not valid to current The Best of the Best™ subscribers.
   ® are registered trademarks of Harlequin Enterprises Limited.

BOB02-R   ©1998 Harlequin Enterprises Limited

**You asked for them—
so you're going to get them!**

SUTTON, ETHAN and **CONNAL** are available,
bigger than life and some of the most intriguing
men you'll ever read about. In fact, they are

TEXANS AT HEART

And only

DIANA PALMER

**could have created men as powerful
and unforgettable as these!**

So here are some bold men who won't be tamed—
until they meet the perfect women.

Don't miss TEXANS AT HEART, available March 2003—
wherever Silhouette books are sold!

Silhouette®

Where love comes alive™